"WE READ HEARTS...."

The boy nodded once. "Will it tell me if I'm brave?" he asked.

"Heart reading doesn't answer specific questions," Dasis said. "What heart reading will do is give you reasons and understandings about many things about yourself. Come sit. Let's see what we can do for you."

Stashie set a slate on her lap and arranged her chalks. "Give me your left hand," she said to the boy. She grabbed his finger so hard that he winced, and then she closed her eyes and her body sagged. The boy's eyes grew wide. His right hand crept to his breast, as if he felt Stashie's invasion of his soul. He trembled but didn't move.

Finally, Stashie's hand moved, and the boy's body relaxed visibly. She grabbed pink and red chalks and, with her left hand, began slashing at the slate. She swirled in some browns and pale whites. After a moment, she flung the slate at Dasis, and released the boy's hand as if it burned her.

Dasis looked at the slate and began to read. . . .

FANTASTICAL LANDS

HEART READERS

Kristine Kathryn Rusch

A ROC BOOK

ROC
Published by the Penguin Group
Penguin Books USA Inc., 375 Hudson Street,
New York, New York 10014, U.S.A.
Penguin Books Ltd, 27 Wrights Lane,
London W8 5TZ, England
Penguin Books Australia Ltd, Ringwood,
Victoria, Australia
Penguin Books Canada Ltd, 10 Alcorn Avenue,
Toronto, Ontario, Canada M4V 3B2
Penguin Books (N.Z.) Ltd, 182–190 Wairau Road,
Auckland 10, New Zealand

Penguin Books Ltd, Registered Offices:
Harmondsworth, Middlesex, England

First published by Roc, an imprint of Dutton Signet,
a division of Penguin Books USA Inc.

First Printing, October, 1993
10 9 8 7 6 5 4 3 2 1

 REGISTERED TRADEMARK—MARCA REGISTRADA

Printed in the United States of America

Back in the days when I thought everything had to be a short story, I tried to cram this novel into twenty pages of text. When Algis Budrys saw those twenty pages at a workshop, he told me I had to look into myself and find the real story. Patrick L. Price, then editor at *Amazing*, told me to tell the entire tale. Dean Wesley Smith, who has been with me from almost the beginning of this, told me to make the story into the novel it deserves to be. I have finally taken all of their advice.

So, this book is for AJ, Pat, and Dean. Thanks, guys.

It's also for Paul Higginbotham and Steve Braungin, my favorite pair of twins.

PROLOGUE

Pardu stopped at the open door and wiped the sweat from his face. The desert's heat shimmered in here, making the room feel tight and close. Pardu stopped as the smell hit him. Rank and fetid, the smell almost overpowered him before he recognized it. Blood and fear and something raw, something his long-dead brother once called invigorating. The smell of the battlefield. The smell of death.

The low murmur of women's voices drifted from the room. A girl cried out, and someone shushed her. Pardu smiled. No one should scream at the birth of a king. He pushed the silken curtain back and stepped inside.

Four women surrounded the naked girl. Her distended breasts rested against her overlarge belly. She leaned against the birthing couch, her legs spread, a large, blood-drenched pillow beneath them to catch the little king. Her eyes were wide, her hair matted to her face. For a brief, breathless moment, she looked as she had in passion: cheeks flushed, eyes glazed and too bright, lips soft and rounded. Then she began to pant, and the pain spasmed through her body and into her face. She didn't know he was there, but the midwives did. They nodded once and returned to their task.

The smell had faded, although the heat was more intense. He walked across the parquet floor and crouched next to the midwife by the girl's feet. The edge of the child's skull pushed against her pubic hair.

"Pardu." The girl's surprised whisper echoed against the curtains. She thought he had forgotten her—and he had, for the most part, since the child had begun to ruin her slender figure. He had other lovers, better lovers, although none had ever borne him a child. And he thought of this child daily, planning great things for the life of his son.

"Push, Lanie," one of the midwives said.

The girl half groaned, half sighed, and the child's head appeared, covered with a milky fluid and bits of blood.

"Again," said the midwife next to Pardu.

"I can't," the girl whispered.

Pardu pushed the midwife aside, and cradled his son's soft, sticky head in his hand. "You will," he said and glanced up. The girl's eyes were frightened. "Push."

She gritted her teeth, and her face grew red with straining. He cupped his son's head and watched as the shoulders appeared, then the entire child, trailing a cord, fell into his hands with a bloody, sucking sound. Pardu glanced for a penis, saw it small and shiny with fluid, then held the child up in triumph.

"My son!" he said.

The midwife snatched the child from him and dabbed the baby's eyes and wiped the slime from its nose. The baby choked, then coughed and wheezed. No cries from this little one. He would be strong, like his father.

Pardu was about to stand when the girl moaned. The moan rose into a scream as one of the midwives pushed on her belly. Another head pushed its way out of her opening, followed quickly by shoulders. Pardu had to move quickly to grab the child before it fell to the pillow below.

Another son, still attached to its mother by the long, kinked cord. Pardu stared at the child, remembering the series of fortune-tellers, the long, pitched battles, the nights he had lain awake agonizing. All he had to do was take the cord, wrap it around the child's neck and squeeze. He had killed enough men in his time. What was one son's life to protect another son's legacy?

The midwife took the child from Pardu, cleaned its eyes and nose and, when it didn't breathe, slapped it. The child wailed, revealing good, healthy lungs.

Pardu closed his eyes. For the first time since he had entered the birth room, he felt ill. Two sons. Twins. The elder would have to rule.

He opened his eyes. The twins rested on pillows, squirming as the midwives swabbed the blood off their skin. Pardu couldn't tell which was which, and soon the midwives wouldn't be able to either. The elder would have no claim, no legitimate claim, because no one would know for sure which child appeared first.

Pardu walked to the door, pushed the curtain back, and motioned for one of his men. "Send the heart readers," he said.

The man nodded and walked across the sunbaked sand to the main palace. Pardu returned to the stifling room. The girl cradled his sons, one against each breast. The smaller baby nuzzled, while the larger suckled heartily. The midwives had clipped the cords and were taking them and the afterbirth outside to dry for the womb casters. One of the midwives remained, wiping up the blood.

The girl smiled at him. A strand of hair curled against her flushed cheek. "We have sons."

He did not smile back. "One of them will have to die."

The other child began to suckle. The girl glanced at both of them and a tear ran out of the corner of her eye. She shook her head, slowly.

"Heart readers," a male voice said. The curtain swished open and two elderly women hurried into the room. They bowed before Pardu and he noted that their white hair was thinning against their skulls. Dust covered their robes.

"Welcome," he said, fulfilling custom.

The women stood. One opened the side of her robe

and pulled a slate from a sewn-in pouch. The other said, "Who do we read?"

Their eyes were shiny raisins against their leathery skin. For a moment, Pardu wondered at trusting the lives of his sons, of his own future, to these women. Then he remembered his sixteenth birthday, when the heart readers had pointed at him, and his first command, when the heart readers had shown him the treachery in Ilande. Heart readers had never failed him.

"You read my sons." He pointed to the babies. The girl clutched them tighter and turned away slightly, as if she could protect them with her body.

The heart reader without the slate smiled. "Beg pardon, sire, but we cannot read newborns."

Pardu clenched his fists together. "I need them read to determine succession."

"Newborns have had no chance to love or to hate," the heart reader said. "They have not cried except in physical pain."

"Newborns have no heart to read." The other heart reader slipped her slate back into her pouch. "To determine succession now, you must see a womb caster or a fortune-teller."

"But they won't tell me who has a pure heart," Pardu said.

"And neither can we," said the first heart reader. "For that we must wait until they have had a chance to live and to love. We're sorry, Highness."

They bowed again and scurried from the room. The girl smiled at him, but her eyes glittered with rage. "Perhaps you should let the babies grow," she said. "I'm sure they'll both have hearts purer than yours."

"I'm sure," Pardu said. He looked at his sons. One had a ridge around his skull, an indentation caused by the birth. The other clutched his mother's breast with one tiny hand. Perhaps if he raised them equally, one would show an affinity for leadership, while the other did not. Perhaps he wouldn't need spellcasters, sorcerers, or heart readers.

He clapped his hands and the remaining midwife

started. "Take the children and find a wet nurse," he said. "I want them raised in the palace."

"I can nurse my own sons," the girl said.

"They are my sons," Pardu said. "They shall be raised my way."

"Pardu—"

He waved his hand and silenced her. "Pay Lanie well," he said to the midwife. "Make sure she can live in comfort if she chooses. Kill her if she tries to so much as see my sons. Is that clear?"

"Yes, sire," the midwife said.

Pardu turned, his boots slapping against the parquet floor. The babies did have purer hearts than he did. Twenty years ago, he never would have thought of killing newborns, or of removing them from their mother.

He slid the curtain back and stepped out into the heat. The sun reflected off the sand and he had to squint against the brightness. He took a deep breath. The air smelled fresh. Perhaps the stench had goaded him into thoughts of killing—the birthing room as a battlefield. The opening gambit in a war that would continue throughout his lifetime if he let it: brother against brother, son against son.

PART ONE

Twenty Years Later

CHAPTER 1

Tarne pulled out his sword the moment he saw the village. He waved the weapon above his head and ordered his men to follow. Then he dug his heels into his horse's side and leaned forward in the saddle, eager to be active again.

His party of thirty men had been riding most of the day. Early that morning, on a ridge to the south, they had met a ragged force of elderly men and boys, armed with hand-carved weapons and a few burning torches. Tarne's men had killed them quickly and left most of the bodies strewn across the path, the heads on poles marking the roadside like torches lining the roads in Leanda. He believed the elderly men and boys defended a village—why else appear on a deserted road in a troop without real warriors?—and he had been right.

He wiped his sweaty brow and tugged at the scarf around his head. The sun was hotter here than it had been at home. His hands, the only exposed part of his body, had turned red, then blistered, and were now lined with painful cracks. He had trouble gripping the reins, but somehow the pain disappeared when he clutched his sword. He glanced back at his men. They were grinning, the smiles fierce on dirt-encrusted faces.

"One more for Leanda!" he called, and the men cheered. Their cry rose above the clip-clop of horses' hooves, the snap of clothing in slight wind. Ahead, the mud-brick buildings became distinct. Mud-brick meant water, and water meant victory.

Women stood outside, clutching children to their

skirts. A cripple stood in the middle of the road, leaning on his staff, a thin dog beside him. Chickens
flapped their wings and scattered from the road as the
troop approached.

"You have no right here!" the cripple called. His
voice broke. Tarne squinted and saw a boy with a
man's shape, one footless leg hovering above the
ground. A boy with a man's shape and a baby's grace,
doing a general's job.

"We have every right," Tarne said. "I claim this
village in the name of Pardu, King of Leanda, and his
twin sons, Ele and Vasenu!"

"We are a peaceful people," the boy said. "We will
barter—"

"You have nothing to barter with." Tarne's horse
bore down on the boy. Tarne could see the boy's
gaunt features and wide eyes, a sign of sickness or
lack of food. "Out of my way, child. The village is
mine."

The boy did not move. Tarne rode around him and
slapped him with the broadside of the sword. The boy
lost his balance, fell, and scrambled on his hands and
knees to the side of a building. Women screamed and
ran inside, dragging the children with them.

Tarne reined up in front of the circular communal
trough, noting the muddy water. More than enough.
The horse reared, and Tarne used the extra height to
see beyond the handful of buildings. A thin trickle of
water ran through what appeared to be a large river-
bed. These people lived amid water, a small amount,
but the rains would start soon. This land was hot, but
water-rich. He was doing well for his king.

Tarne needed a base. The village was small, but the
buildings were solid and built in a semicircle. His men
could handle women, children, and a crippled boy.

"We will camp here," Tarne said. He patted his
horse, calming it. "Secure quarters."

The men brought their horses around. Some went
farther into the village, while the rest scattered.

Tarne dismounted. His body shook. He had been
expecting battle and it had not come. Funny that he

should have thought it would. The old men and boys were the last line of defense. The healthy men and women—the fighters—had to be long dead, or gone, fighting in another section of the country. Only a crippled boy had stood in Tarne's way. Although, he had learned, sometimes a crippled boy was enough.

Tarne led his horse to the building where the boy leaned, watching the activity. Tarne brought out his sword, placed its tip under the boy's chin. "I rule here now," Tarne said.

The boy glared at him, then spat on the sword's blood-flecked blade.

Tarne pushed harder. A trickle of blood ran down the boy's neck, followed by another. Tarne smiled a little. The men were securing their quarters. "Should any of my men die or become injured, I will come to you first, do you understand?"

A girl came to the doorway of the building. Her thin arms hung from the sleeves of her oversized dress, and her bare feet were covered with dirt. Black hair curled around her face, and touched the tips of her budding breasts. Her eyes, as dark as her hair, snapped, not with fear but with anger. "Leave him alone," she said.

"Stashie." The boy's voice sounded raspy. "Go inside."

Another woman screamed, and a man laughed. The girl didn't take her gaze from Tarne's face. "He hasn't harmed you. Leave him alone."

Tarne hated her lack of fear. The courageous ones were the ones who hurt him on all of his campaigns, who interfered with his actions, made his command difficult.

"Stash—"

The boy's voice faded into a whistle of air as Tarne shoved the sword through the boy's throat. The girl stepped back as the blood gushed. The boy flailed, pulling at the blade, and finally stopping. His body slouched, but he remained upright, his chin supported by the sword blade. Tarne pulled the sword out, feeling a tug as the boy's body held, then toppled forward.

Now the girl was frightened. Tarne could smell it

in the sharpening of her sweat. He let go of the horse's reins. He pushed past her and went inside.

The building was cool and dark. He blinked once, letting his eyes adjust, then saw the older woman clutching a young girl in the corner of the room. He brought the blade up. The woman scuttled back, shoving the child behind her. The girl—Stashie?—had come up beside him.

"This frightens you, doesn't it?" he asked.

She crossed her arms in front of her tiny breasts. Her body shook.

"Doesn't it?"

"Yes," she whispered.

He pushed the blade closer to the older woman. Blood dripped on her dress. The woman pressed the child against the wall, and backed up as far as she could. Tarne brought his blade closer. Outside, a woman yelped, then wailed, and the sound continued, echoing in the small room. He pushed the blade's tip against the woman's throat.

"Don't!" Stashie grabbed his loose arm, and he pushed her back. She gasped as she slammed into the wall. The older woman clutched her neck, and he couldn't tell if the blood he saw there was from a wound he had given her or from the boy.

Stashie shook herself and then stood. This time she put her hands behind her back, as if she had to hold them to control herself. "I'll—" Her voice shook. She paused, cleared her throat and started again. "I'll do anything you want if you leave them alone."

He smiled again. She had courage, this one, even when she was frightened. Too bad she belonged to the enemy. Too bad he had to break her spirit. "Anything?"

"Yes," she said.

The woman pushed at the blade—hard—causing Tarne to move the tip and lose his balance. She held her throat and pushed the child ahead of her. Stashie grabbed Tarne's sword arm and tried to hold it, but he was much stronger. He swung around, this time pinning the child against the wall. "I've killed children before," he said.

Stashie and the woman stopped moving. The little girl was breathing heavily. Light from the door glinted off the tears on her cheeks.

"It's all right, Mama," Stashie said.

The woman shook her head. "Better that we die, Stashie, like Tylee did."

Tarne watched them. He had seen such struggles before, and each time, they had left him excited.

"Put your sword down," Stashie said, "and I'll do whatever you want."

Tarne didn't move. "Who was the boy outside?"

"My brother," Stashie said. "Tylee."

Tarne nodded. Not a lover, then, as he had expected. And she still lived in her mother's home. A virgin. Even better. Her spirit would be easier to break. He eased the sword down. "Get them out of here."

The woman grabbed the child, holding her tightly.

"But it's our home," Stashie said.

"It's my quarters now." Tarne moved the sword, and wiped the bloody blade on the woman's dress. "And you said you would do anything. I assume that means without complaints."

Stashie glanced at her mother and the girl. "I'm sorry, Mama."

"We'll be all right," the woman said. She slunk along the wall, clinging to the child, until they reached the door. Then they ran outside.

Stashie watched them go. Tarne sheathed his blade.

"They're gone," Stashie said. The little tremor had returned to her voice. "What do you want me to do?"

CHAPTER 2

Stashie woke a little after dawn. She huddled on her side, hugging her knees to her chest. The night before she hadn't so much slept as passed out. Tarne had held her down, sticking his large body in hers, rubbing her, burning her—

—and she hadn't made a sound. She had promised. Without complaints. Her mother and sister were somewhere in the village, and as long as Stashie cooperated and didn't complain, they would live.

The pallet scratched her back. She opened her eyes and scanned the room. It looked so different with all four pallets sprawled in the middle of the floor, the table pushed against the wall, and the jars in front of the fireplace. Tarne had insisted on inspecting everything, and he had drunk at least half of one of the wine jars. His mouth had tasted sour.

Stashie spat, and then looked again. Tarne was not inside. She could hear his voice, faint and commanding, outside. He was talking to the men. She rolled off the pallet.

Her entire body throbbed. Tarne had ripped the strand of flesh under her tongue, and had bitten her all over. His large fingers had left bruises on her wrists and hips. She trembled as she stood up. She had never been completely naked before—always dressing half-in and half-out of clothes. Her mother had said that as long as Tylee . . .

Tylee. She closed her eyes, but that only made the picture stronger: his neck spurting blood, his body flailing. Worse, worse than it had been when he had come home from the fighting, his foot swollen and infected, and his screams as his mother and the witch woman cut the foot off. Tylee. She wondered if he was still outside, leaning against the wall, if his spirit had heard her spirit scream when Tarne touched her.

The water jugs were gone. She grabbed the jug Tarne had drunk from before, picked up her torn dress and wiped the jug's mouth. Then she tilted the jug and drank, wincing as the liquid stung her bruised lips and tongue. The wine tasted sweet, sweeter than she could have imagined, than she could have hoped for. It tasted of the nights before the wars, when she, her mother, and Tylee played with baby Kalie, and talked of the future.

Stashie let the jug stand and wiped her mouth with the back of her hand.

"You're awake."

Tarne's voice made her start. She whirled, trying to cover her nakedness with her hands.

He smiled. "You don't have to hide. I've already seen it."

She didn't move. He came up beside her, and tucked a strand of hair behind her ear. "I let you sleep this morning," he said. "But from now on I expect you to have breakfast ready for me when I get up."

She swallowed. He leaned over and kissed her, biting her lower lip. "I also expect you to stay out of the wine unless I tell you that you may have some."

"How is my mother?" Stashie asked.

Tarne shrugged. "Fine, so far as I could tell. Get dressed. I've already eaten with my men, so you won't have to worry about feeding me until lunch. Clean this place up and then come find me. Is that clear?"

Stashie nodded. He ran a hand through her hair one more time, then left her. She grabbed her dress and looked at it. He had ripped it along the seams and down the middle. She wouldn't be able to salvage it. She would have to wear something else.

She reached into the clothing sack and took her mother's good dress. It was loose and hung about her ankles. She had always been smaller than her mother. Stashie cinched it with a piece of rope and straight-

ened the room, placing Tarne's things in a pile near
the door, as if he were going to leave soon. Then she
rearranged the furniture, leaving the soiled pallets in
the middle of the floor. The blood would never come
off the center pallet. She considered rolling it over,
but decided to let it stay, symbolic of the night Tarne
killed her brother.

The sun was still low in the sky when she finished.
She set aside some bread and cheese to break for
lunch, then went to the doorway.

The smell hit her first: rich in decay, almost fetid,
the stench of blood and feces, and the beginning of
something rank. Bodies littered the street all over the
village, and she longed to run forward, to see if her
family were among them. But she had promised to
obey Tarne, and he had promised not to hurt them.
He was a soldier, and a soldier was a man of his word.

Slowly, ever so slowly, she looked to her left, and
saw Tylee, still slouched against the wall, head half-
severed by Tarne's sword. The shaking started again,
and for a moment she couldn't control it. The night
before, she had let her brother's murderer touch her,
use her. All she had to do was reach past him, and
grab his second's knife and stab him in the back. She
hadn't. She had let him live.

And she would let him live tonight too.

There were too many men, too many things that
could go wrong. If she wasn't strong enough to kill
him, he would turn on her and destroy the rest of her
family. *You understand, don't you, Tylee?* she
thought, wanting to crouch beside him. *Please understand.* But Tylee didn't move. His eyes were swollen,
and looked as though they were going to burst out of
his face. His skin had become pallid except where the
blood had settled along the bottom of his legs.

He wouldn't have understood. He would have
fought the whole way, resisted as best he could—as
he had, when faced with Tarne's sword.

And yet, Tylee had tried to save her.

She had killed him by angering Tarne.

She brought her head down. The street was deserted, except for the bodies and the flies. If someone didn't clean up, the entire village would smell so bad, everyone would have to leave. Tarne and his men had disappeared. They were off doing—something, she didn't know what. Someone had to clean up. Tarne had told her to clean up the house. Tylee had always been part of the house. Taking care of him was the least she could do.

Stashie stared at his body for a moment. She couldn't do the death magicks, and neither could anyone else in the village. The last mage had gone off to defend the pass. Tarne was here, though, so Stashie could assume that he managed to clear the pass. The last troop had to be dead, just as the troop before it—the one that Tylee had survived. Most of the village was dead, although Tarne didn't know it yet.

She didn't even want to try the death magicks, for doing them badly meant cursing the soul. Better to leave Tylee unprotected than damn him. She would, if she ever escaped this, find a death mage to perform the ritual for her brother.

She had neither the strength to raise him above the ground, nor the kindling to build a proper fire. The kindling she had left came from the scrub beside the river. The branches were large, but too green. She kept them beside the house in case of emergency. Emergency. Her smile was bitter and she made herself focus on her brother's body.

The river moved in a trickle, so she couldn't send him down the mountain. She would have to use the third method of caring for the dead, the least preferred method. She would have to bury him. He would understand that she was not slighting him.

Stashie went back inside and brought out the flat rock her brother had used for digging. She crouched before his body and began to scrape at the sand. The rock dug into her palms. The muscles in her arms pulled and the soreness from the previous night made her back ache. The work would be hard; she might not finish before Tarne returned. But she would tell him that she was doing as he asked—she was cleaning the house.

She dug for the rest of the morning, until the blood ran from the blisters on her hands. The sun shifted and glared on her back. Sweat dripped along her face, and stained her mother's dress. Beside her, Tylee watched with what seemed like amusement. Stashie had always ridiculed death ceremonies, thinking they had nothing to do with the person who died. Yet Tylee's body rested against the wall like a broken wine jug. Her mother would grind down the jug, reuse the sand in new jugs. Stashie's burial of Tylee seemed the same, a way of reusing part of him by placing him in the earth.

The hole had become Tylee-sized, and deep enough to swallow her hand to the wrist by the time she heard pounding of horses' hooves. She turned, stood, and wiped her palms on her dress. Tarne rode in, followed by three of his men. He looked so big and powerful on his horse. The memory of his suffocating weight made her want to use the knife more than ever.

He waved the men on, and reined up beside her. The horse was breathing heavily and covered with sweat; they must have ridden for miles. Tarne dismounted and looped the horse's reins to a chink he had made in the wall. His foot narrowly missed Tylee's body. Stashie flinched.

"What are you doing?" His movements were deliberate. He didn't face her, but already she knew the tone. Displeasure.

"I-I'm cleaning up as you asked." She had been planning that sentence all morning. Still, her voice shook.

"I said nothing about the garbage outside." He kicked Tylee. The body fell, Tylee's head lolling back. "I left it here for a reason."

His words angered her, but she stifled the anger, held it back, hoping she could salvage something of this, keep it from hurting the rest of her family.

"Bring me lunch," he said and grabbed a long piece of kindling from beside the house. He sat down on the rim of her shallow hole and took out his knife. When she didn't move, he looked up at her. *"Now,"* he said.

She darted into the house. The coolness felt welcome after the burning of the sun. Her skin throbbed and she knew that, had things been normal, her mother would have yelled at her for remaining in the sun too long. Tylee would have agreed, then put ointment on her, soothing the burning, and little Kalie would have kept Stashie amused until it was time to sleep.

Stashie took the bread and cheese she had set out and placed it on a ceramic platter her mother had made. Then she poured some of the remaining wine into a small misshapen cup that she had made a long time ago, when she had tried to imitate her mother.

Everything in the house had a memory attached to it. And Tarne's actions were destroying those memories, tainting them with new, awful ones. Even if he left, she would have no home now. Only a place where the ghosts of her past surrounded her, attempting comfort and failing.

She set the wine jar back and hurried outside, afraid that she had been too slow, that Tarne was even more displeased. He was standing when she emerged, leaning on the kindling like Tylee used to lean on his walking stick. Tarne's eyes sparkled. He acted as if he had been waiting for her.

"Set the food down," he said.

She did, placing it at the ground by her feet.

"Hold this." He handed her the kindling. The stick he had chosen had been a long one. He had whittled both ends into sharp points. She clutched the wood, feeling it dig into her already sore palms.

He waited until she was looking at him before he withdrew his sword. "I leave the body of a traitor where other traitors may see it," Tarne said. "Sometimes that subtle warning isn't warning enough. So I take more drastic measures."

With a single, quick movement, he sliced the remaining threads in Tylee's neck. Stashie jumped back,

expecting more blood and finding it even more horrific
because there was none. Tylee's head rolled down the
slight incline and landed in the hole, upside down.
Tarne extended his hand.

Stashie stared at him, afraid to move. She knew
what he wanted. He wanted the kindling. He would
put Tylee's head on it, and display it throughout the
village. She couldn't let him, but she didn't dare stop
him. So she did nothing.

"Hand me the stick," he said.

She clutched it tighter. "Let me bury him. He didn't
harm you."

Tarne smiled, but there was no kindness in it. "You
are a child, aren't you? He did harm me. Sometimes
words are much stronger than weapons."

"We have no magic for him," she said. "No proper
way to prepare his body. Isn't that indignity enough?"

"No," Tarne said and snatched the stick away. He
heaved it over his head, and in a fluid motion, shoved
the end of the stick through the opening in Tylee's
neck.

The loud, squishy sound made Stashie want to turn
away, but she couldn't move. Tarne grabbed the lower
part of the stick, bracing it with his palms, then lifted
it upright. Tylee's hair moved as if blown by a breeze.
His eyes had a startled expression and she wondered
if it was new.

Tarne carried the stick to the edge of the road. He
used his entire weight to force the pointed end into
the ground. Tylee's head swung for a moment on the
pole, then the movement stopped.

Tarne gazed up. "The first one," he said, with some
satisfaction. "Maybe by the time I leave, they will
alternate with the torches."

He came back and picked up the cup at her feet.
With two swallows, he finished the wine. He grabbed
the plate, broke off a piece of bread and offered it to
her.

"I don't want to eat," she said. Her voice sounded
broken and hoarse.

"You will eat," he said.

She shook her head.

He set the bread in her hand. "When I say eat, you will eat. You have no choice, girl. You disobeyed me once. Don't disobey me again."

Stashie took the piece of bread and swallowed it, although it choked her. Tarne broke the bread into large hunks, and ate them. She chewed each piece that Tarne handed her, swallowing constantly, trying to keep what food she had already eaten down. She couldn't look at her brother's head, and she couldn't look at what remained of his body, lying at Tarne's feet. So she stared at the plate, watching the bread and cheese become crumbs. All those days of work, all the time her mother had spent preparing the bread, trading for the cheese, only to have it eaten in a single meal. A loaf of bread was supposed to last for days. She wondered if Tarne would consider it disobedience when the time came and she told him the last of the supplies was gone.

When they finished, Stashie said, "My mother and sister, are they—?"

"I grant you no favors." Tarne stood and brushed the crumbs off his pants. He left the plate on the ground beside Tylee's legs. "Their welfare is no longer your concern."

Panic shot through Stashie's system. "You said you weren't going to hurt them."

"You said you weren't going to disobey me." Tarne untied the horse from the building. "I expect the hole covered by the time I get back, dinner ready, and you naked on the pallets. Do you understand?"

"Yes, sir," Stashie said.

"Good. The orders are simple. Follow them." He mounted the horse, pressed his boots into its side, and rode off.

Stashie watched him go. As the horse passed the pole, Tylee's head moved slightly from side to side, as if saying no. As if he were telling her to disobey Tarne again. She took a deep breath to keep her food down, turned her back on her dead brother, and went inside the house.

*   *   *

Stashie waited until Tarne was asleep before rolling off the pallet. She moved silently across the floor and lifted her dress from the sack she had placed it on. She slipped the dress over her head, and allowed the thin sliver of moonlight to guide her to the door.

She had to push gently, careful not to make a sound. Tarne sighed in his sleep and rolled over, but did not wake. Stashie crept out to see if her mother and sister were all right.

The moon was full and round, illuminating the village with the thin light of a rainy day. The bodies looked like grotesque shadows, parodies of the persons who had died. Stashie slipped across the road, watching for movement other than her own. She moved from building to building, peering in window after window. Mostly, she saw Tarne's men, sleeping on pallets with the village women, much as Tarne slept with her. But none of the women were her mother.

She had walked past most of the buildings when she saw the tent that had been erected near the river. A light created shadows in the interior. Two of Tarne's men sat outside it, sleeping from the angle of their heads. She moved sideways across the sand, her bare feet whispering against the ground. The men didn't look up. When she reached the back of the tent, she peered beneath the small gap between the peg and the ground.

Two candles burned on the table, spreading wax across its surface. The older women and very young children slept on the floor. They huddled together as if for comfort. Stashie stared until she saw her mother and Kalie, leaning on each other in the far corner of the tent. He hadn't touched them. He probably didn't even know who they were.

She rolled away from the tent before anyone inside saw her. Then she made her way back, slowly.

The moon's light had grown brighter. The corpses on the street looked as if they had changed positions. A large shadow covered the center of the road. Stashie followed the shadow to its source, and found herself looking at Tylee's head, great and angry in the moonlight.

He seemed to be ordering her to take him down, to fight back. But she had no reason to rebel. If she fought Tarne, she would lose what remained of her family. The village she had loved was already gone.

Tylee frowned. *Then I have died for nothing,* he said. *I have wasted my life, trying to protect people like you. Cowards, who don't know how to protect themselves.*

She wanted to deny it, but the image of Tarne sleeping on what had been Tylee's pallet came back to her. It would have been so easy, so very easy to slip that knife into his back. And if Tarne died, maybe his men would leave. If Tarne didn't die, they would punish her, but leave her family alone. She had disobeyed Tarne that afternoon, and he hadn't gone near her mother. He had tortured Stashie with Tylee's body, but had left her family alone.

We can't sit by while they take our land, destroy our homes, kill our families, Tylee said. *We have to fight back, Stashie. It's the only way.*

"The only way," she whispered. She walked along the shadow, stepping over the decaying bodies. Tylee peered down at her, watching her move. His eyes had a glow that was more than moonlight. The glow warmed her, helped her make her choice. When she reached the pole, she grabbed its rough wood and yanked with all her strength.

It took several good pulls before she was able to loosen it. Then the weight of Tylee's head nearly forced the pole—and Stashie—over. She took two lurching steps to regain her balance, then tipped the top of the pole into the hole she had dug that afternoon.

She had covered the hole poorly. The dirt was still loose. She scooped out what she could with her hands, then grabbed Tylee's hair and began to separate him from the wood.

She gritted her teeth and closed her eyes, pretending she was working with clay instead of her brother's decaying head. She twisted the pole and pulled backward. It slid slowly. Finally, Tylee's head pulled free, and she tossed the pole away. She placed Tylee's head in the hole she had scooped, apologizing to her brother for the indignity that he had suffered.

She scooped out the rest of the dirt as best she could. The hole wasn't as deep as she would like, but it would do. She grabbed Tylee's body and pulled it over to the hole, arranging his limbs carefully and aligning his head with his neck. Then she covered him. In the morning, she would gather rocks and cover the grave while Tarne was away.

When she finished, she was sore, with bruises on top of bruises. The eastern sky had a dim light and she could see the open sores on her hands. They didn't matter. Nothing mattered except that Tylee was finally at peace. Maybe Tarne would ignore the whole thing, and leave her alone.

She hoped so.

She went back inside, pulled off the dirty dress, and set out some food for Tarne's breakfast. Then she crawled onto the pallet, lying as far from him as possible, and fell into an exhausted sleep.

Pain, sharp pain, snapped her awake. She tried to roll over, but she couldn't move. She was pinned on her back, with her arms above her head and her legs spread. Ropes bit into her wrists and ankles. She opened her eyes and saw the sun still low in the eastern sky. Something scratched her back and she looked down.

She was naked and tied spread-eagle on top of Tylee's grave.

Tarne stood over her, some of his men behind him. He seemed twice as big.

"Good," he said. "You're awake."

He crouched beside her. She could smell wine on his breath. "I told you not to disobey me again." He stroked her cheek with one hand. The calluses on his fingers scratched. "I admire courage and spirit. I hope I have enough if I ever have to defend my homeland against raiders. But I know how much damage rebellion does. As a leader, I can't tolerate it."

He kissed her more gently than he ever had. She turned her head away and spat. The spittle formed little bubbles on the dirt.

"I have to punish it," he said. "And you, like your brother, only seem to understand extreme punishment."

Her heart pounded against her chest. If he had her, then what had he done with her mother and Kalie? "My mother didn't do anything—"

"She's not the one tied to poles in the ground." He got up, and opened his trousers. His member was long and hard and red. He stroked it, once, then stepped over her leg and crouched between her knees. He took a glass of wine from one of his men and poured it on himself, then shoved inside of her. She tried to squirm away. It hurt worse than it ever had before. She bit her lower lip, but didn't scream.

He pounded into her again and again, each time burning more. She couldn't move; she was tied. And around her, the men gathered and laughed. Tarne's face turned as red as the wine. He shuddered and pulled out.

"Don't disobey me again," he said, and smiled at her. Her body throbbed. She nodded, relieved that it was over.

"You promised before," Tarne said. "This time, I'm going to make sure you don't forget. I have things to do, but I told my men that they could enjoy themselves. You'll make sure they have a good time."

Another man got between her legs and shoved inside her. She whimpered. Tarne's smile grew. She wouldn't satisfy him by showing pain. She wouldn't. She stared at the top of the pole and, as man after man used her, she reminded herself that Tylee's head was no longer there.

She had set him free.

It took nearly a week before she could move. The women in the tent had tended to her. She could barely remember who treated her wounds, and how their fingers had soothed. When she became more conscious, she wouldn't let anyone touch her and treated herself. Finally the pressure of too many people got to her, and late one afternoon, she crawled out of the tent.

The guards looked at her with surprise, but watched her go. She didn't look at them, didn't want to speculate if they were among the ones who had used her. She would go to Tarne and demand to see her family. He owed her at least that.

She stopped beside one of the buildings, winded and hardly able to walk. With one hand braced on the mud-brick, she looked up—

—and saw not one, but three heads on poles lining the street. Tylee's was barely recognizable, decayed and covered with dirt. But she did recognize the others immediately. Her mother's face had frozen in a cry of pain and her sister's, her little baby sister's, in one of anguish.

Stashie sank to the ground and buried her face in her arms. She didn't move for a long, long time.

PART TWO

Ten Years Later

CHAPTER 3

Tarne lay on his stomach on the soft mat. The masseuse's fingers kneaded his back, easing the tense muscles. The heat was less intense here. The brick walls of the palace's new wing and the gentle movement of six large hand-held fans kept the air moving. Fresh water stood in small pitchers in corners of the room. All he had to do was snap his fingers to get a drink. He loved it here. For an hour a day, he could pretend that life was easy, that he had no cares but rest and the maintenance of his body.

The masseuse slapped oil on his back. The liquid, cool and slick against his skin, smelled faintly of roses. He closed his eyes and smiled. Roses had thrived in one of the towns on his last campaign. He missed the traveling, the feeling of absolute power as he took over a place, altered it, made it his. He loved the first drink of water from the streams, the first touch of the liquid wealth he had brought back to Leanda. He had owned, over his lifetime, at least fifty towns, holding them for a week, a month, until he had to move on, and allow the occupying forces to take over. But by then, he would always be restless and ready to conquer a new place.

He would be restless here, if he allowed himself.

But he couldn't allow it, not when he was this close to true power. His reigns in those towns and villages had been temporary, his leadership an illusion supported by force. Yet all those campaigns, all that work, all those days riding in the harsh desert sun had given him the credentials he needed, the experience he needed, to become an adviser to the King.

A trusted adviser, whose power would grow as the King grew older and more feeble.

The masseuse spread oil along his naked buttocks, down the backs of his thighs. Her hands were gentle, and he felt a slow arousal build. He so loved this hour—

"Sir?" The deep male voice sounded a little embarrassed. Tarne bent his head and looked toward the door. A thin man stood there, his hands clutching the edges of his blue robe. One of the King's runners.

The masseuse kept rubbing Tarne's legs. Her touch distracted him. With a quick movement, he caught her wrist and she stopped.

The runner took a step into the room. "The King bade me to come, sir. Scouts say horsemen approach to the west, and they bear the King's colors. He believes his sons are coming home. You are to dress immediately. He would like you to greet them."

A shiver ran down Tarne's back, even though the room had grown hotter. The arousal left him, as did the calmness, and he shoved the masseuse's hands away. "Thank you," Tarne said, dismissing the runner.

The runner nodded and backed into the hallway, facing Tarne until he could no longer make eye contact. Tarne stood up and walked across the rugs to the room hidden by a single curtain. The baths were inside, the pool empty. He stepped in the water and submerged himself to the shoulders.

He used to marvel at the presence of so much water in a desert. The wonder had left, though, as he accepted his new post. Now the bathwater felt tepid, thick, and dirty. He would find no calm here, not this afternoon.

He wiped the oil off his shoulders, climbed out, and dried himself with a large towel. The twins were back. They weren't due for a visit for another year. Even then they wouldn't be ready to rule. No one had trained them yet in the art of war. All they had learned so far were diplomacy, mathematics, statecraft, and languages. They were supposed to be touring Leanda and its colonies, learning about the land's peoples and customs. The King had ordered the trip and only the King could cancel it.

The shiver returned and ran through Tarne's entire body. The King had said nothing, and planned to send Tarne to greet them. The old man was shrewd, shrewder than Tarne gave him credit for.

He threw the towel aside, pushed back the curtain and returned to the other room. The fans continued to sway, but the mat was gone, as was the masseuse. A servant had left Tarne's riding clothes on a pillow near the door. He clenched his fists and loosened them three times. Perhaps the horsemen were not the twins. Perhaps the King wanted his trusted adviser to deal with a potential problem. Perhaps the King was not being cunning, but simply cautious.

Tarne hoped so. He needed the King on his side.

The air had a gritty, acrid feel. If he closed his eyes, Tarne could almost believe he was on a campaign, his troops behind him, waiting for a command. But nothing surrounded him except desert. The palace and the walls of the city were behind him. Ahead, he could see the small cloud of dust that the watchers said hid horsemen bearing the King's colors.

Tarne touched his sword. Any treachery and he, and the ten men behind him, would end the threat immediately.

He half wished a threat would materialize. He hadn't realized, until he felt the horse's muscles ripple between his thighs and the sword rest against his hip, how restless he had actually become. He had never been good at waiting. He didn't know why he had expected to be now.

The air pulled the moisture from his skin. He leaned forward and squinted to see the riders. Shapes appeared, horses bounding in the dust cloud. Tarne turned.

"See anything?" he asked. His second, Melie, rode only a half-pace behind him. The other nine men were too far away to hear.

Melie tugged at his scarf. Small grains of white sand had lodged in the wrinkles around his eyes. He looked as if he had been riding for a few days, although he had left the palace with Tarne. "The entourage seems large."

Tarne looked back at the dust cloud. The group would have to be large to create that much disturbance in the desert. His hand brushed the hilt of his sword. He was glad he had chosen this particular nine to support him. They had all fought with him on various campaigns, each man exceptionally gifted in the art of war. If the force they met turned out to be hostile, all Tarne would have to do was bark a single command and these men would fight as a unit.

They had done so numerous times against large odds and won.

Tarne reached a small rise, picking the location for its slight strategic value. Here, in land as flat as the desert surrounding the palace, any break in the landscape provided an advantage. Tarne signaled his men, and they flanked him in a formation both ceremonial and protective.

And he waited.

The cloud of dust came closer. Eventually he made out a group of about twenty riders. Three led, bearing flags that fluttered with the breeze. Two rode behind, followed by a column of riders three across. The flags were rectangles, the right size and shape to be of Leanda, but the light and the dust made the colors impossible to determine.

A drop of sweat ran down his back, followed by another. The heat burrowed under his skin. He had waited like this in Anleon just before ambushing a group of tribesmen. When that attack started, he had been sluggish, dizzy, almost faint from lack of movement and lack of water.

He hoped the wait here would be shorter.

The droplets of sweat covered his back by the time he could make out the flags' colors. Deep brown and black. Leanda's colors. He did not relax, having been a soldier long enough to suspect a ploy. But he moved his hand away from his sword and shifted his shoulders slightly, easing the kinks in the muscles. The two men riding together had the same build. As they got closer, he saw that they had the same features.

Vasenu and Ele, the King's twin sons. One of them would rule Leanda when the King died. Unless Tarne did something.

He urged his horse forward, forcing himself to abandon the thought to overthrow. Throughout Leanda's history, several groups had tried to destroy the aristocracy. None of them had succeeded. None even had popular support. The people in Leanda lived well, and the King made sure they credited him with their good fortune. It was the people in the conquered lands who hated the rulers of Leanda. And it had been those people who had tried to kill a king or two. They had failed and died, often at the hands of the very folk they had thought they were acting for.

His men followed him. Quickly they covered the distance between themselves and the arriving group. Both groups stopped on a flat plain in full sunlight. Tarne touched a hand to his forehead, then his chest, bowing his head in a ritual greeting.

"You may look." The voice sounded like the King's, only richer. Tarne brought his head up. The two men had ridden up between the flag bearers.

Up close, the King's sons were not identical. Their build and features were the same, but thirty years of different use had made them dissimilar. The twin on the right—Vasenu, judging from the "V" embroidered on his scarf—sat straight in the saddle. His shoulders were wide and firm, his gaze piercing. Ele, the other twin, moved with quick, jerky motions. Frown lines had formed around his mouth, and his hair refused to lie smooth.

"Your father bade me to guide you into the city." Tarne's grip tightened on the reins. Damn the King. He had known, and he had planned. "I am Tarne—"

"The general my father promoted." Vasenu spat out the word "general" as if it were foreign to his tongue. "I know who you are."

Ele glanced at his brother, then smiled at Tarne. "We appreciate your guidance." Ele's voice had the richness Tarne had heard before. Vasenu sounded like the King, too, only Vasenu kept his voice pitched higher, as if something squeezed it from within.

Tarne snapped his fingers. His troop fell in behind the twins' riders. He rode up front, before the flag bearers, as if his presence would protect them all.

I know who you are. Tarne frowned. He hadn't seen the twins since they were young boys. His promotion had come after they began their tour of the conquered lands. He wondered what the twins knew of him, if anything. Had the King discussed his choice of advisers? Tarne couldn't imagine the King committing information that sensitive to paper. Perhaps rumors, gossip, and stories circulated in the conquered lands.

He nodded once. Of course. Stories of him in the conquered lands would not be good ones. He had killed a fair number of people, destroyed uprisings by threatening, maiming, and breaking a few obvious leaders. His strategies had worked. The places he overtook had no history of rebellion, no record of discontent. His methods had been effective. They had worked well enough to bring him to the King's attention and, now, to this post.

Tarne almost turned back to ride beside the heirs, but he did not. Let them think they knew him. They would be surprised when they found out that they did not.

Tarne did not see the twins again for the next three days. He had arrived in the sitting room just past dawn, as servants shaded the windows. The room was near-dark and felt cool; only a little light filtered in through the cloths. Tarne took his usual seat off to the side, near the candle stands and a small, rarely used brazier. The room was quiet, the cushions empty. The water pitchers were full, though, and five servants waving long fans looked as if they had been in the room for a long time. The other advisers hadn't arrived yet and the King, as usual, was late.

The King had not broken routine since his sons had arrived. Indeed, if Tarne hadn't escorted the twins to the palace, he wouldn't have known they were in the area at all. The King never mentioned them, and Tarne did not either, fearing that any breach of that unspoken confidence would be a failed test.

Wydhe, one of the other advisers, arrived and took his seat. He was a large man with sallow skin, who had spent most of his life observing instead of participating. Still, his observations were sound; his advice good. Tarne found it amazing that a man with so little experience could be so astute.

A third adviser, Apne, paused in the doorway. He had grown up with the King and had managed to remain, over all the years, the King's most trusted adviser. Nothing Tarne could do could dislodge Apne from his position.

Apne spoke quietly to someone Tarne couldn't see, then came inside and sat. Tarne caught a faint whiff of sandalwood, and knew that Apne had spent his night in the women's quarters. Rumor had it that Apne tried out the women for the King, making sure there would be no surprises—too much violence, or inexperience, or bad technique. A job many of the other advisers envied, but Tarne was glad he didn't have. He liked to train women his own way, imprinting them with his own style. A king's tester should remain invisible. Tarne glanced at Apne, a small, stick-thin man with few distinguishing features. He would be able to disappear from a woman's mind. Tarne knew that he would not.

The King entered the room and closed the door. Tarne tensed. The King hadn't had a meeting of his top three advisers for a long time. The King grabbed a soft pillow, and brought it over, facing the three men. He used to stand during the meetings. But recently, he began sitting, as if standing had become too much effort.

Yet he looked fit enough. His color was good and his body trim. In the past few weeks, he had lost the excess weight he had been carrying, and that made him appear even younger. He leaned back, resting one ankle on a knee. "Three days ago," he said, "my sons arrived with news of the northern conquered lands. Apparently, we have a lot of discontent there. Our people saw signs of a growing, organized rebellion."

"Your sons?" Apne said. Tarne stifled an urge to turn. If anyone knew of the twins' arrival, it should have been Apne.

"I have asked them to join us," the King said. He snapped his fingers and a side curtain opened. The twins entered and stood at attention behind their father. This time, the identifying clothing was missing and Tarne had to search for the strands of unruly hair to pick out Ele.

"I want you to tell them what you saw in the north," the King said without looking at his sons.

"We stumbled—" they began in unison and then looked at each other. Vasenu nodded once and Ele continued. "We stumbled into a meeting in a tavern our first day in one of the provinces. We made no attempt to hide who we were, and when they saw our colors, they scattered. We had a few followed. The meetings were held at a different place every night. One of our scouts managed to get close enough to overhear some of the conversation. The group was planning the overthrow of our local provisional government. We warned the government before we left the area and gave them what names we had."

"So far there has been no trouble," Vasenu said. It took Tarne a minute to realize the other twin was speaking. "But we found similar meetings in several other towns. We're afraid that we would have an uprising on our hands before we even knew it."

"We're always prepared for trouble," Tarne said. His hands were clasped tightly in his lap. He hadn't worked in the northern province. Goddé had taken most of those lands. Goddé believed in working with the people instead of smashing rebellion. If he had used Tarne's methods, the quiet little meetings wouldn't be happening.

"All this news could have been sent with a messenger," Wydhe said. "Why are you here?"

Neither brother moved. Ele clasped his hands together.

"I asked them to return," the King said after too long a silence. "I think it's time to start another phase of their training."

Tarne felt Apne's gaze on his back. Vasenu smiled, but the smile didn't reach his eyes. "Father believes that we've seen enough of the realm. Now we have to learn how to rule."

"It's a test," Ele murmued. He hadn't moved, but his knuckles turned white. Tarne studied Ele's face. The twin was frightened. Tarne knew what fear looked like, perhaps better than he knew any other emotion.

"So you still plan to give us one ruler," Wydhe said.

"Joint rule doesn't work." The King didn't move. "The experiences of my father and his father before him have shown us that."

Tarne squirmed. He had not paid a lot of attention to the history of Leanda, believing instead that he would be better off learning everything he could about the present, and manipulating it to his own benefit.

Vasenu and Ele stood behind their father, shoulders touching. They looked secure enough, loyal enough. Yet the King's words meant that one of them had to die. A little tremor ran down Tarne's back. No one went voluntarily to his death. Perhaps, for the first time, Tarne had a legitimate way to seize some power. If he associated himself with one brother—it didn't matter which, just as long as the brother accepted Tarne—then he might be able to control the succession.

Tarne smiled just a little. The King noticed. "A problem, General?"

"Yes, sire," he said. "I'm still concerned about the unrest in the north. Perhaps if we learned a little more . . . ?"

Then he leaned back and let the discussion proceed around him. Control the succession. Finally, he had a war to fight here at the palace. And the war was a covert one, played out in the human mind—his favorite battlefield.

CHAPTER 4

Stashie rested her elbows on the rolled-up rug. The sand scratched her legs. Her chalks and slates leaned against her thigh. Twilight gilded everything with cool shadows. She could barely see Dasis, arguing with the innkeeper a few buildings away.

Stashie shook her head. She could tell from the inn-keeper's stance that no amount of argument would change his mind. He would rent out their room to a paying customer. Dasis's pretty face and soft voice no longer charmed him. He wanted money or something neither woman would give.

The town was small, a few mud-brick buildings and a half hundred tents. The town was losing its riches. A small pool, dirt encrusted, its underground spring dying, was its only means of support. The bazaar's customers had trailed off in the few months that Dasis and Stashie had been there. No one wanted to come to a place that was water poor.

A hand touched her shoulder. Stashie jumped. Dasis gazed down at her. Dasis's curly hair framed her face, making her seem rounder, almost matronly. "We have to talk, Stashie."

"He wouldn't help us, will he?"

"No," Dasis said. She sat down beside Stashie in the dirt. "He said to go to Leanda. He said there would be no more bazaars this far east for at least two seasons."

"We could go north—"

"There's unrest." Dasis took Stashie's hand. Dasis's fingers were warm. "They'll want fortune-tellers, not heart readers."

Stashie pulled away. "I can't go to Leanda."

"I don't see any other choice, Stash. The money here has dried up. No one can afford a heart reader. And the bazaars are gone. We have to go where the clients are, and they're in Leanda."

"Then you go." Stashie clasped her hands in her lap. Her palms still bore the scars of that day, all those years ago.

"Don't be stupid, Stashie. We have to go together."

Stashie shook her head. The twilight had grown to darkness. Behind them, someone had lit torches. Shadows danced across the street. "The troops are there. People—" her voice broke "—I can't see. I couldn't read up there, Dasis. I couldn't help them. Please."

Dasis put her arm around Stashie's back, but Dasis's body remained rigid. She couldn't understand. She never had, not even after she had found Stashie that first day, beaten beyond recognition, starved and dehydrated from a trek across the desert. Dasis had tended Stashie, saved her life, and had never allowed Stashie to tell her the entire story. *Those things are best forgotten,* Dasis had said. Stashie had loved her then. Stashie loved her now. But a bitterness had grown between them, a bitterness composed of an untold story and unhealed pain.

"I think we're in more danger being hurt here, in a province, than we are in the country proper, Stashie." Dasis squeezed Stashie's shoulder, then let go. "Let's try. The border is only two days away. We'll go to the first town we find, and leave at the first hint of trouble."

"Promise?" Stashie asked.

Dasis nodded. "I promise. Will you come with me?"

Stashie got up and wiped the dirt from her skirt. "I'll think about it," she said.

Buildings shimmered like a mirage during the sun's peak. Stashie wiped the sweat from her forehead. They hadn't found a town. They had found a city.

Leanda's flag flew from the gate. Her heart pounded. Inside the gate, she would find soldiers. Too many soldiers.

Dasis walked slightly ahead, her back bowed with the weight of the rug. Her hair had matted to her head and her skirts were covered with sand and dust. Still, her steps were light and her mood strong.

Stashie kept her eyes on the flag. Its black-and-brown design flashed gold in the sunlight. The colors made her tremble inside and, if she closed her eyes, she saw the flag as she had last seen it, flying from a staff between her mother's and brother's heads.

"This looks big enough," Dasis said. She was staring at the city's walls, uncountable numbers of buildings behind them. People thronged around the edges, and if Stashie squinted, she thought she could see uniforms.

Stashie nodded. Big enough for soldiers, big enough for violence. She had become a heart reader because she thought she could stay away from the wars Leanda made. Heart readers catered to the curious at bazaars. They also performed services for the rich, and sometimes determined lines of power. But by staying in the provinces, Stashie could guarantee that she would never work for the powerful or the rich. She just hadn't counted on the need to keep traveling. Most people had their hearts read only once. They would wait years before someone read it again.

The dust from the road blew into her face. Sweat ran down her cheek. She felt grimy. Dasis had decreed that they needed to make money that day or they wouldn't have a room for the night. Stashie wondered if she would make it into the city at all, let alone work at the bazaar.

The city's walls were made of mud-stone. Small, rounded viewspots perched at regular intervals in the brown surface. The gate stood open and, inside, Stashie could see teeming masses of human beings moving in various directions. She could also smell horses and sweat not her own.

Dasis squeezed her arm. "Wait here," she said.

She set the rug down beside Stashie. Stashie reached into her large, oversewn pocket and felt the reassuring slate of her board. In the other pocket, her chalk box balanced the weight of her dress. Dasis carried food and water in her pockets. Stashie drew for them; Dasis read. Somehow that gave Dasis the most power between them.

Dasis had walked up to the wall and disappeared around its far side. Stashie watched with an added degree of worry, waiting to see her partner's skirts, swaying with a slight breeze. But she saw nothing. She imagined Dasis talking to one of the guards. He would be in uniform. He would *(tie her up—the ropes chafing against her wrists—)*

"Stashie?"

She started. Dasis was beside her, a smile on her face. She looked small and round and childlike. "The bazaar isn't far from here. And it's an open one."

Stashie nodded, feeling drained. An open bazaar was good. No one to bribe then, to let them set up their rug. She picked up the rug and settled it on Dasis's back. Then they walked through the gate, together.

They unrolled their rug in the heat of the afternoon sun. Around them, the bazaar was at the height of midday activity. Goats bleated. Pigs squealed. Children laughed and conversation rose like sand in the wind. Stashie took out the poles and the small canopy they kept wrapped inside the rug and, with Dasis's help, assembled it. The canopy gave them needed shade and allowed them to work the entire day without heatstroke.

Because they arrived so late, they had had to take a space at the very edge of the bazaar. The bazaar itself was located on a side street which opened into a wide alley. Through the cracks between the buildings, Stashie could see the main thoroughfare—horses, carriages, people on foot, and people in sedans being carried by servants. She had never been in a large city and the sights entranced her more than she had thought possible.

Dasis tugged on her sleeve. "Stashie, let's finish setting up."

Dasis had placed their change pouch in the center of the rug. She sat at the edge of the shade. Stashie pulled the slates from her pocket, grabbed two rags and set them beside Dasis. Then she took out her chalk box and opened it.

The journey had damaged two of the chalks, breaking them in half. The colors were mixed, runnier than usual—thanks, probably, to her sweat. But they would do. She sat beside Dasis, legs crossed, palms resting on her knees and waited.

They didn't have to wait long. A thin, nervous-looking man with a scar under his chin trampled sand on the rug.

"Heart readers?" he asked.

Stashie nodded.

"One gold piece for a short reading, two for a long, and three for an in-depth look at your heart," Dasis said.

The man fished two gold pieces from his pocket. As he reached to place them in the pouch, Stashie touched his hand.

"Have you ever had your heart read before?"

"Stashie!" Dasis hissed.

"It's part of the procedure," she said calmly. Dasis knew the rules of the trade. She also tended to ignore them when she was hungry. Stashie had long ago learned the price of breaking rules.

"No," the man said. "But I was told that if I were to know myself, I needed my heart read."

"A heart reading does not show you the future. It does not give you luck. It only allows you to see through the masks into your own heart. And that can be painful. Do you understand?" Stashie kept her voice soft, even though her words were harsh.

The man nodded.

"Then sit," Dasis said and waved to a place in front of Stashie.

The man dropped his gold pieces into the pouch

and sat cross-legged in front of Stashie, knees touching her knees. Stashie set the slate on her lap and took his left hand, tracing the fingers and the lines until she felt a spark. She traveled through his arm into that spark, deep inside him, feeling his heart—being his heart. Inside him, she felt deep pain, cold, and warmth. If she wasn't careful, she would get lost inside him. She had to find her way back out. For a moment, she didn't know how. Then she remembered.

She willed her own hand to pick up a piece of chalk. She scratched the chalk along the slate, each movement bringing her out of his heart. Gradually she returned to her body, noting that her hand was finishing a sketch.

Chalk dust filled the air. Blue, gold, and red lines marked the slate. Her fingers hurt. She let go of the man's hand, and the sounds of the bazaar returned— talk, laughter, the rumble of wheels. Dasis took the slate from her, and Stashie had to lean back so that she didn't collapse.

Dasis studied the slate for a moment. Stashie leaned over to listen. What she drew never made sense to her. She only saw lines and squiggles, the same thing that the customer saw. Dasis wasn't able to reach into the heart and sketch it, but she could interpret the heart that Stashie saw—and would be able to do so as long as she and Stashie remained heart-bound lovers.

"Your heart is sore," Dasis said. "It has witnessed so much pain that it is beginning to frost over. There is a small red core in the center—a new love, perhaps, that can melt this frost if you let it. But you must let it and want it. The danger from the red is that it will burn you completely and the small, ancient pile of ash that I see toward the edge of your heart will become a group of live but dying sparks."

The man clutched his hands together. "I thought you didn't tell fortunes."

"We don't," Dasis said. "I tell you what is there now and where it might go. Any advice I give is a woman's advice, not a mystic's."

He glanced down at the slate. Stashie could see the

disappointment in his face that he could not see what Dasis did.

"Your heart is at a crisis point. It could become cool or burning hot—filled with passion or leached of love. Your choice."

The man reached for his gold pieces, as if he thought of taking them back, and then stopped himself. He stood rather shakily, and nodded his thanks. Then he disappeared into the crowd.

Dasis wiped off the slate. "I'd forgotten what new ones were like."

"At least there's gold," Stashie said. "And perhaps a place to sleep tonight."

Dasis nodded. She gave the slate back to Stashie.

"But, Dasis?" Stashie took the slate and set it beside her, then wiped her face with the back of her hand.

"Mmmm?"

"Don't ever start a new customer without the warning. It's not fair."

"It's fair when we need the money."

"No," Stashie said. "For if we lie, the money will be tainted. Promise me this, Dasis."

Dasis frowned. Stashie could see the anger in her partner's ·face. "I promise," she said. "Although it will probably cost us a good percentage of our day's earnings."

"Thank you." Stashie watched as a young family approached their rug and then turned away.

The rest of the afternoon went quickly. They read the spidered heart of a young woman ("cracked and about to shatter," said Dasis); the small, dried-out raisin-sized heart of an old man ("never loved," said Dasis); and the diamond-shaped heart of an elderly matron ("warmth lost to cruelty," said Dasis). As the sun began to set, they had six gold pieces in their pouch, more money than they had ever seen at one time.

"See?" Dasis said as she wiped off the last slate. "The city will do us good."

"The money will do us good," Stashie said. She closed her chalk box. "I don't like it here." She stood up and went for the canopy when she heard shuffling behind her.

"Heart readers? I thought only the King had heart readers."

Stashie whirled. Soldiers. Three of them clustered at the edge of the rug. She gripped the wooden canopy bar and willed herself not to shake. Dasis set her slate down and managed to look serene.

"Heart readers are common in lands south of here. Would you like us to do a reading?"

Stashie didn't move. She couldn't touch them. To touch one of them would send her screaming away in revulsion.

The spokesman laughed. "To see if we're little princelings? No, thanks."

He turned on his highly polished boots and walked away. The others followed. They moved with military precision and exactness. Stashie hadn't seen anything like that in ten years.

Dasis shook her head and stood up. She froze when she saw Stashie. "Stash?"

"I won't read for them." The words emerged slowly. Stashie wasn't even sure she spoke. "I don't care how much they pay us."

"Stashie, they're just clients—"

"No. They're not. And I will not sit there, calmly holding hands and linking up with the heart of one of those . . . things."

"They're too young to be the men who hurt you."

A splinter dug into Stashie's palm. It almost felt good. "They're the same kind of men. I will not touch them."

"It would be brief, and we could charge more."

Stashie glared at Dasis. She had tried to explain what happened once, but words were inadequate for the experience. Dasis had grown up in peace; her village had surrendered with few lives lost, conquered by someone other than Tarne. She had understood the words Stashie used, but not the depth of the pain.

"I don't care how much gold they give us," Stashie said. "I will not touch a man like that. Not ever."

She turned her back on Dasis and slowly, one concentrated movement at a time, tore down the canopy.

CHAPTER 5

Pardu lounged in the open doorway of the pavilion. A manservant stood beside him, swirling the hot dead air with an oversized fan. From his pillows, Pardu watched the desert. It had gained a tame look over the years, even though he knew it was still dangerous. Every time he saw the landscape, it took his breath away. He owned that land, and the land beyond it. Towns and villages and people all fell under his rule. He had seen more than half of the conquered countries, and none was as beautiful as the desert outside his windows.

He picked up a silken handkerchief and coughed into it, noting as he pulled his hand away the blood that flecked the soft blue cloth. Blood now for the past three months. The royal physicians said he would be fine, but the physicians cared more about their posts than the truth. He knew he was dying. He recognized it in the blood, in the increasing weight loss, in his growing exhaustion. He had sent for his sons because he knew that in a short time, he would either be dead or the gibbering fool his father had been during his last year of life.

And unlike his father, Pardu wanted to have the succession question settled before he died.

He closed his eyes and his brother's form loomed up in front of them. Tall, razor-thin, a voice like a trumpet, and so cunning. They had been inseparable from birth and then, that last day, when Pardu had brought his sword down—

He opened his eyes, and stared at the sand. All for land. Land and power and water, things his father had told him were important. Things that had never seemed to matter much after that last downstroke of the sword, the spurting of his brother's blood. No matter how much beauty he saw in the landscape, it didn't make up for the loss of his brother's counsel, his brother's company. His brother's love.

And now he was asking his sons to make the same choice. Death for one, power for the other. He should have killed one at birth, before he came to love them both. No barren landscape was worth the life of a son. Power seemed futile as death sucked the life from his bones and ate him away, inch by inch.

Perhaps he could share that with his sons, get them to work together, as they had always done. They were stronger together than they were separately. And when one died, the other would remain, strong and hearty and in control of his world.

Pardu picked up the handkerchief again, coughed, felt the blood spatter inside his mouth. Everything tasted of iron these days. He wanted to lie back, let the servants tend him, and his sons rule.

He wanted to die in peace.

CHAPTER 6

Radekir had been watching the new couple for nearly an hour. She sat cross-legged on her table, dice scattered around her, her turban-wrapped head already too hot. She hadn't seen heart readers for nearly a decade, not since her own partner had left her. The taller woman, slender and willowy, particularly caught Radekir's eye. Her movements contained a measure of fear, as if she expected something—or someone—to harm her.

The heat would be thick and the morning would be slow. Radekir pushed off her table and wandered through the throng of marketers toward the heart readers. Normally she enjoyed the small crowds. She eavesdropped on conversations, watched people barter and concentrated on reading movement. She had to. Dice reading was a fake magic, like so many at the bazaar. Her talent lay in picking the right details, reading people correctly, guessing at their characters and their futures. Most people who frequented the bazaar knew that the magicks were mostly fake. She wondered what they would do when they encountered the heart readers.

She snitched a pomegranate off one of the tables and then held up the fruit for the vendor to see. "I owe you one reading," Radekir shouted. The vendor smiled and nodded. He knew the readings were faked, but he also knew that he would probably get a mead from Radekir later.

Radekir sighed and pushed through the throng again. Body against body already sweating in the heat. She remembered the magic of heart reading, the way the sight flowed from her to her partner, the gasps of pain and shock as the readings rang true. Once they had read for a military governor who wanted to know if his second in command was capable of treachery. The second had been capable of it; whether or not he committed it was another matter. But she still recalled that moment of power when her actions held the key to a man's decision, when her magicks gave her the power she normally lacked.

She stopped before the heart readers' rug, uncertain about what to say or do next. She had come because she was drawn, not just to the profession, but to the frightened woman. The other woman, the rounded, more matronly one, smiled when she saw Radekir.

"May we help you?"

Radekir shook her head. "I came to wish you well. I'm Radekir, the dice reader. That's my table over there."

"I'm Dasis," the woman said, "and this is my partner, Stashie."

The tall woman turned. She froze when she saw Radekir and her gaze scanned Radekir's length. It took a moment for Radekir to realize that the other woman was trying to determine Radekir's gender. When Stashie realized that Radekir was female, she relaxed.

"Have you worked the bazaar long?" Dasis asked.

"Long enough," Radekir said. "The business is good. The townsfolk come through often and the soldiers change every few days. A lot of people travel through, which, I imagine, would be good for heart readers."

Dasis's smile became more sincere. "You've worked with heart readers."

Radekir nodded. She didn't want to admit her former status as a reader. That always led to questions about why she no longer read—and she didn't want to answer those.

Stashie came closer. Her face was beautiful: skin dark, eyes black, set deeply in high cheekbones. "You said a lot of soldiers go through here."

"And they spend money on fortunes."

Stashie bit her lower lip and looked away.

"You don't care for soldiers," Radekir said.

"Stashie's village was overtaken when she was younger. She lost her family," Dasis said.

Radekir kept her gaze on Stashie. The other woman's entire demeanor had frozen, as if that past moment still held her in thrall. "There are ways to keep the soldiers away," Radekir said.

Stashie tilted her head so that Radekir knew she had Stashie's attention.

"They're quite superstitious and tend to spread rumors among their ranks. If we start a story that you're bad luck to people in uniform, they'll stay away."

Stashie took a deep breath. Dasis frowned. "But the soldiers are the ones with the money."

"Sometimes," Radekir said. "But what is the worth of money gained at great personal expense?"

"We barely have enough to make it through the week," Dasis said. She sat down on her section of the rug and smoothed her skirts around herself. "We take the money we can get."

Stashie flinched. Dasis didn't seem to notice. Radekir wanted to reach out to Stashie, but didn't. Not yet. "Well, it's an idea," she said, "and I will help if I can."

"Thank you," Stashie whispered. Radekir thought she could see her own attraction reflected in Stashie's eyes.

Radekir nodded. She didn't want to get into the middle of something too personal. Or did she? A heart reader and an attraction. It boded well for the future.

The twilight brought a slight breeze that shifted the desert sands and took the force of the heat from the city. Radekir pocketed her gold and her dice, leaving her table to welcome the morning sun. The day had been better than she had hoped, and part of the reason had been her proximity to the heart readers. New people approached the heart readers continually, fill-ing their pouch and telling others of the new fortune-telling method. The newness spilled onto Radekir's table and she cast more fake fortunes than she had in days. She felt good. No matter what she was doing, she loved being in the bazaar.

She tied her pouch to her skirt, and was about to leave when a hand brushed her shoulder. Stashie stood behind her, eyes sunken into her lovely face.

"Let me get you some dinner," she said.

A little thrill ran up Radekir's back. "Let me cook," she said. "Your partner mentioned that you were short of money."

"We got enough today," Stashie said. "Dasis gave me coins enough. We should stay in public, though."

"She'd know if you and I did anything. You wouldn't be able to read."

Stashie's eyes widened. "Where did you learn so much about heart reading?"

"I was a reader myself once," Radekir said—and then mentally kicked herself. She wasn't going to admit that.

But Stashie merely nodded. "Then you understand why we can't meet in private. A partner's trust is almost as important as a partner's fidelity."

"Your partner doesn't understand you." Radekir tapped her pouch, then tucked a strand of hair beneath her turban.

"She understands what she needs to." Stashie touched Radekir's elbow, then pulled away as if she had been burned. "Let's go. Take me somewhere good."

They walked through the darkening streets. Tavern keepers were placing torches into their wall holders, the flames casting a bit of light in the narrow passageways. Most of the women had disappeared with the sun; only one night woman crossed their path. A half dozen soldiers laughed and joked along a side street. When Stashie saw them, her entire body became rigid. Radekir tried to touch her, but Stashie pulled away. The soldiers stole a torch from one of the tavern walls, and kept walking. Stashie didn't move until they were out of sight.

"How long ago did they hurt you?" Radekir asked quietly.

Stashie let out a breath that she had held for a long time. "Before I met Dasis. I was just a girl."

"Dasis said they killed your family. How did you survive?"

Stashie wrapped her arms around herself. "I made them kill my family. I didn't listen. I disobeyed. He let me live as punishment, I think. Then I escaped."

Radekir heard the reluctance in Stashie's tone, and realized that she wouldn't say much more. Radekir decided not to push. Dasis had probably pushed and that was why she seemed to know nothing of her partner's anguish. If Dasis did know, then she was too insensitive to be with such a fragile woman.

They stopped in front of the tavern without the light. "The soldiers won't come back here," Radekir said, "and the others won't find it without its light."

Stashie nodded and shoved her way in.

The open door sent a flood of light, noise, and food scents into the street. Radekir blinked once, then followed Stashie in. As she had suspected, they were the only women. Men turned from their positions on the benches, saw Radekir's turban and looked away, dismissing them because they were not night women. The tavern keep came forward, hands twisting in front of his stained shirt.

"Women use the back door," he said.

Stashie tensed. Radekir touched her arm. "We did not know," she said. "We won't make the mistake again. We would like some dinner."

"The back room," he said and waved a hand. "Through that door."

Radekir took Stashie's elbow and led her to the back. Four other women—all from the bazaar—sat at a round table, eating quietly. Radekir led Stashie to the bench beside the fireplace.

Radekir blessed her own skill at reading people's bodies. Stashie's spoke more than her mouth did.

"You've never been separated before?"

Stashie shook her head. "None of the provinces do this. Except—"

She frowned. Radekir waited. When Stashie said nothing else, Radekir said, "They did in your village."

Stashie swallowed. "After the soldiers came."

One of the night women came through the side door. She held a tray in one hand, two steaming dishes perched on top of it.

"I need your coin first," she said, extending her other hand.

Radekir reached into her pouch, but Stashie stopped her. "I said I would." She placed two gold coins in the night woman's hand. "Enough?"

"Enough to get you some mead, too." The night woman set the bowls down, revealing a rich, thick stew. She set a loaf of bread beside it. "I'll be back."

Stashie broke a piece of bread and scooped it into the stew. Her movements were quick. Radekir recognized a deeper hunger than she had seen. Radekir also took bread and dunked it in the stew. "You had a reason for wanting dinner with me," she said.

Stashie nodded, her mouth full. She continued to dunk and scoop, speaking around her food as she did. "I want to know about the soldiers."

"What makes you think I know anything about the soldiers?"

Stashie chewed for a moment, then licked her fingers. "You know more than I do."

The night woman brought the mead and set it beside them. Radekir took a sip. It was warm and honeyed.

"I want to know why they're here and what they've done and if they—" Stashie stopped herself. She grabbed more bread and scooped the remaining stew from her bowl.

"And if they what?"

Stashie shook her head. "I just want to know about them."

"To know if you have to fear them?"

Stashie jerked her head up. Her eyes had almost a

glaze to them. "I will always fear them. I have to know if I can read from them, if they will leave Dasis and me alone if I cooperate with them."

Radekir took another bite of stew. The meat was real, not gristle, and it added a depth of flavor that she wouldn't have expected in a tavern. "The soldiers come to the bazaar for recreation. They sometimes torment fruit sellers and people they need to bargain with. As I told you before, they're very superstitious. They treat fortune-tellers with a kind of awe. Luckily, most soldiers do not stay in town long enough to realize that the fortunes are fake."

"Readings aren't faked," Stashie said quietly. "We tell the truth about people."

"And you don't think the soldiers would want to hear truth about themselves."

Stashie took the mead cup and hid her face. Radekir reached out and touched her hair. It was as soft and silky as it looked.

"They're not very deep men," Radekir said. "Once they realize that you do not foretell the future, they will probably leave you alone. All they want to know is if they'll die on the next campaign or if they'll become a military governor or if they will find a fortune and escape. They don't care whether or not they have the capacity to love someone."

Stashie set the mead cup down. "So you're saying that if we do our job well for a few soldiers, the others will leave us alone."

"I think so." Radekir smiled. "I'd offer to do a dice reading for you, but the dice tell me nothing. All I know is what I observe from others."

"And what do you see when you look at me?" Stashie's face held an openness that Radekir hadn't expected. She ran a thumb along Stashie's soft cheek, wishing that she could touch this woman in other ways.

"I see a frightened woman," Radekir said, "who has never dealt with her fear. I see a strong woman, who has survived things that most of us have never dreamed of. And I see a beautiful woman, who believes that no one understands her."

Stashie's eyes glistened. She moved her face from Radekir's touch. "You don't read hearts anymore."

"My partner left me," Radekir said.

The words hung between them for a moment. Then Stashie wiped her fingers on her skirt and stood up. "Thank you for talking to me," she said. "I will see you tomorrow?"

Radekir nodded. She watched Stashie thread her way through the tables to the back door. Once Stashie left, Radekir picked up her own stew bowl. The food was still warm and her appetite had grown. Perhaps Dasis had helped Stashie once, but she was helping her no longer. The women had grown apart. All that held them together was their profession. Radekir could see many things. She could see relationships that were about to die.

But she couldn't tell if others were about to start. She had never heard of heart readers switching partners. She didn't know if it was possible. The lore said nothing about it. Heart readers were bonded sexually and emotionally. That bond allowed them to combine their talents and see into the hearts of others. First loves always had a magic to them that second loves never seemed to have. But perhaps second loves could form a stronger bond. Perhaps the magic was not necessary.

Radekir smiled. It was something to think about while she was at the bazaar, watching Stashie work from across the distance of a few tables. Perhaps Radekir would remember. Or perhaps she would find out.

CHAPTER 7

Tarne stood with his hands clasped behind his back, unused to the feeling of servitude. He waited in the heat outside Vasenu's pavilion. The sun beat on his unadorned head and sweat trickled down his back. He wasn't going to ask again if Vasenu knew that he had arrived. The princeling was acting the upstart, letting Tarne know his place.

The pavilion stood alone on the palace grounds, a hastily erected tent made of fine silks, filled with whatever riches the servants could find. Tarne had heard that the brothers' old rooms within the palace were being redecorated to suit the adult men rather than the boys they had been. Ele's pavilion was on the other side of the grounds, as if someone had wanted to keep the brothers separate.

By the time the servant summoned him, Tarne's entire body felt as if it were going to melt. As he followed the servant into the cool darkness, he had to blink twice. This pavilion smelled of sweet incense—probably something Vasenu had picked up on his travels. Tarne suppressed a sneeze.

The hallway was filled with braziers and cushions—standard-issue furniture. Apparently Vasenu had not had time to make the pavilion his home. The servant led Tarne through an oval-shaped opening that led into a wide chamber. Flowing silk covered the walls. A thick pallet rested on wooden slats and pillows were scattered about the room. The colors were light, reflecting instead of blocking the sun. The servant bent at the waist and backed out of the room. Tarne waited, inspecting with his eyes.

Off to the left stood a half-open door. Through it, he could see clothing and boots. This apparently was Vasenu's sleeping chamber, a barren place, even for a man newly returned from campaigns.

"You wished to see me, Tarne?"

Tarne whirled. Vasenu stood against the silk-covered walls, hands clasped, as if he had been there all along. Tarne wondered at the man's silent movements and thought perhaps he had underestimated the rooms after all.

"I came to discuss your father," Tarne said.

Vasenu pulled down a cushion and sat on it. Even though he had taken the subordinate position, he still seemed to be the one in control.

"My father sent you?"

"No." Tarne wished he had something to do with his hands. He felt awkward, standing in the center of the room, looking down at the princeling.

"Then we have nothing to say to each other," Vasenu said.

"On the contrary, Highness, I think we have much to discuss."

Vasenu tilted his head. He assumed the regal posture as easily as his father did. "I'm waiting."

"Your father brought you home for a reason. It is time, I think, to discuss the future, yours and your brother's."

"Your point?"

"I can help you. With my men and the people behind me, I can guarantee that you will have your father's place."

Vasenu's smile had no warmth. "And you will retain your position as second in command."

"Yes," Tarne said.

"And my brother?"

"I think we can get him to agree to this."

Vasenu nodded. "Get him to agree." He stood up, clasped his hands behind his back, and paced. "You can't use the tactics you used in some of the southern villages, because my brother has no women for you to rape. Your other techniques won't work either because, presumably, my father would already be dead and you wouldn't touch me. So murdering family is out. Pray, then, how would you coerce my brother into supporting my reign?"

"I think 'coerce' is the wrong word—"

"No." Vasenu stopped walking. "I've seen the results of your campaigns. Ruined families, destroyed villages. If that is what you believe conquered lands should be, then you have no right being in the position you are. My father has never been to these places. He sees only that there are no uprisings. But there are few children and even fewer families. The land is barren and produces little. And what it does produce, the villagers use for their own subsistence living. All they have is the water which the military governors send to Leanda by the barrel."

"Those are the results of war," Tarne said.

"Those are the results of a harsh military leader. A man who respects no one but himself."

Tarne held himself rigidly. "I have done good work for your father."

"You have done good work for yourself."

Tarne felt a frustration he hadn't felt since he conquered villagers. Vasenu had that same power the rebels had. The rebels that Tarne had broken. Perhaps that was why Vasenu fought him. He knew that Tarne could break him, too.

"I never campaigned in the northern lands. And now there's talk of uprising."

Vasneu nodded. "We worry about it because the north is the only conquered section that brings a profit to Leanda. The southern lands are a drain on our economy. Ironic. We went after them because they were rich in fruits and foodstuffs. Even the herd animals are gone."

"Your father and I—"

"Don't speak of my father again." Vasenu had softened his voice and somehow that made him seem more threatening. "He is alive and well, the firm ruler that he always was. You come into my chambers with an offer of treason, a way to betray both my father and my brother, and you do it in my father's name. You are a destroyer, Tarne, and for that alone, I would hate you. But you are working at destroying my lands and my home for your own personal gain. I would never work with you. I could never trust you. I find it hard to believe that my father does."

Tarne felt as if he had been slapped. He took in a slow breath, to keep himself calm.

"The audience is over," Vasenu said. "You may leave my chambers."

Tarne didn't move. Vasenu stared at him. For a moment, Tarne's hand fluttered near his sword. Then he let his hand drop. It served no purpose to kill this young man. At least, not while his father was alive.

Tarne turned and stalked out of the room into the incense-filled outer chamber. He didn't need direct combat with a princeling. He still had Vasenu's brother to visit. Only he wouldn't approach Ele as directly. Tarne's failure with Vasenu had been a lack of subtlety.

Tarne wouldn't make that mistake again.

CHAPTER 8

Dasis sat cross-legged on the rug. The heat rose through the sand, burning her legs despite the rug and the thickness of her skirts under her thighs. The morning had been long. The customers had been few and the flies heavy; she had brushed a number off her face in the past half hour alone.

Stashie had said almost nothing all morning. She had greeted the two customers they had, but otherwise sat in silence. Dasis had tried to draw her into conversation, but Stashie had replied in monosyllables.

Ever since the night before, Dasis had wanted to talk about Radekir. When she had returned to their room, Stashie had said nothing. When Dasis asked her, Stashie had smiled and said that they shared dinner and Radekir had assured her she had nothing to fear from the soldiers. Somehow Dasis didn't think that was all that had happened.

Dasis glanced at Radekir. The dice reader was sitting on her table, her turbaned head facing the crowd. The woman seemed too friendly, too nice. Dasis had seen something else in Radekir's eyes, something that made Dasis believe Radekir wasn't telling the entire truth.

Dasis hadn't told Stashie the entire truth either. The palace was just outside the city, and Dasis had heard that the King was looking for heart readers. The bazaar had been a good excuse to come to the city—it had paid off—but it had been merely an excuse.

She heard Stashie's slight intake of breath, and she turned, following her gaze. A soldier stood at the edge of their rug, his hat clasped in his hands. He was young—no more than sixteen or so. His face still had the rounded look of baby fat and a scraggly attempt at a beard dotted his cheeks.

"Hello," Dasis said. Stashie's hands dug into her thigh, pinching skin.

The boy nodded once. "I hear you can read character."

"We read hearts." Dasis stifled the urge to push Stashie's hand off her leg. "Sometimes that gives an indication of character."

"Will it tell me if I'm brave?" the boy asked.

"No." Stashie's tone was harsh.

The boy crushed his hat between his hands and was about to turn away. Under the protection of her skirt, Dasis did push Stashie's hand aside. "Heart reading doesn't answer specific questions," Dasis said. "You have to go to fortune-tellers for that. What heart reading will do is give you reasons and understanding about many things about yourself."

"I've been to fortune-tellers," the boy said. "They all tell me something different."

Dasis nodded, refraining from making a comment on fortune-telling. "Come sit," she said. "Let's see what we can do for you."

Stashie's face turned white and she pushed herself backward a little on the rug.

"He's a boy," Dasis hissed.

Stashie nodded and bit her lower lip. She set a slate on her lap and arranged her chalks. "Give me your left hand."

The boy sat in front of her and did as he was told. Stashie's fingers were shaking. She grabbed his finger so hard that the boy winced, and then she closed her eyes. Dasis watched, fascinated as she always was by Stashie's movements. The true magic seemed to come from Stashie's half of the work: the unreadable vision, marked down by chalk. That Dasis could understand that vision seemed less a miracle to her than the fact that the vision appeared.

Stashie's body sagged. She once said that she disappeared into the subject—lost in the other self. When

Dasis first saw this, she had grown frightened. She knew that Stashie was barely in her body. Sometimes she thought she witnessed a little death each time Stashie read. In the early days, Dasis would hold her breath until Stashie moved again.

Dasis found herself holding her breath this time. Stashie had been so reluctant to go inside the soldier. Maybe she would have trouble returning.

The boy's eyes had grown wide. His right hand had crept to his breast, as if he felt the invasion. He trembled but didn't move. Some subjects cried during this part. Others struggled. But Dasis had never seen one pull away. She didn't believe that breaking the union was possible.

Finally, Stashie's hand moved. Dasis let out the breath she had been holding. The boy's body visibly relaxed.

Stashie grabbed pink and red chalks and, with her left hand, began slashing at the slate. She swirled in some browns and pale whites. The boy watched her too, eyes wide. His right hand gripped his knee, but he managed to keep his left one steady.

After a moment, Stashie flung the slate at Dasis, and released the boy's hand as if it burned her. Her entire body was rigid. Dasis looked at the slate.

The heart Stashie had drawn was full and bruised. Lines of white ran along the bruises like scar tissue and the brown swirled in the middle as if the bruised areas had once been worse.

"Come here," she said softly, ignoring Stashie's distress.

The boy slid across the rug to sit in front of Dasis. He chewed on his lower lip.

"You have loved freely, but your love has been badly returned," Dasis said. "People have hurt you, over and over again, and still you love. Some of these bruises are fresh—and are probably the reason you became a soldier, right?"

The boy nodded. His eyes were red-rimmed.

"You have a very strong heart that bears its bruises well. You came to us asking if you were brave. Anyone who risks loving after being hurt as badly as you have is brave. I don't know if you will survive battles or show yourself to be a superior warrior, but if you follow your heart, you will always show an incredible measure of courage."

A tear slipped out of the corner of one of the boy's eyes. He swiped at it, nodded, and clasped Dasis's hand. "Thank you," he whispered. He took four gold pieces from his pocket and threw them into the pouch. He reached for Stashie but she flinched away from him. "Thank you both very much."

He grabbed his hat, stood, and wiped at his face once more. Then he summoned dignity as if it were a shield, stepped off the rug, and disappeared into the crowd.

Dasis smiled and turned to Stashie. Two spots of color dotted Stashie's cheeks. "You made me touch a soldier," she said.

"He was just a boy."

"Now. And then he'll go off and he'll kill children and what kind of heart will he have then? Bruises and scars and bravery. None of that will matter once he learns how to kill." Stashie got to her feet.

Dasis rose too, reaching for her. "Stashie—"

"Don't say anything. You don't understand. You'll never understand. You seem to think that all people are the same and they deserve the same treatment."

"I can't understand unless you talk to me," Dasis said.

Stashie studied her face for a moment. The color in Stashie's cheeks had risen to a flush. "I tried. But every time I think you grasp what I'm telling you, you invite a soldier over to have his heart read—or you make me come to a place that I don't want to be. This partnership is failing, Dasis."

Then Stashie whirled, skirts twirling around her, and ran, her bare feet leaving light prints in the dirt. Dasis gripped her own skirts and held tightly, watching Stashie push her way through the crowd, moving blindly. Dasis waited until she couldn't see Stashie anymore, then she eased back down, picked up the soldier's slate, and ran her fingers along its edges.

"They destroyed some part of her, you know."

Dasis looked up. Radekir was kneeling on the rug, her eyes wide against her dark skin. "What do you know of Stashie?"

"Only what she told me. Enough to realize that those soldiers from her past stole something precious from her, something she believes she'll never get back."

"They killed her family." Dasis's voice felt tight, almost as if she were defending herself against this woman.

"We all lose family," Radekir said. "But something happened to Stashie, or it happened in such a way as to take something else from her."

"She didn't tell you?" Dasis couldn't resist the question. Radekir acted as if she had known Stashie for years.

"I don't think she's told anyone."

"And you don't think I was wrong, making her read."

Radekir shrugged. "Insensitive, perhaps."

Dasis dropped the slate. "He was a child. He was just a baby when Stashie was hurt."

"He wears the same uniform."

Dasis's entire body felt tense. If she didn't control herself she would hurt Radekir. "What makes you think you understand my partner better than I do?"

"I observe people. You look at slates."

"You have to watch people to make your dice reading sound plausible." Dasis picked up the slate and wiped it furiously with her rag.

"That's right." Radekir's voice was soft. "But you glance at slates and think you understand the entire race. You wouldn't even be able to see without Stashie."

"What do you know about that?" Dasis said. "I had talent long before I met Stashie."

"But there's a reason she became your partner, isn't there?"

Dasis stood up and set the slate in a pile under the canopy. "Get off my rug," she said without turning around. "You're not welcome here anymore."

"Because I tell you the truth?"

"Because you want something." Dasis finally turned around and found that Radekir was standing too. "You don't care about me and you certainly don't care about Stashie. You want something from her, something you can't get on your own."

Radekir's eyes were level with Dasis's. "Are you sure about that? Or are you just jealous?"

"Get off the rug." Dasis kept her voice low.

"She's as welcome here as anyone else."

Dasis turned. Stashie stood behind her. A streak of dirt crossed her face, and in her hand she held a cluster of dates.

"Don't bully her just because she's decided to be my friend, Dasis." Stashie took one of the dates and tossed it to Radekir. "Ignore her. She gets jealous easily."

Radekir held up the date and smiled just a little. "I don't want to create problems," she said.

"The problems were already there."

Dasis looked at Stashie. The words had a finality to them that Dasis hadn't expected. She felt a slight coil of fear then, a trembling that surprised her.

Radekir noticed the expression. "I need to get back to my table. I've left it unattended too long."

Stashie tossed her another date. Radekir caught it, smiled, and winked. Then she pushed her way into the growing throng to return to her table.

"What do you mean that the problems were already there?" Dasis asked without taking her gaze from Radekir.

Stashie sat down and spread the dates on her lap. She took one and bit the end. "You don't understand me, Dasis. And you don't work with me."

"I can't work without you," Dasis said.

"No," Stashie said. "You tell me where we're going to go and how much money we're going to make. You demand that I work with soldiers—"

"If we don't, we invite suspicion."

"Then let's leave. Let's go somewhere where they won't suspect our politics just because we refuse some business."

Dasis wished that Stashie would give her a date. Just one, to share in the simple way she had shared with Radekir. "I don't know of anywhere like that anymore, do you, Stash?"

Stashie studied her hands. "There's got to be. Maybe in the north—"

"Rebellion's brewing in the north. Do you want to experience another war?"

Dasis regretted the words the moment she said them. They hung in the air like a death knell. Around them the sounds of the throng seemed to grow louder: people laughing, the snatches of gossip, voices raised in barter. If Stashie said anything, Dasis didn't think she'd be able to hear her.

Stashie sighed and reached out, her hand holding a date. Dasis took it and sat beside her.

"Why are we so mean to each other?" Stashie asked.

"I don't know," Dasis said. The date felt warm in her palm. She suddenly wasn't as hungry as she thought she was.

"There was a time when we could only do nice things for each other and we never fought. Do you remember?"

"I remember." Dasis closed her eyes. Stashie had been so small when they met. Stick-thin and all eyes. She didn't speak for the first several days and after Dasis had decided that Stashie couldn't speak at all, one morning she whispered her thanks. That had been the beginning. The entire time they had been together, Dasis had taken care of Stashie. And now that Stashie no longer wanted her to, Dasis didn't know what to do. "I think you want different things now, Stash."

"You mean Radekir."

Dasis opened her eyes. Stashie was glancing at her sideways, her expression unreadable.

"Maybe Radekir. But no. I meant in everything. You no longer want to read."

Stashie finished her date and set the pit aside. "I don't know what I want," she said quietly. "Maybe nothing at all."

Dasis nodded. She had squeezed her date until the juices ran along the inside of her palm. She took a cloth and wiped her hand, mixing chalk dust with the date juice.

"I didn't tell you what I heard," she said, not wanting to destroy the moment, but no longer able to hold the secret. "The king needs heart readers."

Stashie was silent for so long that Dasis was afraid she hadn't spoken loudly enough. "You knew that before we came," Stashie finally said.

"I had heard, yes."

"And even though you know what anguish that man has caused me, you still thought we could go in there and read." Stashie's voice rose with each word. "That's just what I was talking about. You don't think, Dasis."

"Yes, I do." Dasis kept her tone level, but she could not look at Stashie. "I thought we could make enough from that reading so we could quit. You wouldn't have to make these choices anymore."

"What made you think I could do the reading?" Stashie asked. "I don't care how much money is there. The reading itself would be impossible for me. Dasis—"

"Heart readers?" The man's voice was deep. He stood at the edge of the rug, his chin lifted, his manner used to command. He wore no uniform, but his robes were made of silk.

"Yes," Dasis said, wishing she could tell him to go away, but knowing she didn't dare.

"I would like to try a reading."

Dasis glanced at Stashie. Stashie cleared the dates from her lap and picked up her slate. The discussion was over. They were going back to work.

"Have a seat," Dasis said. And as she explained the procedure, she held herself rigidly, forcing herself to concentrate on the work, not the tension between herself and Stashie.

CHAPTER 9

Ele was resting by the baths. Tarne hesitated for a moment, then wandered over. He had been purposely avoiding Ele, uncertain how best to approach him. Vasenu's reaction had left Tarne shaken; he didn't want to alienate the other brother too.

All of the pools were empty. Ele was the only person lounging on the piles of cushions beside the water. The air was humid here, inviting people to slide into the baths and ease the tensions of the day.

Tarne sat on a pile of cushions. Ele's eyes were closed, his hands clasped on the back of his head. A servant was waving a fan and another had brought drinks to set beside the baths. Ele's skin was red and smooth; he looked as if he had been in the waters a long time.

Tarne half closed his eyes and rested for a moment. He didn't want it to look as if this move was deliberate. He wondered if Vasenu had said anything to his brother.

Ele rolled on his side and looked at Tarne. Tarne wondered how he had ever confused the brothers. Ele's face wasn't as harsh. He looked younger, as if the strains his brother had endured hadn't touched him.

"My father's most trusted adviser has time to rest?" Ele's voice, however, had the same mocking quality that Vasenu's did.

"We all need to rest," Tarne said. He closed his eyes all the way, as if he had no interest in conversation.

"I've done nothing but rest since we've returned. Do you know if my father will speak to us soon?"

A wisp of salty steam rose from the baths and enveloped Tarne, making him even hotter than he was. He longed to remove his uniform and truly rest, but he didn't dare. "I'm sure he will."

Tarne kept his voice calm. So Vasenu hadn't spoken to his brother. No one had. And despite what Vasenu said, the King still hadn't told them why he brought them home.

"My father is ill, isn't he?" Ele asked. "He looks very fragile."

Tarne frowned, then opened his eyes. The King had lost weight recently and his chronic cough seemed to have grown worse, but Tarne had never thought that meant the King was ill.

"He has been more tired than usual."

"Vasenu says he looks different because we haven't seen him for so long. But it seems to me as if he's withering away. He was always such a big man and now he seems so slight."

Tarne rubbed his eyes. The baths were too hot to sit by fully clothed. "Some of that is the effect of age and time."

Ele sighed and rolled onto his back. "You don't see it either."

"There is nothing to see." Tarne snapped his fingers at one of the servants, beckoning him closer so that the fan could drive away the steam. "Why are you so worried about this? Do you want to know what will happen when he dies?"

"I heard a story," Ele said, "that when Vasenu and I were born, Father hired heart readers to tell him which of us to kill. The heart readers couldn't read newborn hearts, so he told them he would wait until we became adults, kill one of us and make the other his heir."

Tarne clasped his hands together, not pushing the conversation, not willing to make the same mistakes he had made earlier. "You're asking me if that's so?"

Ele hadn't moved. "Is it?"

"I don't know. I was on campaigns in those years. I don't know what your father plans for his sons."

"But you're his most trusted adviser."

"Yes," Tarne said. He chose his words with caution. "But even my position is threatened should the King get sick and die."

Ele raised himself on one elbow and looked at Tarne. "So what do you plan to do?"

Tarne thought for a moment. He could answer truthfully and jeopardize walking into a trap, or he could take his time, work slowly to see if Ele was truly operating alone. "I plan to wait to see what happens when your father dies."

"No military uprisings? No coup?"

Tarne smiled. "If I were planning that, do you think I would tell you?"

Ele shook his head. "Vasenu said that you wanted one of us to work against the other so that you would have a place of power once Father died."

Tarne made himself remain still. So Vasenu was talking. Tarne had made a more serious mistake than he had thought. "Such a move would probably make sense," Tarne said, "when it became clear that your father had only a little time left. It's not clear now. Your father seems healthy to me."

"Are you saying that my brother lied?" Ele's voice had risen in pitch to that of a man expecting a fight.

"I'm saying that your brother might have misunderstood a conversation. He doesn't like me much."

"He saw the results of your campaigns in the south."

"So did you." Tarne snapped his fingers and the other servant came over. He took a drink off the tray. "Do you hate me too?"

"I think war brings out sides of men that we wouldn't normally see."

Tarne sipped the drink. It was cool. "I think you're probably right. But you didn't answer my question."

"If my brother and I hate you, you have no future here once my father dies, isn't that so?"

Tarne shrugged.

"So I am better off saying that I respect you to prevent some sort of subversive military action."

"There will probably be such an action anyway," Tarne said. "Leanda has never been ruled by a pair of twins, even though each ruler has once had a twin brother."

Ele wiped sweat from his face. "You're saying that my brother and I will war against each other?"

"If your father doesn't settle the succession question before he dies."

"If my brother and I war against each other, which side will you be on?"

"The side that wins."

Ele stared at him. Tarne smiled and set his drink on the parquet flooring. "Neither you nor your brother has military support," Tarne said. "Like it or not, the future ruler needs me."

"Things have time to change."

"Do they?" Tarne stood. "You're the one who said that your father looks ill. Was that just a pretense to get me into this conversation?"

Ele glanced away.

"I thought not," Tarne said. "I knew something had to be wrong for your father to call you back so soon." He walked over to Ele's cushions and looked down at the young man. "With or without you and your brother, I will retain my power," he said softly. "I'm the one with the military support. Remember that."

Then he walked away, feeling calmer than he had in days. This conversation went as the other one should have. Smoothly. Points made and measured. Vasenu might dismiss Tarne out of hand, but Ele would think about it.

And that was all Tarne needed. Just a little bit of thought from one brother.

Tarne smiled. He had started everything moving. Now all he had to do was follow it through.

CHAPTER 10

Pardu kept his eyes closed, unwilling to face the morning. The night had been long; he spent most of it pacing and spitting up blood. His pillows were damp with sweat, even though the heat of the day hadn't yet begun. He had never been this sick before, and the physicians were more concerned with their own reputations than with healing him.

As if he could be healed. His own father had died this way, withering into nothing, spitting out his insides day after day after day. Pardu recognized the pattern. He would have to choose for his sons because he didn't want them to make the same mistakes that he had.

He still remembered that morning. His brother, Megle, had brought in a fortune-teller in an attempt to negate the heart reading. Pardu still remembered his frustration, his feeling that the succession fight would never end. Whether he started the argument or not, he no longer knew, but he did know that Megle had pulled his sword first. Pardu had shoved his sword through Megle's heart almost before he realized what he had done.

He wiped the sweat from his eyes and staggered off the pillows, nearly losing his balance as he tried to stand. It would be a long day with his pretense of health. He sighed, then directed a servant to bring in his bath.

When his bathwater arrived, it felt tepid. He climbed in anyway and relaxed against the cedar sides of the tub. The room reflected his restless night. The pillows were in disarray and his clothing strewn about the floor. He would have to direct someone to do a thorough cleaning when he went out to face his day.

A knock at the door startled him. He had not ordered any breakfast and no one else would disturb him in his rooms.

"Yes?" he called.

"Father, I would like to speak with you." Vasenu. His voice was more powerful than Ele's.

"Come," Pardu said.

He didn't bother to cover himself up, but remained stretched in the cool bathwater. Vasenu stepped in. He wore the long, flowing robes of a king's son. His feet were encased in sandals, and yet he still had that military power and precision Pardu had noticed when the twins rode in. Vasenu glanced at his father, then looked straight ahead. But Pardu still noticed the slight shock in Vasenu's expression, shock at his father's condition.

"Why couldn't this wait until I held an audience?"

"Because I need to speak to you away from Tarne's presence. Are we alone?"

The cool water had grown chill. Pardu grabbed a towel and eased himself to a standing position. "We're alone. Sit and relax, Vasenu."

His son grabbed a cushion and folded his long body onto it. His expression, touched ever so slightly with fear, made him look like a little boy again.

"I know that you and Tarne are close," Vasenu began.

Pardu waved a hand. "No apologies," he said. "Just tell me what you need to say."

Vasenu nodded. Pardu wrapped a towel around his too-thin body and stepped out of the tub. When he grabbed a robe and slipped it over his head, Vasenu began to speak.

"Tarne showed up in my rooms a day or so ago. He asked me my plans after your death and told me that together he and I could defeat Ele and ensure my kingship."

The robe felt too hot, but Pardu left it on. He sat across from Vasenu. "Why bring this to me?"

"Because he's talking treason. He's talking as if you're going to die."

Pardu smiled. "I am going to die. Everyone does."

"But—"

"And if you look, you will see how very ill I have been. Then you will understand why I called you home."

Vasenu's face paled. "People thin with age."

"But they don't cough blood and have night sweats. My father died this way," Pardu said. "I think it is a family curse to have twins and to die off the battlefield."

"So you brought us home to settle the succession issue."

Pardu nodded. He was beginning to shiver under the robes, although he could feel the heat of the day touch his face like the warmth of an oven. "And to ensure that you were here when I died."

"Tarne knew this?"

Pardu clenched his hands. His sons shouldn't be this unobservant. "I told Tarne nothing. He just spent the time to figure this out."

Vasenu took a deep breath, held it, and glanced around the room as if he were seeing it for the first time. "Still," he said slowly, "Tarne should not have talked to me about taking rule away from my brother."

"Of course he should have." Pardu wrapped his robe tightly around himself, wishing he had the strength to stand. "And he should have spoken to Ele about the same thing."

A slight movement of Vasenu's head told Pardu that his assumption had been correct.

"Tarne's first priority is always to keep Tarne in power," Pardu said. "As long as he has that, he will be a good adviser and a strong ally."

"He told Ele that he had the military support to stage a coup."

Pardu suppressed a sigh. "And he does. The military is familiar with him. They don't know you, so why should they support you? I thought you had more sense than this, Vasenu."

"I didn't expect to find out that you were dying." The pain in Vasenu's voice sounded young, childlike. He had known from birth that Pardu's death meant the loss of his entire family. Pardu had given him that much.

"Expect it now and make plans," Pardu said. "For the kingdom is more important than any of us. We guard thousands of lives, ensure that hundreds of homes remain stable, that the land is rich. Our work matters more than our lives, do you understand?"

"Tarne doesn't understand that," Vasenu said. He still hadn't looked at Pardu.

"No, he doesn't." Pardu kept his voice soft. "And that is why he cannot take leadership from you or Ele. I have trained you two to take my place. You must not disappoint me."

Vasenu looked at him then, eyes lined with tears. "Who will take your place?" he asked softly. "Have you decided that?"

Pardu shook his head. "You haven't been here long enough for me to determine—if I can determine. But I can promise you this. I will live until this question is settled."

"You have no control over that," Vasenu said.

Pardu smiled, but the smile had no warmth. "My father died without determining succession. My brother and I tried fortune-tellers, heart readers, and agreements. None worked. So one afternoon I killed him. And the family's rule goes on."

Vasenu leaned back as if he had been slapped. "I couldn't kill Ele," he whispered. "We've been together since we were born."

"You do what you have to do," Pardu said. "If we don't settle this, either you'll kill him or he'll kill you."

"Or Tarne will take over."

"Which, at the moment, seems more likely." Pardu leaned against the cushion. The little strength he had summoned had left him. "Leave me now," he said, "and let your brother know that I wish to speak with him. We must get this process started."

Vasenu nodded and stood. He bowed once, then left. Pardu waited until his son's footsteps had faded before collapsing backward against the softness. He needed to think. Perhaps the traditional route was better—the route he had started on and then abandoned. If he called in heart readers and determined which son had the pure heart, he would have to kill the other.

Pardu sighed. He loved them both. He couldn't kill one, not even to save the other. He had lied to Vasenu. The country was not the most important thing to Pardu.

His sons were.

CHAPTER 11

Stashie sat in the shade, leaning against the cool mud-brick of one of the shops. The noonday sun beat on her sandaled feet, warming her instead of overheating her. She popped another grape into her mouth and glanced at Radekir.

Radekir had her eyes closed and her breathing was heavy. She always rested during noontime. The heat was nearly unbearable. Only a handful of customers appeared at that time, and they always had a specific goal in mind. People did not come specifically for Radekir's readings. Customers always stopped at her table on impulse, and impulse diminished as the sun climbed.

Stashie had started taking her breaks with Radekir. Few clients approached the heart readers during the noontime as well. Dasis believed that was because Stashie was away from her post; Stashie believed it to be the same cause as Radekir's. Dasis never left the rug, so Stashie usually brought her food.

"What're you staring at?" Radekir murmured.

Stashie started. She had been thinking so hard, she hadn't realized that she was still looking at Radekir. Radekir opened one eye and smiled. "You've been quiet lately."

"What happened between you and your partner?" Stashie asked.

Radekir opened her other eye and pushed herself upright against the wall. She took another grape and spent so long chewing it that Stashie thought she hadn't spoken loud enough. Finally, Radekir sighed. "Why do you want to know?"

"Because the only other heart readers I've ever met were the couple who trained us. They had been together for forty years. I never met someone who had split with her partner."

"I'm sure you have. Most of the people in the bazaars have tried heart reading at least once."

"I know that." Stashie slid her feet into the shade, and immediately felt cooler. "But most of them didn't have the skills. You had the skills. What happened?"

Radekir pulled a grape from the stem. She rolled the grape in her fingertips, then threw it and caught it repeatedly. "I was young," she said. "I thought all the magicks were real. So I went off on my own."

"You—?" Stashie leaned forward. "But I thought your partner left you."

"No." Radekir's voice was flat. "I left her, thinking I could do so much better on my own, without her constant nagging and pushing. I didn't know then just how good things were."

Stashie sucked on a grape. The fruit was cool against her tongue. "And now?"

Radekir smiled, but kept her gaze away from Stashie's. "Now I wish I had a partner, just to share this life with, to make it less stressful on me."

Stashie froze. If she wanted to get away from Dasis, here was her opportunity. She could leave her partner and get a new one. "Do you think you could read with a new partner?"

"I don't know." Radekir spoke softly. "I've never met anyone who has tried switching partners. But nothing in my training said it was impossible. Did anything in yours?"

Stashie thought for a moment, then shook her head. "No one even mentioned it."

Radekir took the last grape and stood up. "Charting new territory is always risky," she said, and walked away.

Stashie watched her return to the dice-reading table. Radekir was a beautiful woman in an exotic kind of way. Her lean body had almost a masculine attractiveness. She had a wisdom that Dasis had never had, and a willingness to understand Stashie. Stashie felt more comfortable than she had in years. And yet . . .

She glanced over at the rug. Dasis sat cross-legged, watching the bazaar's patrons pass. Stashie's heart still leapt when she saw Dasis, still felt that moment of warmth that she had never felt with any other person. In the training, she had been taught that the heart readers' bond was a sexual one, but Dasis had always insisted that there was more. If Stashie decided to go off on her own and leave Dasis behind, she might lead a life like Radekir's. If Stashie went with Radekir, she might never read again.

Stashie closed her eyes again. A small breeze rippled against her skin. No matter how much she loved Dasis, Dasis continually hurt her. This reading for the King made Stashie's stomach turn. She could barely hold the hand of a boy almost young enough to be her son because he wore the King's uniform. She couldn't imagine being in the same room with the man who had created the policies that killed her family. She would murder him herself.

Her fingers dug into the dirt. She used to dream of murdering Tarne, of catching him while he slept and running his own sword through his heart. Then she would rip off his head and stake it in the center of the village for all the world to see. Even that would have been too good for him.

A hand touched her leg. She jumped. Dasis bent over her. "No time to sleep, Stashie. We have readings to do."

Stashie glanced at the rug. No clients waited. She took a deep breath to still her heart. "I'll be over in a minute."

Dasis nodded and walked back to the rug. The crowd had grown thicker. The smell of bodies in the heat mixed with the smell of horses. Voices rose along with the dust. Stashie stood up and adjusted her skirts. The food and rest had left her drowsy. She started across the road when she bumped into someone. She tried to move around, but her arms were held fast.

"Mistress?" A man's voice. She looked up. Not a

man, but a boy. The boy soldier who had asked them to read. She shook herself free, stifling the urge to brush the sweat of his fingers from her arms.

"What?" she snapped.

The boy took a step backward. "I wanted to thank you for the reading. It has made a difference."

Stashie swallowed. Very few patrons came back with thanks. Most left angry and never returned. The boy did have the strengths that Dasis had seen in his heart drawing. "You're welcome," she said.

"If there's anything I can do . . ." His heat-flushed face had a look of sincerity.

Stashie paused and it seemed as if everything around her did too. The dust motes froze in the air; conversation stilled; even Dasis appeared motionless on the rug. "Yes," Stashie said. "Do you know of a soldier named Tarne?"

"I've never met him, but I know of him. He's the King's chief adviser."

The information seeped into her like water in the parched ground. "So he's always with the King."

The boy nodded. "He used to campaign, but those days are done. He's heading the military now and staying beside the King."

The dust motes rose and fell in the sunlight. Laughter braying from the far side of the bazaar carried across the air. Dasis leaned forward and opened the pouch. "Thank you," Stashie said, amazed that she could sound so calm. "I knew him when I was a young girl, and I wondered what had happened to him."

The boy stood awkwardly in front of her and it took Stashie a minute to realize that he was waiting for her to excuse him. Amazing the power that her readings sometimes gave her. She reached out to touch his hand, then pulled back. "I'll tell my partner that you came back," she said. "She'll appreciate it as much as I have."

The boy smiled. Stashie ducked into the crowd, allowing it to be a momentary buffer between herself and Dasis. Tarne was with the King. And the King needed heart readers.

CHAPTER 12

Tarne took his customary seat in the audience chamber. He had always hated the room. The main palace had two levels: one above ground and one below. The door to the audience chamber opened on the upper level, but the parquet floor sloped until the main, wide portion of the chamber was deep underground. Behind the chamber itself were tunnels, catacombs, and the dungeons, providing a dozen different ways for the King to escape in case of attack. But Tarne never felt safe here. He always felt as if the walls were closing in on him, as if the ground above would fall in.

The room itself had a damp chill in the late afternoon. The other advisers felt it too. Tarne watched them enter, wrapping their robes tighter around their bodies. They took their seats without looking at him. The advisers rarely met in the large room. They had their own chamber with its familiar privacy. This type of gathering was usually reserved for heads of state. Tarne's intelligence network should have informed him of such an arrival, but since it had not, he assumed that something else was happening.

A young boy servant, hands trembling, circled the room, lighting candles. He left a small trail of smoke behind him. Tarne watched, the closed-in feeling growing stronger. The boy disappeared through one of the side doors. Half a dozen guards entered from the main door and positioned themselves around the room. Tarne frowned. He hadn't given the order for those guards to appear.

The huge wooden doors swung closed behind the guards. The bang echoed in the overlarge chamber.

One of the elderly advisers jumped, then glanced about the room to see if anyone had noticed. Tarne met the old man's gaze. The old man blushed and looked away.

Fifteen men, most of whom Tarne had little time for. Fifteen men who owned the most land or who had helped the King with some major project in the past. Tarne sighed. All of them looked as confused as he did. The King usually confided in at least one of his advisers.

Another young servant entered through one of the side doors and lit the candles behind the dais. He then added extra cushions and disappeared again. After a moment, the royal physicians entered from behind the dais. They stood behind it, backs against the wall, hands clenched at their sides. The chief physician, Wydhe, was flushed as if in anger. Tarne's frown grew.

Finally the King's door opened, and Tarne felt a moment of relaxation before he saw who emerged. The twins. They wore full-dress uniforms, spit-polished boots, and the crest of their official rank as heirs. Vasenu wore red robes over his uniform, Ele, black. Their expressions were as solemn as the physicians' had been.

With a flare of trumpets from one of the back rooms, the King entered. He looked thinner than usual, his face paler. His robes were red and black— the official uniform for greeting heads of state. The advisers rose as a group and bowed. The King waved them back to their feet. He sat cross-legged on his cushion, followed by his sons. The advisers sat too. Only the physicians remained standing.

"I have called you," the King said, "to determine the most important question facing our land. I am dying. We need to establish succession."

As if to prove his point, he leaned forward and coughed. His entire body shuddered. Ele placed a hand on his father's arm, but the King shook it off.

"The physicians," he continued when he could get his breath, "have lied to me and to us, fearing that my mortality would cost them their jobs. Now that they are convinced that they will remain employed even though I have gotten ill, they are willing to comment on my health. "Wydhe?"

The chief physician's flush looked darker. Tarne suppressed a smile. He wished he could have been present for Wydhe's tongue-lashing. The man had always been too arrogant. Tarne would have liked to have seen his downfall.

"His Highness suffers from chronic cough, fever, and fatigue," Wydhe said. His voice squeaked in the upper register. "He has lost weight and appetite, and has difficulty sleeping. The symptoms are not serious in and of themselves, and we thought them signs of overwork. But when his Highness began coughing blood, we knew that his time here was limited. His father died of a similar disease. We know not what causes it nor have we any cure."

"There are women in the city that do healing," Delanu, one of the older advisers, said. He sat just behind Tarne, and Tarne resisted the urge to turn and face him. "Perhaps they are familiar with this disease."

"We tried such a thing with my father," the King said, "but it did nothing."

"As this disease progresses," Wydhe said, "the body rots and the mind goes. This process varies from individual to individual. The King could be with us for another week or several more years."

His words rang in the silence. None of the advisers moved. Finally, Wydhe returned to his place against the wall. He looked as if he had swallowed a foul-tasting drug. Tarne knew that Wydhe had spoken the truth about the disease; Tarne had seen it eat his own men from time to time. He wondered, however, what type of persuasion it took to get Wydhe to admit there was a disease that he could not cure.

"When my sons were born, I thought it wise to wait until they were of age before deciding who would succeed me." The King took both of his sons' hands. "I figured that one of the boys would show an aptitude for leadership and the other would not. I trained them equally, gave them the same advantages and advice. Ele and Vasenu are truly twins, however. Their skills are equal in all areas of leadership and both have expressed a desire to rule. Therefore, I must choose and choose wisely."

A younger adviser, Janu, stood for permission to speak. The King nodded at him. "We have discussed allowing both boys to share the rule. Why are we no longer considering that?"

Ele and Vasenu both sat straighter. Tarne held his breath. He wouldn't be able to run things as he had hoped if both sons ruled.

"After the heart readings, the fortune-tellings and the womb castings, my father found himself unable to choose between me and my twin brother. He set us up to rule together. We were fighting before his body grew cold. Our fight nearly caused the country to rupture. So he challenged me to a duel—and I killed him."

The words reverberated in the large room. Ele looked as if he had been slapped. Tarne clasped his hands together tightly. He remembered the tensions from that period. He had been just a young boy, but his father spoke repeatedly about the evils of civil war. His father had been a mere peasant and saw things from a peasant's perspective. Tarne understood the potential behind devisiveness.

The King coughed again. The sound wrenched through him, causing him to double over in agony. Neither son reached for him, nor did the physicians. The advisers sat on the floor below and stared, as if they could not believe his ill health. The cough hadn't been this serious before. The disease was progressing faster than Tarne had first thought.

The King took a deep lungful of air and sat up. No one else moved. He scanned the room, his gaze dispassionate, as if he had suddenly realized that his worth to this group of people had diminished. "I have called you here," he said, his voice stronger, more commanding, "not to make a decision, but to abide by one. Heart readers will determine which of my sons has the pure heart. The impure son will renounce his claim to the throne. If he does not do so, he will be put to death. There will be no campaigning and no favorites."

With this last statement, the King looked at Tarne. Tarne did not blink or flinch. Let the old man think what he wanted. Tarne would do as he pleased.

The King did not drop his gaze, either. "By the magicks that exist and the powers that surround us," he said, "I curse any man who interferes with this simple changeover in leadership."

Tarne struggled to keep his expression level. He did not believe in magicks or curses. He had been cursed hundreds of times before by people with more magical gifts than the King, and he had never felt the results of those curses. The King needed better safeguards than a simple curse to protect the ruling son.

The King held up his sons' hands. The princelings looked at him, identical expressions of surprise on their faces. "I need your public agreement to this," he said.

Vasenu took a deep breath and faced the advisers. "I will abide by the heart readers' decision." His voice was clear and firm.

Ele glanced at his imprisoned hand, then at his father. "I will abide by the decision also."

The King nodded, apparently satisfied. Tarne nodded too. Ele was reluctant. The weakness was clear.

Tarne unclenched his fingers. The King was truly blind. He had only one son who had the strength for leadership. Vasenu. Ele would never be able to rule on his own. He would need assistance, guidance. Ele would need Tarne. Vasenu would dismiss Tarne and strip his powers.

The heart readers had to declare Vasenu impure. And then Vasenu had to die.

CHAPTER 13

Dasis's hands were shaking. She reached out for Stashie who leaned against the door to the inn. "You're not angry with me?" Dasis asked again.

Stashie shook her head. The street was nearly empty. A few shopkeepers had come outside to prop open their doors and a handful of soldiers had walked by. The bazaar hadn't opened yet and most people were still asleep. The sun was a pink nub on the horizon and most of the torches had burned low.

"I don't understand." Dasis clasped her hands together, trying to keep them warm. The morning air smelled of baking bread and horse manure. "Two days ago you didn't want to do this."

"I hadn't thought it through," Stashie said. "With the money we get from the King, we can leave this place and find something better. Maybe even make a home."

Her words sounded convincing, but her expression remained flat. Dasis knew that Stashie wasn't telling her something, but she would wait until Stashie felt safe enough to talk to her. "Come with me then?" Dasis asked.

A light flared in Stashie's eyes and then died. "I'll do the readings. Don't ask me to do anything more."

Dasis nodded. She had pushed too far. She took Stashie's hand and pulled her into a hug. She was warm, but her body was unyielding. "I'll be back by evening. You'll be okay?" Dasis asked.

Stashie eased out of the hug, and smiled. "I can't remember when I last had a day free. I'm looking forward to it."

Dasis believed that. She released Stashie and began the slow walk to the edge of town where the King had set up a place to screen heart readers.

Dasis didn't know how many would try. In her entire life, she had only known a few heart readers. She wondered how long the King had been searching and how far the others had to travel.

Soldiers passed her, always walking in formations of four. Innkeepers, removing the spent torches, never gave the soldiers a glance. Even in the wealthy sections, where mud-brick houses stood instead of tents, soldiers paced the streets. Dasis had never realized how many soldiers there were in the city.

By the time she reached the edge of town, the sun had moved halfway up the sky and had burned off the morning chill. A small building surrounded by soldiers stood by itself. That fit the description of the place she had to go to. She was a bit surprised that no line waited outside, no one else was trying. Or perhaps there were so few, they were already gone, and she was too late.

She walked up to the soldier near the door—a boy not much older than the boy she and Stashie read—and stopped. He wore a half-cut uniform that left his legs, arms and most of his shoulders bare, but sweat still poured down his face. That and his light skin told Dasis that he had been raised in the northern lands and was not yet used to this climate.

"I'm a heart reader," she said.

"Where's your partner?"

Dasis had been waiting for that question. "I handle the business side of our partnership. She will be here for any readings. I understood there would be none today."

The young soldier said nothing, but instead pounded on the door with his right fist. It swung open a hair's-breadth. He leaned inside and said, "One more." The door closed.

The soldier looked straight ahead. Dasis waited, even though she had not been told to. After a few moments, the door opened again and two women emerged. Their skin was withered and burnt brown, and their slates, hidden in their robes, made them look heavier than they were. Dasis did not recognize them, but before she had a chance to say anything, the soldier shoved her inside.

The room was dark and smelled of incense. Somehow they had trapped the morning coolness inside. Dasis felt the sweat on her arms turn to goose bumps. Someone took her elbow. She started. Another soldier.

"This way," he said.

He led her through a small corridor into a room lit by two dozen candles. Three men sat inside; the two at the table looked the same. Dasis squinted for a moment before she saw differences—a line beneath one man's eye that didn't appear beneath the other, a quirk of the lips, a different hairstyle. Then she saw their robes and her heart nearly stopped. The King's sons.

The other man came forward. He was small and dark and wore the robes of a government official. "Where's your partner?"

"In the city," Dasis said. "She will only come for readings."

The man glanced over his shoulder at the sons. They watched without saying a word. "And why such a restriction?"

"She's afraid of soldiers." Dasis kept her voice level. "Soldiers murdered her family in front of her eyes when she was just a girl."

"And she wants to read for the King?" One of the brothers spoke. He had stepped forward, his polished boots making a scuffed sound against the dirt. She could see his clothing a bit more clearly now. A "V" had been embroidered on his shirt collar. Then she could name him.

"She doesn't want to read for the King, sire," Dasis said with a small courtesy. "She believes that we will be paid enough that we will not have to work again."

"And you believe this too?"

Dasis met his gaze. She hadn't seen such strength

come from a man's eyes before. "I *hope* that we will earn enough."

"How would you feel if my brother were to inherit because of your reading?"

Dasis looked from one to the other. Her mouth had gone dry. She forced herself to swallow. She had promised herself that she would answer everything truthfully. Shadows flickered across the men's faces. One of the candles near the far wall guttered. "I doubt things would change much for my partner and me, no matter who inherited," she said, her voice soft.

Vasenu smiled. Ele leaned his head against the wall, his expression hidden in darkness. The other man glanced at the brothers, visibly distressed. "Your name, mistress?" he asked.

"I'm Dasis," she said. "My partner is Stashie. You can find us at the bazaar."

She felt the dismissal and turned to go.

"Wait." The voice sounded almost like Vasenu's, but without the deep control. Ele. "We're not done with this woman."

She stopped and waited.

"Turn around, mistress." The other man sounded exasperated.

Slowly Dasis faced them. The tension in the room made her queasy. She glanced from one man to the other. They had powers she never even dreamed of. They could take her and make her disappear, and not even Stashie would know where to find her.

"Don't be afraid." Vasenu had come closer. He pulled over a chair and rested his foot on it. "We just want to know where you're from and how long you've been reading."

Dasis nodded. She swallowed again, and nearly choked on the dryness in her throat. "I come from Eother, one of the border towns. Stashie joined me shortly after her family died. Together we had a gift for seeing things more clearly than most people, so when some heart readers came to town, my mother took us to them. The readers didn't even do a reading of us. They pulled us aside and asked us if we wanted

to train. We did. We have been traveling now for ten
rainy seasons."

"Have you ever read for the King before?" Ele
again, his mouth hidden by shadows. He looked almost like a ghost man, a reflection of his brother. He
made Dasis nervous.

"No," she said. "We've never even been here before. Until now, we have avoided places with
soldiers."

"What changed?" the other man asked.

Dasis looked at him, unable to believe he had asked
the question. "There aren't many soldier-less places
left."

Her words hung in the room. Vasenu cleared his
throat. He looked as if he were having trouble suppressing a smile. "Would your partner be able to read
in front of soldiers?"

Dasis nodded. "She read a soldier a day or so ago.
She found it difficult, but possible."

Vasenu studied her for a moment. Dasis willed herself not to squirm. She forced herself to breathe regu-
larly. Finally, he nodded.

"We will do trial readings tomorrow. Bring your
partner."

The soldier who had escorted her in took her elbow
again. This time the dismissal was an actual one. Dasis
was about to promise that she would bring Stashie,
but the men were no longer looking at her. They were
engaged in a conversation, the words too soft for her
to hear. They were discussing her. She didn't want to
know what they were saying.

She let the soldier lead her back to the door. When
she stepped into the burning sunshine, she took a deep
breath. The goose bumps stayed on her arms and she
rubbed them to let the warmth seep in. She had been
nervous in the dark with those powerful men. Perhaps
Stashie wouldn't be able to read.

Perhaps Dasis had made the wrong choice, after all.

CHAPTER 14

Ele dipped his feet into the cool waters of the salt baths. The bath chamber was wide and dark, lit only by a few candles. The splashing echoed in the large room, and when he stopped moving, he could hear water dripping.

These baths always calmed him. They took the tension from his body and eased his tired muscles. Vasenu preferred the warm baths, but Ele thought the cool more appropriate to the climate—pulling the sweat from his body, easing the heat. Sometimes all it took was to get his feet wet and he would relax.

This time, however, it would take more.

He slipped into the water, felt it buoy him up and cradle him as if he were a baby. Only he had never been cradled as a child, never been held by someone who loved him. He didn't know who his mother was and his father had never held him, not once in thirty years. He and Vasenu used to huddle together for warmth and affection.

The kindest thing his father had ever done was to spare both brothers. The kindest and the cruelest.

The saltwater caressed Ele's skin, making him tingle. Still, he could feel the tension run like shivers through his body. For his entire life, he had felt the competition with Vasenu. He had striven to work harder, to perform better, to fight better, while Vasenu had done the same. They were equals in everything. And that had frustrated Ele, although not as much as watching the heart readers that morning.

He closed his eyes and mouth, rolled over and tried to submerge himself in the water's coolness. He couldn't go under very deep. His lungs expanded, feeling as if they might burst. Still he held himself down, wanting to test his limits, to know that he had pushed as far as he could.

Heart readers. Ignorant peasant women with a gift for flaming superstition. He and Vasenu had lived the same life. How could one have a pure heart when the other didn't?

Finally Ele came up for air. His expulsion of breath resounded around the room. Droplets flew, landing on the parquet floor. The candlelight seemed brighter now. He wiped the water from his eyes and rolled over onto his back.

The heart readers would find nothing, and his father would die. The country would be torn apart. He and Vasenu would fight each other, and everything he loved would disappear. No wonder tension shook him. No wonder he felt as if he were losing control. He was. His choices had narrowed.

He stood and shook the water out of his hair, then wandered to the side of the bath. He could, he supposed, renounce his claim to the throne, deny everything he had worked toward since he was a tiny boy. But would his father be proud of him then? Or would he think Ele a coward, striving only to save his own life?

Ele pulled himself out of the water and allowed the hot air to pull the drops off his skin. He buried his face against his damp knees. All of his choices required that he lose something: his throne, his brother, and his father. But Ele had been raised for this. He didn't know why he was having so much trouble.

Vasenu wasn't having any trouble. He knew his choices and he seemed comfortable with them. He had never once said to Ele that they should both rule, that they should continue to work together, just as they had always done.

Ele shook his head. He and Vasenu were probably equals in this too, in how much they wanted the power, in how much they wanted to compromise, and in how much they were willing to let someone else determine their fate.

CHAPTER 15

Stashie sat in the dirt, her skirts pulled over her legs and her knees against her chest. She leaned against the mud-brick wall of the building. Half a dozen women sat near her, and soldiers stood at the door. The brick was cool but the air baked. A trickle of sweat ran down her face, stinging as it traveled. She felt old. Her skin had pulled tight against her bones and her entire body ached.

She knew what caused the feeling. Fear. Too long buried fear. Dasis told her that nothing would happen during the readings, and Stashie supposed she was right. But that didn't stop her from trembling as she thought about sitting inside that small room, surrounded by soldiers, being forced to touch them.

A tremor ran down her back and she hugged herself tighter. They had been sitting in this line for nearly two hours. Dasis had tried to make conversation, but had given up a long time ago. She too leaned against the building, her eyes closed as if she were sleeping. But Stashie knew that she was listening. Dasis's body was too still for sleep, her breathing too uneven.

Other heart readers waited as well. Dasis had recognized one couple, the pair inside the building now. She said they had worked her village during Dasis's childhood. The others varied in age and size. A pair of old crones sat in the back, so enfeebled by age that they needed help to stand. Sometimes Stashie wished that the others would get the position. Other times, she hoped that she and Dasis would be able to read. She would make Dasis happy and get revenge at the same time.

Another bead of sweat ran down her cheek, feeling almost like a tear. She didn't wipe the bead away, preferring to let the sweat and dirt mar her features. She didn't need to look good for these soldiers, only to read well.

As if reading well mattered. All of the heart readers, if they were truly heart readers, would give the same reading of the same heart on the same day. It was a fixed magic—one based on truth instead of on lies like Radekir's. Stashie and Dasis had a gift, a gift of sight. The only thing these readings would show the King was which of the heart readers were frauds.

A hand clamped on Stashie's shoulder. She started, a scream trapped in her throat. She made herself look up very slowly.

A soldier looked down at her, his dark eyes dispassionate in his dust-covered face. "Wake your partner. You're next."

Stashie nodded, not trusting her voice. She shrugged her way out of his grasp and turned to Dasis. Dasis was already rubbing her eyes. She grabbed Stashie's hand and squeezed it, as if in reassurance. Stashie couldn't be reassured. Not now. And not by Dasis, who wanted them here.

Dasis stood and pulled Stashie up. Hand in hand, they followed the soldier into the cool building.

It took a moment for Stashie's eyes to adjust to the darkness. A table sat in the middle of the room, with two stools behind it. A dozen men lined up against the wall, leaving open areas shielded by sheer curtains. If she squinted, Stashie could see shapes moving behind the curtains and knew that she was being observed. A shiver ran through her. Perhaps the King was there. Perhaps Tarne was. The thought made her hands turn cold. Dasis must have felt it, for she squeezed hard.

The soldier pointed toward the table. Stashie gazed at it, her entire body motionless. They couldn't read behind a table. Dasis dropped her hand and grabbed the table's edge as if to move it aside. But there wasn't room. She let the table go and climbed on top of it, sitting cross-legged on her usual side.

"Stashie," she said, her whisper half a command.

Stashie forced herself to swallow, then came forward, placing her palms on the table. The rough wooden surface dug into her skin. She would rather have been on the ground, feeling the cool earth against her legs. But she had no choice. She hoisted herself on the table and sat beside Dasis, trying to ignore it as her entire body shook.

Dasis set out the slates and Stashie put her chalks in her lap. "We're ready," Dasis said.

Stashie took a deep breath. A soldier came forward, an older man, lines creasing his sun-darkened face. His eyes held no warmth and his expression showed his disdain for the entire procedure.

"Give my partner your left hand," Dasis said. They had planned that Stashie would not speak. She knew that she couldn't trust her voice.

He held out his left hand and Stashie took it. His fingers were calloused and hard *(digging into her already battered flesh with a strength she thought no man could have)*. She made herself take a deep breath, then she plunged into him.

He struggled like no subject ever had. She had to fight her way into his heart, fight past the barriers into his very soul. *(The calluses scraped her like knives as his fingers moved across her skin, tweaked a breast, held her shoulder firmly while another soldier towered above her, sunlight glinting off his armor. She wished she had no feeling from the legs down. She wished she had no feeling at all. . . .)*

Her memories, not his. She pushed, pushed again, and was suddenly inside. The pain rocked her, as did the need for affection. The need was so deep, she sank into it, wanting to fill it, then remembering *(the armor, the way they used her—)*.

She yanked herself out, felt her hand grab chalk. The hand was moving. She had to concentrate on the movement. Gradually, she became aware of her eyes, her entire body, the chill in the damp room.

Then she looked down. Brown marks. Yellow chalk. A touch of red. A small line of white. Stashie released his finger and shoved the slate at Dasis. She took three deep breaths to calm the nausea and resisted the urge to wipe her hand on her skirt.

"You've fought many years long and hard," Dasis said, "and saw things that your heart can't accept. Your heart is hidden beneath calluses as thick as those on your hand. Only a line of color here and there indicates the open passages into your soul. Soon your entire heart will be covered, protected, guarded. No love will get in and no love will get out."

A flush rose in the soldier's face. Stashie could see his building anger. Her trembling grew.

"Witch magic and lies," he hissed. "You planned this with the others. They told you what to say."

Stashie backed away toward the edge of the table. If he touched her, she would scream. She would grab a slate and bash it over his head, then she would take Dasis and run. Her hands reached the edge of the table and she nearly lost her balance.

He leaned against the table, his hands only inches away from Stashie's legs. "I don't know why we give women this power. I don't understand what true witchcraft they practice—"

"Quiet, Denlu," another soldier snapped with the voice of command.

Denlu froze and stood upright. Dasis caught Stashie's arm and held her in place.

"You are here because your King commands it. And you will listen, no matter how much it pains you."

"Yes, sir," Denlu said softly. He backed away from the edge of the table and returned to his post against the wall. Dasis put her hand against Stashie's spine and pushed her forward. Stashie's heart pounded against her chest. The pain in her joints grew.

"The next," Dasis said, her voice calm as if nothing had happened.

A young boy soldier stepped forward. His eyes were red rimmed, as if the last reading had touched him. Stashie glanced at Denlu before taking the boy's hand. The older soldier leaned against the wall, hands clasped behind his back, eyes staring straight ahead. Only the flush in his cheeks showed his continued anger.

Stashie took the boy's hand and felt the nausea rise again. She swallowed to suppress it, and followed the path up his arm.

He was easier than the other soldier. She found hope inside him, warmth. It felt so good to be warm. But beneath the hope, need. And the need trapped her. She let him hold her for a moment. Then she realized where she was. A soldier.

Her consciousness skittered backward even before her fingers began to move. She raced out of him, landing in her own body before her hand had completed the drawing. She felt the colors flow, felt relief when they stopped.

Blue. (*His hands were smooth, like Tylee's before the war, before battle had taken his leg, his head.*)

Pale pink, suggesting a softness.

Green.

Black. (*The color of dried blood around Tylee's neck. The fear and anger in his wide-open eyes. . . .*)

Dasis yanked the slate from her. Stashie dropped the boy's finger, caught Dasis's worried glance. Stashie bowed her head and gripped her knees hard to control herself. The memories hadn't been this strong in years. But then, she hadn't been around so many soldiers in years.

". . . a lot of fantasy," Dasis was saying. "Wishing that you could be loved, when in fact you are not. For to love, you must give in return. And the blackness covering your heart suggests that you are giving not love, but anger."

The tears lined the boy's eyes, and in spite of herself, Stashie felt compassion. Why had she chosen this profession? Why had she chosen to show people their insides and cause them such pain? Because she had had so much pain inflicted upon her?

She wiped her hands on her skirt and glanced at Denlu. He was staring at her, hatred so deep in his eyes that she recoiled from it. Dasis set the slate down and the boy returned to his post against the wall.

"Next," Dasis said.

"No." Stashie sounded harder than she expected. The room, which already held an abnormal silence, seemed to grow quieter. "These people are not willing to be read and we're doing a disservice to our profession by exposing them in front of their peers. We read volunteers. If there is a real and true volunteer, a man who *wants* his heart read, we will gladly help him. Otherwise, we have shown you what we can do. We will not inflict pain upon any others."

Dasis grabbed her hand. "Stashie."

Stashie looked at her. Dasis's eyes were wide. It was as if Stashie's fear had left her and rooted in Dasis. Stashie felt strong, stronger than she had all day. "We made vows when we became readers," she said. "We promised that we would never misuse our power, never inflict it upon the unwilling. And we're breaking that vow here."

Denlu's flush had faded. Stashie's words seemed to have startled him and calmed him. The boy wiped a tear from his eye. The soldier who had shushed Denlu nodded once. "You are free to go. But do not leave the city in case we need to contact you."

Stashie didn't need to hear anymore. She stuffed her chalks into her pocket and pushed the slates at Dasis. Her hands were shaking more than they ever had, and she was filled with a curious elation. She had stood up to soldiers and there had been no consequences.

At least, not yet.

CHAPTER 16

Stashie. Tarne frowned and leaned away from the curtain. Stashie. The name brought images of his last campaign. He stared at the woman as she packed the chalk into her skirt. Her movements were agitated, frightened, but her voice had been strong. He had to squint to see her eyes. Her eyes had the look of the ancients in them. He had known her once. He was sure of that.

The small observation room had grown hot. He knew that the princelings were in their rooms also, and that Pardu was looking on. He wished the King would trust him on this, would listen completely to Tarne's advice. But Pardu had his own ideas about this succession. He was trying to remake the past, trying to undo the death of his own brother.

The fact that he had murdered his brother.

Strange the things that dying caused a person to do. Tarne had seen that hundreds of times. The fear of death, the threat of death, and the act of dying all brought out the depth of character in each person. And Stashie . . .

Stashie had fought him.

He let out a breath of air. He remembered now. She had been a wisp of a girl, angry that he had killed her brother. He had had to teach her respect, and when she didn't learn it, he had had to punish her. The punishment had broken other women, left them gibbering in the streets. Some had never recovered. Stashie had passed out, near death, so bruised and bloody that the sight of her excited Tarne all over again. He had taken her again, all broken, thinking that that was how it felt to fuck the dead.

Only she hadn't died. He had thought she had crawled off into the desert to die, but somehow she lived, and sat in front of him, in the position to decide the very thing the King had denied him.

And she had been frightened. Very frightened. Tarne saw it in her shaking hands, in the stilled expression as she held Denlu's fingers. Tarne could smell fear, and Stashie had never lost hers.

He could use that.

He smiled a little as the next pair of heart readers entered. That fear would allow him to manipulate the proceedings in the very way the King didn't want, but in the way that would benefit Tarne the most. The secret was to pick them in a way that didn't make the King suspicious. Or Vasenu.

And he needed to completely terrorize Stashie. To bring back that fear and loathing that he had engendered so many years ago. If he did that, and threatened her again, she would cooperate. Her spirit wasn't completely broken, but it was damaged enough. He could use her. He knew he could.

CHAPTER 17

Pardu rubbed his eyes. His throat tickled from an afternoon of suppressing coughs and hiding his presence. Even now, in the spaciousness of his resting room, he felt the silence that had bound him through all the readings. Vasenu, sprawled on the divan, looked as tired as Pardu felt. Ele was half asleep on a pile of pillows, and Tarne—Tarne looked as if he had just discovered a state secret.

The resting room had been designed for afternoon naps. It was half underground, to retain the day's coolness, but windows faced the east and north, to catch a breeze. Servants with large plumed fans waited in the corners for Pardu's waved orders to start the air moving. He did nothing.

Pardu placed a pillow against his back and willed himself to be strong. The decision to use a heart reader had seemed so easy once. Now it felt as muddled as anything else. All of the readers had given the same interpretations of the guards' hearts. Moreover, the readings were consistent with the personalities of the men. Yet Pardu knew his sons, knew their personalities. He was using the readers to save himself a decision, just as his father had tried to do.

"I see no difference between the readers," Vasenu said. Ele opened one eye, and Tarne didn't even look over at him. "We could pick any of them and get the same result."

"No," Tarne said. "They think we're convinced now. They could come in and lie to make things go the way they want."

"So bring in all of them," Ele said. "That makes the most sense anyway."

Tarne shook his head. "They could plot together."

"You see conspiracies everywhere," Ele said, closing his eyes and leaning back.

"That's because he creates them." Vasenu's voice was flat.

Tarne gazed at Vasenu over Ele's head. Pardu could feel the hatred crackling in the room. "My job is to protect the King. I'm supposed to foresee problems."

"And he foresees them well," Pardu said. The tickle in his throat grew stronger and he coughed, just a little. He kept his breathing shallow so that he wouldn't have to cough again. He beckoned for water, and a servant left the room to get some for him.

The others said nothing. They were waiting for him to make the decision. He had put them on this path. He could, he supposed, take them off it. He could command his sons to work together or he could choose one. He could banish Tarne and pray that the kingdom survived his death. Or he could work with superstition and command, and see if the power of tradition would save all that he had worked for.

"Heart readers are not supposed to be biased," Pardu said.

"Heart readers are human," Ele said, hands clasped in his lap. He was pretending disinterest, but his responses gave him away.

"What of the girl who interrupted her reading because she felt as if she were compromising her principles?" Pardu asked. "She would give us an unbiased reading."

"No, she wouldn't," Tarne said. "Her family died in the wars. She hates us."

Vasenu nodded. "I heard her partner's interview. The girl is terrified of soldiers and of the house here."

"Then what has she to gain no matter who comes to power?" Ele asked. "Unless, of course, she conspires with good old Tarne here."

Pardu stood up, swayed for a moment, then caught his balance. The room seemed hotter than before. The girl hated them, and yet she had read and stood up for her principles. She had risked the soldiers' wrath to stand up for herself. Her family had died in the wars, so of all of the readers, she had the most understanding of war, and the most reason to prevent it happening again.

The servant came back into the room, carrying a pitcher and a hand-designed glass, part of a gift set from a neighboring country. Pardu took the water, grimacing at its warmth, and drank. It seeped down his aching throat, made the tickle momentarily stronger, then he felt it melt away. So little time, and such a major decision, one he would never see the results of. He wanted to keep living and here he had to plan for dying.

"We will go with the girl and her partner," he said, handing the glass back to the servant. "Their reading will determine which of my sons has the pure heart."

"And what if we both do?" The softness of Ele's tone belied the seriousness behind it. Pardu could hear his son's fear.

Pardu took a deep breath, then turned slowly. Ele had opened his eyes and he was leaning forward. Vasenu hadn't moved. Tarne's secret smile was back and it sent a shiver of unease down Pardu's back. "In all the history of our family," he said, "when twins are read, only one is pure."

"Things can change," Ele said.

"Not that much." Pardu sat back down, but a trickle of fear danced across his back. He remembered his brother's eyes, wide and frightened as the sword pierced him the final time. If the reading didn't work, his sons would face the same dilemma. Pardu hadn't had the courage to spare them that on the day they were born. And he didn't have the courage now.

Tarne was watching him as if he were trying to decipher Pardu's thoughts. Pardu would have to do something about Tarne as well. The man had served faithfully, but he wanted too much power. Somehow, Pardu had to prevent that.

"I want the girl and her partner," Pardu said. "And

I want the reading to take place as soon as possible, so that the decision will be made, and we can prepare for it."

"I still don't see why we can't decide it for ourselves," Ele mumbled.

Pardu sighed and looked away. Because otherwise, he thought, one of you will decide in a moment of passion, a moment you will regret for the rest of your overlong life.

CHAPTER 18

Stashie walked as fast as she could. The streets were narrower, more oppressive. As they got farther into town, the number of people grew. Stashie twisted so that she didn't have to touch them and half ran to avoid soldiers. Dasis had to struggle to keep up, but Stashie didn't care.

"You said you wanted to do this," Dasis said, her voice a whine. "You said you were willing to give it a try."

Stashie continued moving, pushing past people on their way to their own business. The heat made it hard to breathe, and when she did, she smelled sweat and fear. She tried to walk without brushing people, but she couldn't. Each touch made her flinch. Dasis kept reaching for her and she kept ducking away.

"You said—"

"I know what I said," Stashie snapped. She kept pushing, wanting nothing more than to return to the bazaar, pack up their rug, and leave this place. "I was wrong."

She barely had the strength to confront soldiers she had never seen before. She couldn't imagine what it would be like to stand in front of Tarne. She would probably freeze and he would have his way with her again. He would take her by the arms, throw her against the ground, push up her skirts . . .

"What happens if they choose us?" Dasis asked.

"Say no." The crowd kept getting thicker. Stashie felt as if she had already walked for miles. She needed something to drink. She needed to get away from people.

"Stash, they might get angry. They might try something."

Stashie stopped and took a deep breath. The air felt hot within her lungs. She clenched her fists and turned, keeping her entire body rigid. "And you don't think they'll get angry if, in the middle of the reading, I declare that I can't do it? Or if I go crazy and attack one of the guards? What would have happened today if that angry soldier had tried something? I would have run screaming from that place or—"

She stopped herself. Dasis had turned white, as if Stashie were hitting her. The crowd gave them a wide berth, two crazy women fighting in the middle of the street on a hot afternoon.

"Or?" Dasis prompted.

Stashie stared at her. Dasis really didn't understand. She couldn't see the pain that being in this city among these soldiers brought for Stashie. "Or," she said softly, "I might have killed him."

"Stash." Dasis used the same tone she would use talking with a small, hysterical child. "You're an adult woman. That happened a long time ago. You would act reasonably."

"Would I?" The street noises had disappeared. Stashie could no longer hear the hum of other conversations, the padding of feet on the dirt. She could hear her heart, though, pounding inside her chest. "I wish I could be as certain of that as you are."

Dasis bowed her head. Stashie pushed her way past the silent people and kept walking, not caring that Dasis hadn't moved. The crowd noises gradually eased back into her consciousness. Snippets of conversation, crying children, barking dogs all added a feeling of unreality. She glanced down at her hands, seeing the scars that had never properly healed. She had destroyed the skin on her fingers digging a grave for Tylee, a grave that Tarne and his soldiers had raped her on. Dasis said such things were a long time ago, as if they were a childhood illness, easily forgotten. Yet Stashie could close her eyes and see Tylee as if he were still alive, laughing with her, struggling, once he came home from the fighting, to exist with only one good leg. She had loved him like she had never loved anyone else, not even Dasis. She had tried to save him, and in doing so, had gotten him and her entire family killed.

She was a grown woman, but she would never act reasonably, not about this.

Finally, she could see the bazaar through the crowd. She shoved a woman aside, pushed past an elderly man. The rug still marked their spot, the place they had planned to return to finish the afternoon's readings. A few feet beyond, Radekir played with her dice. Stashie didn't glance back. She didn't care if Dasis saw her or not. She half walked, half ran the rest of the way to Radekir's table.

Radekir saw her, smiled, and got off the table. She reached out her hand. Stashie ran the rest of the way, wanting to take that hand, wanting someone to understand her. But when she reached Radekir, she ignored her hand entirely and slid into a hug, needing to feel a warm body against hers, a safe body, someone who wouldn't hurt her.

Radekir's hand caressed her hair. Tears rose in Stashie's eyes.

"It didn't go well," Radekir said, her tone making the question into a statement.

Stashie shook her head. She stepped out of the embrace, took a deep breath to explain, and the air hitched in her throat. She tried to speak, but the words wouldn't come.

Radekir grabbed her hand. "Come on," she said. "This isn't the place for this kind of talk. It wouldn't be good for business."

She grabbed her money pouch and led Stashie along. Stashie stumbled behind her like an obedient child. They walked to an inn, and Radekir led her up the dark, damp backstairs into a small room filled with pillows and dominated by one grimy window.

Radekir closed the door and shrugged. "Not much, but right now it's home."

Stashie felt wrapped in a cocoon of silence. She

stood by the door, unable to move. Radekir came to her and placed a hand on her cheek. "Did they hurt you?" she asked.

Stashie shook her head, then leaned into Radekir's palm. With her free hand, Radekir smoothed Stashie's hair away from her eyes. Stashie let herself ease into the touch, a soft touch, with no harsh memories of that awful afternoon, of those hands ripping her flesh, digging into her most private parts. She started to pull away, but Radekir held her.

"Shh," Radekir murmured, her lips against Stashie's ear. "It's okay now."

She kissed Stashie's ear ever so lightly and Stashie moaned. Radekir's lips moved down Stashie's neck, soothing the panic and awakening a warmth that Stashie hadn't felt in a long time.

"Relax," Radekir whispered. "I'm here. I'll take care of you."

Radekir's hands stroked Stashie's body, opening her blouse, releasing her skirt and letting it fall to the floor. Stashie felt the tension leave the places that Radekir touched, felt a kind of calm grow in her, a calm mixed with a passion that was building from the center of her stomach.

Radekir stepped back, her gaze very serious, as if she were waiting for Stashie to say no. Stashie said nothing, but waited in her silence, waited for Radekir to touch her again. When Radekir didn't move, Stashie reached forward and untied Radekir's blouse. It fell open, revealing her small, slightly upturned breasts. Stashie's finger caressed a nipple, and Radekir watched, her mouth open. Then she leaned forward and placed her lips on Stashie's. Stashie brought her hand up and pulled Radekir in tighter, and the kiss built. Their hands roamed all over each other, their clothing fell to the floor, and then Radekir again pulled away.

"You're free to go," she said. "In fact, you probably should."

Stashie gazed at Radekir's body, rosy with passion, and forced herself to listen. She should return to

Dasis, to the rug and the baking heat. But she didn't want to. She wanted to feel loved and understood for the first time ever. She wanted Radekir.

"Let me love you," Stashie said.

Radekir smiled and stepped back into the embrace, her body warm and comforting.

Stashie kissed her, letting the passion build, feeling as if the silence had been broken, forever.

CHAPTER 19

Dasis stood at the edge of the crowd. She was breathing hard and she was bruised from shoving her way after Stashie. Dasis felt as if she had made some kind of terrible mistake, as if in talking with Stashie she had hurt them worse than she had ever done before. And now she watched, from the safety of her rug, as Stashie let another woman hold her and soothe her.

Dasis wanted to run over to Radekir's table and pull her away, but she couldn't. Stashie would turn and see Dasis waiting there. Stashie would know that Dasis loved her, that Dasis was her partner, and that Dasis would help her.

But Stashie didn't turn. Stashie didn't even acknowledge Dasis's presence. Stashie let Radekir touch her, caress her, and she didn't even pull away.

Radekir's gaze met Dasis's over Stashie's shoulder. Dasis started to move forward, but the hatred in Radekir's eyes stopped her. If she stepped in at this moment, Stashie would be even angrier with her, and Radekir would back Stashie up. Dasis didn't move; she barely even breathed. She just watched as Radekir stepped back, took Stashie's hand and led her away.

Into the inn. Into her room.

To talk. All Stashie would do was talk. Dasis knew that. She had to trust her partner, to believe in her, and to love her no matter what.

Dasis sank slowly on the rug and buried her face in her knees. She had pushed Stashie away. She had forced Stashie to do something so horrible that Stashie would never speak to her again.

But Stashie had said she wanted to. She had had a

chance of mind. Dasis would have argued for the reading, but she wouldn't have forced Stashie. Stashie had claimed she wanted to go on her own.

She would wait for Stashie, and then when Stashie returned, they would talk. They would leave the city, if that was what Stashie wanted. They would even quit reading hearts if they had to. Only Dasis never wanted to face this kind of pain again. She didn't want to ever sit through another afternoon and worry that her partner would never return.

The sun had set before Dasis moved again. She had to wait until she felt Stashie's hand on her shoulder, until her partner came and comforted her. At times, Dasis wasn't sure why she needed comforting. She thought that Stashie had needed the comforting, had in fact received it. And then the pain would begin again, deep and rich and flowing.

Finally, the crowd noises dimmed, and then the sounds of the other bazaar folk packing their belongings began. A few of the people passed by her and some stopped. She could hear their breathing, feel the warmth of their bodies beside hers. When she didn't move, they went on, perhaps afraid of her stillness or perhaps they had seen Stashie's betrayal. Either way, she didn't want to talk with them, didn't need their sympathy.

She could tell the sun had disappeared when the ground radiated more heat than the air. She should have moved then—Stashie wouldn't return to the bazaar, she would return to the inn—but Dasis couldn't gather the strength. She shifted her position a little, eased the discomfort on her buttocks, and never raised her head.

Stashie had arrived too thin, bruised, and starving at Dasis's door. She never forgot the first time she saw Stashie: eyes wide and haunted in that cadaverous face, mobile mouth frozen in a position of pain. Dasis believed she could give Stashie what she needed, could help Stashie through whatever anguish had shredded her. That first night, though, Stashie said nothing, and as the weeks passed, she only dropped tidbits of information, as if the memories were so potent that just mentioning them would triple the pain. Finally Dasis had stopped asking, believing that Stashie would tell her when Stashie trusted her.

All Stashie had ever said was that soldiers had murdered her family, and had tried to destroy her. No details, no descriptions, nothing to aid Dasis's understanding of the trauma that had led Stashie to her.

Stashie sharing Radekir's touch bothered Dasis, but not as much as the thought of Stashie talking with Radekir, sharing information that Stashie had never tried to tell Dasis.

Dasis sighed, then froze. Footsteps crunched along the dirt path. Heavy footsteps. Unfamiliar. The sound of booted feet. Not Stashie at all.

Dasis didn't look up, but tried to make herself as tiny as possible. She knew better than to be out at night, in the open like tavern women. She simply hadn't thought, hadn't realized what the implications of the growing dark were.

The footsteps grew closer, then faded as the rug absorbed them. Dasis's heart pounded. She half expected Stashie. When the hand clamped on her shoulder, she did n't jump, but looked up slowly.

She had expected to see one person. She saw seven. All soldiers, their faces hidden by the darkness.

"Your name is Dasis?" one of them asked, and she thought she recognized his voice from the afternoon.

"Yes." The word scratched out of her throat, as if she had been sitting there for days instead of hours.

"And you have a partner named Stashie?"

The curious calm that Dasis had felt a moment before blossomed into something else, something that would overwhelm her if she let it. "Yes," Dasis said, repressing all of the questions, the panic-filled thoughts: *Is she all right? Have you hurt her? What have you done with her? Don't you know she fears you?*

The soldier might have seen the expression on her

face, for when he spoke, his voice sounded lighter than it had before. "You're to come with us."

"Where are we going?" Dasis's hands were shaking. As soon as she noticed it, the trembling spread through her arms and legs.

"To the building you were at earlier today for the auditions."

"Stashie's not here," Dasis said.

"We don't need her." Another soldier spoke. His voice had a harshness and an implied violence.

"We read hearts. I can't do that alone." Dasis stretched out her legs, startled to discover that her feet had gone to sleep. She couldn't run, not then. She would stumble across the dirt, fall, and make things worse.

"You're not coming to read," the first soldier said.

"Then why are you taking me?"

"The King's adviser would like to speak with you." The other soldier, the one whose voice added panic to the already edgy feeling in Dasis's stomach, took a step toward her. Dasis pushed herself backward, her hands touching the polished toe of a boot behind her. She looked up. Five more soldiers flanked her. She was completely surrounded.

"He needs to speak to both me and Stashie." Dasis's voice cracked, and a flush filled her cheeks. She hadn't wanted them to know she was frightened. That was the worst thing: To let them know how much they were terrifying her.

"You're coming with us," the first soldier said. "It's treason to say no to an adviser of the King."

"I don't go anywhere without my partner."

"And yet your partner's not here."

"She will be," Dasis said softly. But the words sounded false, even to herself. She knew, deep down, that Stashie wouldn't reappear. She might never appear again.

The grip on her left arm lessened, then a fiery pain slashed through it as the blood began to flow again. "We'll have you back," the violent one said, "long before your partner even realizes that you're gone."

The words made Dasis ache. They had no idea how likely that was.

"Enough talk," the kind one said. "We're taking you with us. We'll have you back soon."

Dasis looked around wildly, but saw no one. The streets were empty. Not even the tavern torches had been lit. People had seen the soldiers and stayed away. No one would help her. She wasn't even sure she could help herself. If she wrenched her arms free, she could run, but what would seven soldiers do when they caught her? She had heard the stories, seen the scars that Stashie bore, even though Stashie never told how she'd gotten them.

Dasis now felt the glimmerings of understanding what she had asked Stashie to do.

They pulled her forward and she made her feet move. Their footsteps around her sounded like an entire army on the march. They smelled of sweat and polish. The grip on her arms remained tight, painful. The men walked with no regard to her shorter stride.

The streets grew lighter and more populous as they walked. Torches hung from tavern doors. People laughed and joked, then stopped when they saw the soldiers. Dasis thought of yelling for help, thought of all the times she had seen the soldiers walking in a tight formation. She had never pitied the person they had dragged away, always assuming that the person had done something wrong. Stashie had known better. Stashie had stayed away from the soldiers, except when Dasis forced her.

They passed the building where Dasis and Stashie had done their reading that afternoon. Dasis tried to stop, but the soldiers pulled her forward.

"You said we were going here." Her voice came out too soft, almost frightened.

The violent one laughed. "We have another place to take you first."

They kept walking, toward the edge of the city, until she felt as if her feet would fall off. Finally they reached the city's outskirts. The palace rose, a fortress against the moonlight. The desert was cold, and Dasis still wore her day clothes. She shivered despite the heat of the seven bodies crowding her.

"You're taking me to the King?" she asked.

By now Stashie would have tried to return to her. Stashie would worry. She would rouse the inn, get Radekir (the thought sent a piercing pain through Dasis's chest), and find help. When they discovered that soldiers had taken Dasis, would Stashie wait? Or would she run? She certainly wouldn't be able to do anything to save Dasis. No one had power against the soldiers. Stashie had taught her that, and since Stashie believed it, she wouldn't even try.

They passed under a gate in the fortress. The desert smell fled, replaced by the scents of horses and too many people. A trembling started deep in Dasis's stomach. She wasn't sure she wanted to know why they had found her and dragged her away. But she knew that she was about to find out.

The soldiers brought her to a tent stationed just inside the fortress. As they pulled the flap back, she recognized the feel of silk against her skin. Sharp incense rose and tickled her nose. She blinked at the lights burning in holders at two ends of the tent. The ground was covered with ornate rugs and a large mound of pillows near the back. A man sat at the only table, his long legs stretched out before him.

"Leave us," he said.

The soldiers let go of her arms and backed out of the tent. She could see their silhouettes flanking the outside.

"You are Stashie's partner," he said. His voice had the deep rumble of a man accustomed to power.

The wariness Dasis felt had slid into confusion. Whatever was happening to her had something behind it. Something old.

"That means you are her lover." He got up, grabbed one of the candles, and placed it on the table. His face flared into view as easily as if he had lit a match beneath it. The sun had given his skin a curiously flat look. The lines around his mouth and eyes were not laugh lines. They had a more sinister depth.

A small white scar ran across his left cheekbone. But his eyes held her. His eyes glittered with a malevolence she had never seen in a person's face before. He draped one arm casually over the large pillow supporting his back. "I'm Tarne. I was her lover once. Her first lover. I doubt that she has forgotten me."

Dasis held herself rigid. She remembered now. Stashie, starved and abused, whispering his name with a hatred that Dasis hadn't heard before or since. Mumbled threats from nightmare-filled sleep. And once, just recently, from the lips of a boy soldier. "Oh, Stashie," Dasis murmured. She now understood why her partner had agreed to seeing the King. Not for Dasis, but for revenge.

"You know something?" His voice remained calm, interested, as if they were discussing whether or not the following day would be hot or if the King had been seen in the bazaar.

"I thought you were stationed outside Leanda."

He laughed. "A long time ago. Does she still speak of me? Is her memory that fresh?"

"She has only spoken of you once," Dasis said. "The day I met her. She hasn't mentioned you since."

He nodded and indicated a pillow. "Let's talk," he said.

She ignored his overture. "What do you want from me?"

"Do you know that Stashie was a virgin when I took her? I had her blood all over me, more than once. Do you find blood erotic?"

Dasis felt as if her heart would pound through her chest. But she wasn't going to let this man see that he had disturbed her. "I assume you brought me here for a reason," she said.

"She was beautiful, full of twice as much fire and passion as she showed this afternoon. She defended her brother and of course I had to kill him. That didn't quench her flames. When I touched her that night, she fought me, then gave in. She liked having a man inside her."

Dasis bit back the retorts that came to her lips. She

would wait until he let her know why he had brought her here. Then perhaps, she would know if she dared risk herself to protect Stashie's honor.

"I've never understood heart readers," he said. "Women touching women, claiming to have a power that men lack."

"There can be male partners," Dasis said.

"But never all-male heart-reading teams. And few men would debase themselves by doing women's work. Magic is a tool for the powerless, wouldn't you agree?"

Dasis felt a spark of understanding rise. "The King believes in it."

"And he is dying. What else could make a man feel so powerless as watching his life ebb from him and being unable to stop it?" Tarne chuckled. "No. Succession should be decided by strength, not by magicks or blood. The King's sons have no power. They were mere children until a few days ago when they discovered that their father was dying. Now they're frightened children."

"What do you want from me?" Dasis asked, even though she thought she knew. With the knowledge came a kind of calm.

"I took Stashie every night, and still she fought me, long after the other rebels in the village had grown quiet." His eyes glittered in the candlelight. "She never told you this. You look interested."

"I find it fascinating when people justify their perversions."

He smiled. "She has found a match in you. Or perhaps you remind her of what she was. Your fire is softer than hers was. I couldn't stop her from disobeying me. I tied her to the top of her brother's grave and I let my men draw blood from her. Twenty-five of them. Some twice. Many women wouldn't live through that."

Dasis shuddered in spite of herself. Never in her wildest imaginings had she thought of this. "She escaped."

He shrugged. "I let her go. She had been soiled. Once a spirit is broken, I don't care for it anymore."

"And yet you brought me here tonight."

"Yes." He stood, walked over to her. He was shorter than she had thought he would be, his head barely reaching the top of the tent. He took her hand, and held it like a lover would. His fingers and palm were lined with calluses. She wondered if he could feel her fear. "You're going to be reading for the King. They'll contact you in the next few days. The King thought Stashie's spark admirable, and Vasenu, his son, thought she would have no reason to manipulate the outcome. You, of course, are part of the package. And they know nothing about me."

Dasis resisted the urge to pull her hand away. His touch made her stomach turn. "What do you want?"

"Have you ever had a man before?" he asked gently. His other hand stroked her cheek, slid down her neck and into her blouse, cupping one breast. She remained still, but couldn't stop a grimace from passing over her face. "No? Then you don't know what it's like to be really touched"—he pulled down her blouse, leaving her breasts free, then ran his hand on the outside of her skirt, digging his finger between her legs—"here, the way a woman should be touched."

"Do that," Dasis said, keeping her voice calm, "and I won't be able to read in front of the King. Our power is based on our sexual connection. I am Stashie's first *lover*. If I weren't, we wouldn't be able to read at all. All you did was abuse her. That's not love."

"Then it shouldn't affect your readings either. I feel no love for a woman like you." He shoved her away from him. She had to take a step backward to keep from falling. "One of the King's sons must inherit to allow the old man to die in peace, and to lull his advisers into thinking that all will be well in the Kingdom."

"You have other plans?"

He glanced at her. His face became flatter somehow, and she knew with a sudden certainty that anger was the only emotion he knew how to feel and how to use.

"I am not going to remain an adviser for the rest of my life," he said, his tone as flat as his expression. "There is power here, and I plan to use it."

"We can't read your heart. There would be no reason to." Dasis didn't move to cover herself. She didn't want to provoke him further.

"You don't have to. You will read the twins' hearts, and then, no matter what you see, you will say that the King's son Ele has the purest heart."

"And if I refuse?"

His smile didn't reach his eyes. "I will make you my woman. I will parade you in front of your friend Stashie. I will beat you and rape you in public. I will let my men use you. I doubt you are as strong as your friend. I think that twenty-five men would take your mind as well as your female purity."

Dasis swallowed air. The image was very clear to her. He would break her spirit—and destroy Stashie at the same time. Stashie had walled part of herself off. She could take the abuse. But she wouldn't be able to watch it happen to someone she loved. "Sounds like hell for you too," she said.

He laughed. The sound had a ring to it that spoke of warmth and good times. She shivered again. The mirth in his laugh frightened her more than almost everything else had. "You're attractive enough," he said. "And it won't take that long to break you."

"Unless . . ."

He froze, clearly not expecting her to speak. "Unless?"

"Unless I like it." She forced the words out, even though they repulsed her.

He looked at her as if he were seeing her for the first time. For a moment, she felt like he saw her as an equal, someone who actually had a chance of besting him. Then he smiled a very slow, measured smile. "Don't worry," he said. "I'll make sure that you won't like it at all."

CHAPTER 20

Stashie rested in the warmth of Radekir's arms. Radekir was longer than Dasis, more angular, her scent spicier. The differences had aroused Stashie, made the lovemaking continue longer than it had in a long time. Stashie was sweat-covered, spent, and more comfortable than she had ever been.

The room had grown completely dark. Stashie could barely see Radekir. Her even breathing was relaxing, and the gentle movement of one thumb along Stashie's spine took the tension with it.

If she hadn't come up here, she would have been sharing a hostile meal with Dasis. They would sit on their bench in the inn and not speak to each other, concentrating on the stew and the other's silence.

Dasis. Darkness. Stashie felt the tension return.

"Radekir?" she said.

"Hmmm?"

"Dasis is waiting for me."

"Let her wait."

Stashie took a slow breath. Dasis had hurt her, but Stashie couldn't stay away an entire night. Dasis would panic, think that something had happened. Stashie couldn't cause that.

"I have to go," Stashie said. She sat up. Goose bumps rose on her flesh as the chill air replaced Radekir's warmth.

"She'll know what happened," Radekir said. "If not tonight, then tomorrow when you try to read. You're not going to change this, are you?"

Stashie didn't move. She couldn't do that—go from one woman's bed to another. She had to talk to Dasis.

Stashie owed her that much. A discussion for all those years they'd been together. They would decide what was going to happen from there.

"I want you to stay with me," Radekir said.

Stashie rolled off the pillows, her feet touching the cool floor. She couldn't do that. She and Dasis had been together too long. And yet, she wasn't happy anymore. She didn't want to read in this city, and Dasis never listened to her. Perhaps it would be better if she left.

"I don't know," she said.

"We could leave Leanda, travel someplace without soldiers, someplace quiet. Do some readings . . ."

"No." Stashie grabbed her skirt. She couldn't read with anyone but Dasis. "There are no places without soldiers anymore."

"I'm sure we could find something." Radekir rose and leaned on one elbow. "Stashie, Dasis doesn't understand you. I do."

"If you did," Stashie said, slipping on her blouse and tucking it into her skirt, "then you wouldn't push me like this."

Radekir didn't move, but Stashie could sense a sudden chill in the room. "I thought you wanted me," Radekir said.

"I do."

"And I thought you wanted to be with me."

"I like you," Stashie said. The darkness seemed to be growing. She had to find Dasis, before Dasis panicked.

"Then stay," Radekir said.

Stashie didn't feel even a pull. She smoothed back her hair with one hand and opened the door. "I'll see you in the morning," she said and closed the door behind her.

A single torch burned in the corridor. The faint smell of smoke filled the air. The dim light made Stashie squint. She adjusted her clothing. Her body throbbed. She felt as if anyone who saw her would know what she had just done.

No one stood in the main hall. It was later than she

thought. As she stepped outside, the midnight chill hit her full force. Goose bumps rose on her bare arms. She rubbed them, willing the chill away. The torches burned low and the streets were empty. Dasis had probably panicked a long time ago.

Stashie let out a small sigh. Radekir had been so warm, so sympathetic, so different. But a moment ago, Stashie wanted Dasis. She wanted the comfort of their familiar relationship; the soft kisses before they dressed, the unspoken understandings that came from so many years together.

She headed down the street toward their inn. She was trembling, and not just with the cold. What if Radekir were wrong? What if Stashie would not be able to read again? Dasis would never forgive her. Stashie would have injured their love and taken away their livelihood with the same act.

Stashie shook her head. She had been stupid. She had allowed a difficult day, old memories, and fears to jeopardize everything she had.

Something white caught her attention. The torchlight was too dim and she wasn't able to see clearly. She was near the area of the bazaar. She recognized the open space, the lack of nearby buildings. It looked alien in its emptiness. When she and Dasis arrived in the mornings, just as the sun rose, people had already set up their rugs and booths.

The white thing shimmered, like the heat visions she had seen when she crossed the desert so many years ago. She squinted, then frowned. It was a rug. Someone had left a rug.

Odd. People who worked the bazaar treasured the few possessions that they had. No one would willingly leave a rug, and the others would go out of their way to retrieve a lost possession. Bazaar people watched out for each other.

She swallowed, then made herself move forward. The rug's shimmer stopped; a trick of the strange light. She had to walk farther than she had planned, almost to the bazaar's outer edge, where she and Dasis sat every day.

Stashie's entire throat had gone dry. She ran the last few feet, then stopped at the rug's edge, eyes closed. The darkness was playing tricks on her. Dasis would never leave the rug. They had woven it together, the year they had started to read. Stashie slowly sank to her knees. If she opened her eyes and looked, the weave would be unfamiliar. Someone else had left the rug. They had to have.

She opened her eyes, hand poised above the rug's fringe. The weave bore a thin plait of blue. Dasis had added it as a touch of whimsy. Whimsy. That had left their relationship too.

Stashie touched the fringe. It felt soft, almost foreign. Dasis had left the rug. Had she left the slates in the room? Would Stashie find pieces of chalk scattered across the road? Was this Dasis's way of saying everything had ended?

Stashie bowed her head. She had wanted to talk first, before anyone had decided anything. She hadn't realized that Dasis would be so hurt.

"Mistress?"

Stashie started. The voice had come from behind her. She had thought she was alone. She rocked on her heels and rose, breathing slowly so that she remained calm.

The man who stood in front of her had a patch over one eye. His silver-gray hair curled around his forehead. She had spoken to him twice before; he vended fresh fruits on the other side of the bazaar.

"I've been waiting for you," he said. "I was beginning to think you were gone too."

"Too?" Stashie's voice broke. She had been too self-absorbed to think that something else might have happened to Dasis. Something that had nothing to do with Stashie.

"Your partner returned shortly after you left," he said. She thought she could hear faint disapproval in his tone. She forced herself to keep breathing slowly. "She waited for you for hours here."

Stashie's shoulders tightened. Dasis had panicked a

long time ago, then. While Stashie rolled in Radekir's arms.

"The sun started to set, and some approached her to get her to pack up, take care of herself. But she didn't even acknowledge them."

The chill seemed to grow. Stashie wrapped her arms around her waist to keep herself warm.

"My partner was bargaining for the last of our produce when I happened to look over here. Your partner was surrounded by soldiers and—"

"Soldiers?" Stashie's voice emerged in a half-whisper.

He nodded. "They took her with them some time ago."

Soldiers. Stashie remembered the sun shining on their armor, the stink of sweat and horses. She remembered the rough, callused hands stroking her skin, and the braying, mirthless laughter. "Did they hurt her?"

"Not while I was watching," he said. "They surrounded her, talked to her, and then took her with them. There were seven of them. There was nothing I could do."

Stashie extended a trembling hand to him. "You waited for me. That was enough."

He took her hand and squeezed it. His fingers were soft and warm. "I would hope someone would do that for me if something happened to my partner. I'm going to have to go now," he said.

"I know." Her entire body felt empty. She bent down and began rolling the rug, thankful to have something to keep her hands busy. "Thank you for waiting for me."

He nodded, then disappeared into the darkness. Stashie rolled the rug, creeping behind it on her knees in the dirt.

Dasis was gone. Taken by soldiers. They would take her into a small room, beat her and rape her, then take her outside and—

No. Stashie shook her head a little. They couldn't. This was Leanda. The people here didn't fear the soldiers, not like she had. She and Dasis had just read for the King. Perhaps he wanted a new reading. Perhaps they needed more information.

Perhaps they had taken her to the room, abused her, and left her for dead. Stashie had to see. She had to know.

Even if she didn't want to.

CHAPTER 21

Pardu couldn't breathe. The air stalled in his lungs—
and it was hot, too hot, even though he was surrounded by darkness. The pillows stuck to his back
and he could feel the sweat pooling around his legs.
Finally, he forced himself to exhale, and the coughs
followed: deep, racking, painful, starting at the bottom of his chest and burning their way up.

"Sire?"

A man's voice. One he should recognize. The curtains had been pulled back and a silhouette stood in
the doorway. A silhouette holding a lamp.

"Sire?"

Pardu couldn't stop coughing. He felt as if he
couldn't get enough air, but he couldn't breathe in.
Inhaling made the coughing worse. He was growing
dizzy—and the pillows, the damn pillows—were stuck
to his skin. He had to get them off. He had to breathe.
He had to—

Cool hands on his shoulders easing him back. A cup
at his lips.

"Drink, sire."

He pushed the cup away, felt liquid splash on his
chest. Immediately he got cold, too cold for the in-
doors, even in darkness.

"Sire, please."

The coughing finally stopped. He took a shallow
breath, hesitant, afraid that the pain would start again.
By the gods, he was cold. He reached for a covering,
wondering why the pillows moved with him. Perhaps
he wasn't as far upright as he had thought. And he
was thirsty.

"Sire?"

He jumped. Someone was there with him. Someone he knew. He squinted. A light sat on the floor, at the edge of a spray of blood. His personal servant, Aene, knelt on the pillows beside Pardu. Aene had blood on his knees, his thighs.

"What happened?" Pardu whispered, feeling the tickle in the back of his throat, fearing it. His mouth tasted coppery and he was so thirsty.

"You were ill, sire." Aene held out a cup. "I brought you some wine."

So that was what had spilled. The wine. Pardu took the cup, amazed at how badly his hands were shaking. He was breathing easier now, but the threat of another cough hung in the back of his throat.

He sipped once, felt the liquid go down and soothe the itch. Then he breathed—in and out—deeply and slowly. Better. He was feeling better.

"Did I spill the wine?" he asked.

"A little, sire. I'll clean off your chest in a moment."

Chest? Pardu touched himself, feeling the ribs poke through, the sticky wine on his too soft, too old skin. "You need to get the floor too," he said. "And yourself. I'm sorry for the mess, Aene."

"It's not wine, sire." Aene's voice was soft. Pardu wasn't sure he heard correctly.

"Not—?"

"No, sire. It's blood. I came in and you were coughing blood. Great gobs of it. Let me send for the physicians. They'll—"

"No." Pardu made himself breathe again. The taste in his mouth wasn't copper. It was blood. He remembered from his youth, all the war injuries, the lost teeth. Blood. His father had coughed blood—great gobs of it, as Aene said—just before he died. "The physicians will give me something to make me sleep. I don't want to sleep. Let's clean this up, and have someone bring water. I want to bathe."

"But, sire, you're ill and the water spirits—"

"Are superstition. And I'm dying, Aene. Even if

I'm wrong and they exist, they can't do much to me now."

Aene lowered his head. "Yes, sire," he said, then rocked back on his heels and stood up. He scurried into the hall, always efficient, always moving.

Pardu leaned back on the pillows. He was exhausted. He ran a finger through the stuff on the floor. Felt like blood. He sniffed. Smelled like blood. He had less time than he thought. Days, maybe hours. His father had become delirious, childlike in his last few days, his mind gone. Pardu didn't remember Aene's arrival, hadn't realized that he had coughed blood, didn't remember spilling the wine. All that was clear to him was the pain, and the feeling of burning, deep within his chest.

He drew up a coverlet, not caring that he stained it with the wine and blood. So little time left. So much to do. Neither son was ready to rule. They didn't understand all the little secrets, all the things that Pardu had kept to himself, never thinking that he would have to share them. If his mind were going, he would have to train them quickly. He would have to use as much time as he had left working with his successor.

Aene came back in, carrying another lamp. The room grew brighter. Darkness still hovered at the edges. Two other servants arrived, carrying a tub, followed by others with steaming water buckets. They poured the water into the tub, then Aene helped Pardu stand.

The dizziness had returned. Pardu swayed, afraid that he would fall in front of these people. But he didn't. Aene half carried him to the tub and eased him inside. The water felt good and soothing. Pardu hadn't realized how much his body ached until he sat down.

One of the servants took a bucket and began scrubbing the blood from the floor. Another took the pillows and coverlet, and cleared out the wine glass, getting rid of the mess from Pardu's bad night.

They would return with more pillows, more coverlets, and then the entire palace would know of Pardu's growing illness. The physicians would want to keep him sedated, the advisers would no longer trust his opinions, and Tarne would take control instead of one of Pardu's sons.

The heart readers. He had planned for them to come in several days. But they were the key to Leanda's future. Their reading would determine which brother would rule. He needed to know sooner. He couldn't work with them both and then cast the other away. And he had to be clearheaded, in case something went wrong with the reading itself.

Aene took a sponge and rubbed it down Pardu's back. The touch felt good. Pardu wasn't sure he was strong enough to do it himself.

"Aene," he said.

"Yes, sire?"

Pardu thought he heard caution in his servant's voice, the tone a person used with an elderly man, a fool, or a child. "Get my advisers and my sons. Bring them to the Assembly Room just after dawn. We'll do the reading then."

"The heart readers?" Aene was so tactful. He was reminding Pardu as cautiously as he could that he had forgotten to give orders about the readers.

Pardu smiled just a little. He hadn't forgotten. "Tarne knows which readers we're going to use. Have him bring them."

"Yes, sire." Aene snapped his fingers. Another servant rose. Aene handed him the cloth and instructed him on how to finish the King's bath.

Pardu sank into the water, letting it warm him. For the first time, he felt old. He would be glad when everything was finished.

CHAPTER 22

She stared at him from across the tent. The candlelight gave her face a haunted quality. She stood, her feet digging into the rug. Tarne smiled. She was breaking, even though she didn't know it yet. He knew the signs. This woman would cry or plead. One moment she would fight him, the next her mind would snap like fine glass.

He didn't want to snap her, at least not yet. He wanted to make her fear him—and he had done that.

She was pretty enough, and delicate in a robust sort of way. Her movements, despite her weight, were dainty and refined. The kind of woman built for bearing children—and the kind of woman who never would.

Unless she was forced.

He adjusted the pillows on the side of the room and untied his shirt. Her words had made him cautious. If he did take her, he might interfere with the reading, and that was the last thing he wanted. No, he would take her later, after it had ended, when she began to think of ways to get even with him. If she persisted, he would snap her so easily that her partner would never know what happened.

"Are you done with me?" she asked.

He smiled and toyed with the ties on his pants. She grew pale. It was enough to let her think he was going to use her. "You haven't made any agreements with me," he said.

"I don't bargain under threat." Her voice was calm, but her eyes were wide—the eyes of a trapped animal.

It was a sight he loved, and one he saw too rarely since he had become the King's adviser.

"You're in no position to bargain."

She shook her head and crossed her arms. "If what you say is true, if the King truly has chosen us, then you cannot harm me, for he would know. And you cannot harm Stashie for the same reason."

"Not before." He made sure his expression remained pleasant and his tone agreeable. "But I can hurt you afterward. Judging from who you are and why we picked you in the first place, you're not willing to sacrifice your happiness or your life to maintain the correct succession."

To her credit, she didn't look away. She continued to stare at him. But she said nothing.

Voices echoed outside the tent, and shadows moved. Tarne froze. Something unusual was going on. He had left orders for complete silence.

He got up and pushed back the flap. The soldiers had gathered in front of the door. Toward the back, more men stood with torches. He had a momentary recollection of a midnight attack more than twenty years previous, but knew that was not what he was facing.

He snapped his fingers and nodded a man inside the tent. He wanted the woman watched. She was cunning enough to make a weapon while he was gone and to use it against him.

"What's the disturbance?" He gave his voice a ring that brought all of the men to attention. They parted to allow the men in the back through. The leader, a good soldier named Waene, bowed in front of Tarne. Tarne touched Waene's shoulder, and he stood.

"The King has commanded that the reading take place in the Assembly Room at dawn."

Tarne felt a shiver run through him. Had the King learned of his plans? Had someone spoken, revealing the heart reader's presence in Tarne's tent? "Did he give a reason for the change of plan?"

Waene shook his head. "Several servants were commanded into the King's private suite not long ago.

They took linens and a bath. There is talk that he vomited blood."

Tarne took a step back and ran his fingers across his chin. The strain of the last few days was taking the King's strength. And with his strength went his life. Tarne needed to act fast. "Has he sent for the readers?"

"He wants you to find them," Waene said.

Luck. Pure luck. Had he sent someone else, then his evening's work would have been discovered. "Find the other one, and bring her to me. I will take them to the Assembly Room at dawn."

Waene clicked his heels and nodded, then pivoted and left. Tarne went back into the tent.

The warmth startled him, making him realize he had been cold outside. The soldier he had sent in stood directly in front of the woman, not allowing her any movement.

"Thank you," Tarne said.

The soldier nodded once, and walked around Tarne, returning to the outside. The woman's expression was even more guarded.

"Did he touch you?" Tarne asked.

She shook her head.

"Could you hear the conversation?"

"We're to read at dawn." Her voice trembled. Something about that disturbed her. Tarne frowned. Perhaps he had been wrong. Perhaps she and Stashie had planned a kind of revenge, after all.

But he didn't know what they could do. Kill the King? Kill his sons? Kill Tarne? No matter what they did, the government would fall into chaos, war would begin, and someone else would remember Tarne's methods of taming the masses.

"We're bringing your partner here," he said. "I want you to tell her what happened this evening."

"And if I don't?"

He shrugged. "Then I will. And I will be much more graphic than you are. I might even demonstrate some of my threats. We know that my presence in her body doesn't hurt your reading abilities."

"No one"—Dasis's voice broke—"has touched her

like that since I met her. You don't know any such thing."

"Something . . ." he paused, walked over to her and caressed her cheek. She flinched but didn't turn away. "Something has changed. You seem a bit more wary than you did, a bit more frightened."

He spoke to her like a lover would, as if he were truly concerned about those things. She didn't move, but her eyes widened, not with fear, but with hatred.

"I am appalled at what I have done." She spoke softly. "I have, for money, forced my partner into a world that almost killed her once. A world that took her family and her innocence from her. I have also, because I will help the King choose an heir to continue this government, supported a world that breeds people like you, encourages them, and gives them places of power."

"And so you are refusing to read?"

"So that you can terrorize another set of readers?" She smiled. Her cheek moved against his palm and he felt a stirring of true desire. "No. I will read. And I will read fairly. That's the only way I can live with the choices I've already made."

"No matter what the cost to yourself and your partner?"

"We've already paid a terrible price. We might as well make it worth our while."

He shoved her away. She hit the table and sprawled against the cushions. Tarne caught the candle so that it didn't tip and start a fire. "You will do as I have told you," he said, keeping his voice as calm as he could.

"I will do as I please."

He set the candle down, hand trembling, then kicked the table aside. She didn't flinch. He brought his hand back to strike her and, at the last second, caught her smile. She wanted him to hit her, wanted him to hurt her. She wanted the King to know that Tarne had manipulated things. She had nearly bested him.

He kicked the table again, snapping its leg. She would work for him. He would use her partner to make her.

CHAPTER 23

Radekir rolled onto the warm spot Stashie had left on the pillows. Stashie had been so tender, so affectionate. Radekir had never expected Stashie to leave. She had thought that once Stashie made love with her, had broken her tie to Dasis, that Stashie would stay. Radekir would become Stashie's protector and they would leave this place. Together.

The darkness was thick around her. She didn't know how long she had been lying there, waiting for Stashie's footsteps, her soft voice saying that she had made a mistake to go to Dasis. Didn't Stashie see how Dasis hurt her? Radekir had the power—and indeed, did—to cure those hurts. What made Stashie return?

Perhaps—Radekir brushed a strand of hair from her forehead—perhaps Stashie had gone to Dasis to end it. And just perhaps, Stashie hadn't told Radekir that because she didn't want to hurt Dasis any worse. Radekir sat up, feeling the pillows slide beneath her legs. Of course, that was it. And here she lay in the darkness, her body tingling from lovemaking, feeling sorry for herself.

She got off the pillows and grabbed her clothes. She slipped on the skirt, blouse and sandals, welcoming their warmth. She hadn't realized she was so cold. She didn't rewrap her turban—she was going out as a woman, not as a fortune-teller—but instead let her hair flow free. The brush of her dark hair along her shoulders and back made her feel younger. She hummed to herself as she grabbed her cloak and let herself out the door.

She dashed through the corridor quickly and found

herself outside faster than she had expected. The night was clear. She could see dozens of stars overhead. They warmed her, even though the night had the deep desert chill. Stashie stood under the same stars somewhere, probably telling Dasis that their times were over. Radekir wrapped her arms around her waist and smiled to herself. She had taken a chance and made the right choice.

The torches were half burned—she must have dozed after Stashie left—and the streets were empty. She didn't like the darkness: it was cold, and concealing. A dozen people could be standing in the shadows, watching her, and she would not know it. The thought made her skin crawl. She walked faster.

The bazaar loomed up ahead of her. Only a handful of torches lit the flattened earth. She could see the marks of hundreds of footprints and the impressions of tables and rugs. The bazaar was safe in the daytime. Now it felt as if a great emptiness had taken everything away.

She shook her head, trying to free the thoughts from it. She should be happy. She was about to get what she wanted. The rest of the night would be difficult, with recriminations and loud words, but from then on she and Stashie would face the future together.

Radekir let herself in the back door of the inn where Stashie and Dasis stayed. The place was very quiet. She had expected to hear loud voices as she came up the street, or at least as she opened the door. But the place felt as if it were full of sleeping people.

The torches had been snuffed in the hallway, making it so dark that Radekir couldn't see her hand in front of her face. She trailed one hand along the wall, counting the doors. When she reached the right one, her hand dipped inside. The door was ajar.

She heard a faint gasping, rapid and touched with sobs. Not the sound of two people making love. More the sound of a frightened woman, all alone.

"Stashie?" she whispered.

The gasping stopped. Radekir pushed the door

open. A faint light came in through the room's only window. The light outlined a woman's silhouette, hunched over, knees drawn to chest, hands covering her face.

Radekir knelt beside her. "Stashie?"

"They took her," she whispered. "They took Dasis."

Radekir's heart stopped beating. She made herself take a breath. "Who did?"

"The soldiers." Stashie's hand gripped Radekir's. "The soldiers came and took her away. I always knew they would come back. They're going to kill everyone I love."

Radekir trapped Stashie's hand between hers. "Be calm, Stash," she said gently. "Dasis is probably out looking for you. She'll be back soon."

"No!" The word burst out like the anguished wail of a young child. "The soldiers have her. I know."

"How do you know?"

Stashie flung her head back. Radekir could see tears glittering on her cheeks. "He told me. He waited for me at the bazaar and said he saw them."

"Who's he?"

"One of the merchants. With the patch. You know."

Radekir closed her eyes. She had to keep breathing. As long as she took a breath, she was thinking.

She knew the man Stashie was talking about. Ytsak had been at the bazaar longer than Radekir had. He was a good man, honest enough to return coins to patrons he thought overpaid him. More than once he had helped out others in the bazaar. Like Stashie, he had lost family very young, and considered the bazaar his home.

"What would make them take Dasis?" Radekir noticed the shift in her tone. She was believing Stashie now.

Stashie shook her head. "Perhaps we did something wrong at the reading. I don't know. I sometimes think it has something to do with me—that they're trying to hurt me again. But that can't be right, can it? I mean, I've done nothing to these people."

"Let me think." Radekir let go of Stashie's hand and wiped her palms on her skirt. She was trembling. Since she had come to Leanda, she had heard stories of people dragged away in the middle of the night, never to be seen again. If she wanted Stashie beside her, they had to settle this. Otherwise, Stashie would always believe deep down that her love for Radekir had killed her partner.

Radekir took the hem of her skirt and wiped away Stashie's tears. "You're probably right. This probably has to do with the readings. They might have wanted both of you."

"Then why not send for us? Why drag her away without me? It makes no sense, Radekir."

"There are always reasons," Radekir said. "We just have to find them."

She got up and went to the table, fumbling until she found the lamp. She took flint from her pocket and struck until the sparks lit the wick. With the light, the room gained a warmth, and Radekir felt calmer.

Stashie's face was blotched from crying. When she looked at Radekir, it was as if she had left her eyes. "We have to find her," Stashie said. "They'll kill her—or worse. I can't take another killing. I just can't."

Radekir smoothed Stashie's hair, but Stashie stiffened. Contact seemed to distress her more. Radekir moved away. First she had to calm Stashie, then they had to take action.

"We need to find her, Stash," Radekir said. "And that's going to take some work and clear thinking. I'll need your help, do you understand me?"

Stashie nodded. Her gaze was fixed on the window.

"It's probably something simple, like the readings, and they're waiting for you. They won't do anything to Dasis. They need the two of you."

Stashie held up her hand. Radekir stopped. Outside, the low rumble of voices and the sound of many feet.

"They're back," Stashie whispered. In one swift movement, she got to her feet and grabbed one of the cracked slates on the floor.

The outside door creaked open. Radekir touched Stashie's arm, but Stashie brushed her away. "No, Stash, not like this. They probably want to talk."

Stashie shook her head once. Her mouth had thinned. She gripped the slate so tight that her fingers had turned white.

The footsteps echoed through the hall. Radekir moved toward the door. Perhaps she could stop things by speaking calmly, by getting to these people before Stashie.

The door flung back and a young soldier came through, his uniform new, his cap under his arm. With a cry, Stashie ran forward. Radekir grabbed her arm as Stashie tried to bring the slate down against the soldier's head.

Other soldiers poured in the room. The slate fell to the floor and shattered. One of the soldiers grabbed Stashie, held her against him. Another grabbed Radekir. A third pushed his way to the front. He was older, his face lined, hair graying. Stashie gasped when she saw him, and Radekir knew they had met before.

"You're to come with me," he said.

Stashie didn't move, but her expression was defiant. "Where's Dasis?"

"Our lord master Tarne has her. He wanted to talk with her."

"Tarne—?" Color flooded Stashie's cheeks. Radekir could feel the reflection of her fear. "What does he want with her?"

"He wants us to bring you. Your reading is at dawn."

The hands on Radekir's arms were too tight. Her fingers were tingling. The blood had left them.

"I want to know what Tarne did with her." Stashie's voice had gained strength.

"He wanted to teach her how to read properly."

Stashie screamed and began kicking. She managed

to hit her captor's knee with a good thud before the others grabbed her and held her still.

"Why is Tarne here? Why is he torturing me?"

Radekir heard the plaintive note in Stashie's voice. It added the word she didn't say. *Again.* Tarne was the one who had killed her family. Stashie's fears had been true.

"He's the King's adviser," the soldier said.

Stashie thrashed. The impact of the situation hit Radekir. They had to get free and then they had to rescue Dasis. Stashie couldn't face Tarne again—and if he had hurt Dasis, then Stashie might kill him. If she did that, she would die, and her friends would die with her.

Radekir brought her knee up and hit her captor in the groin. He released her arms. She grabbed part of the shattered slate and brought the sharp edge down onto the hand holding Stashie's arm. The soldier howled and let go. Stashie brought her fist back and connected with another soldier's stomach. Radekir stabbed a third soldier in the arm. They backed away from Stashie. Radekir grabbed Stashie's hand when something crashed against her head. The pain shimmered along her spinal column, around her shoulders, into her chin and jaw, then back up into her head. The world was going dark, but she fought it, reaching for consciousness, clinging to Stashie's hand in hers. The hand slipped free—and blackness overwhelmed her.

CHAPTER 24

Dasis watched the man in front of her. He had braced himself in front of the tent's flap, his entire body poised as if to spring. She felt the cushions, soft against her back. If only she could get him to hit her, to leave marks on her sensitive skin. Then she might be able to use his own actions against him, and might be able to protect herself and Stashie.

Tarne flung the table leg aside. "You'll be reading at dawn," he said. "I'll be back for you."

He started to leave, then stopped before raising the flap of the tent. He smiled and Dasis braced herself. "Your partner will be arriving here first. Tell her that I look forward to seeing her again."

Dasis didn't respond. He left the tent, and she watched his shadow move along the outside until it completely disappeared. Then she let out the breath she was holding.

Her entire body started shaking. She grabbed the light, its flame flickering with her trembling movements. The warmth seeped into her skin, soothing her as much as she could be soothed.

She had done this. She had caused it. If she hadn't wanted so badly to earn them a little more money, a chance to quit reading if they wanted to, the opportunity to find a place and live there permanently, then she wouldn't be here now, waiting for Stashie to come.

If they found Stashie—and if she survived the soldiers' touch.

Dasis didn't know how fragile Stashie was. If the things Tarne told her were true, Stashie had once had great strength. All Dasis knew was the woman who froze at the sight of a uniform, who spoke in a whisper when she wanted something—as if she had no right to ask—and who flinched whenever anyone raised an arm in anger.

He claimed he liked to break spirits and perhaps he had broken Stashie's. He certainly knew ways inside Dasis's.

The candle was growing too hot against her palms. She set it down, and got up, looking for weapons, any way to save herself and Stashie once Tarne returned.

The tent was a mess. It smelled of sweat and leather. The pillows hadn't been changed in what looked like months. They were stained and covered with dirt. The table looked makeshift, and the chair had not been sanded. Clothes hanging in the far corner were not the robes of a king's adviser, but a uniform, clean and neatly tailored. This was not Tarne's tent. He had used it to meet her. Burning it would not destroy his possessions, but someone else's.

She walked over to the uniform, her legs shaking unsteadily. She had to control herself. If Stashie saw how frightened she was, Stashie might crack. Dasis needed them both in order to save them.

The uniform was made of a material that Dasis didn't recognize. She touched it lightly, then felt along the pants, in the cuffs and pockets, for a weapon, anything—a knife, a piece of flint. But she found nothing. The scabbard was missing, and there was no sword. She combed through the filthy pillows, looked under the rugs, and scanned the rest of the place. Nothing. The only weapons she had were the table leg that Tarne had broken for her and the candle. Perhaps if she made a torch and thrust it in the face of the men who were coming to get her . . .

She pondered that for a moment, then returned to the chair. She needed to talk with Stashie. If her plan didn't work and they had to do the reading, would she be willing to risk Tarne's wrath? If she couldn't report him or stop the reading, would she be harming or helping herself by picking the brother that Tarne wanted? She sat on the chair and rubbed her fingers together. Dawn seemed a long ways away.

After a while, she moved the table leg over beside the light. She was prepared now. She could act if she had to.

Outside, voices rose in laughter. She shivered, wondering what they planned. She picked up the table leg, held it firmly. The flap opened and hands pushed a woman inside.

Stashie.

Dasis dropped the table leg. Stashie landed on her hands and knees, hair flipping over her face. Dasis ran to her and crouched beside her.

"Stashie," she said.

Stashie glanced up. Her eyes were glazed over, and blood trickled from the corner of her mouth. "Dasis?" She sounded as if she couldn't believe it. "Dasis?"

Her hand cupped Dasis's face. Then Dasis pulled her close and they held each other.

"I thought they killed you," Stashie whispered.

Dasis cradled her and rocked her back and forth as if she were a small child. "No," she said. "They haven't hurt me, at least not yet."

Stashie drew in a hitching breath that sounded as if it held tears. "I thought they killed you," she said again. "And it would have been my fault. I'm sorry, Dasis."

Dasis pulled her back so that she could see Stashie's face. "It's my fault," she said. "I was the one who insisted we come here."

She wiped the blood from Stashie's mouth and kissed her gently, avoiding the bruise. Stashie pulled away. "But Tarne—"

"He didn't hurt me. He just tried to scare me," Dasis said. "I don't scare that easily."

"You mustn't let him touch you. If he touches you, I wouldn't know what to do."

"He didn't touch me." Dasis took Stashie's hands. They were trembling. "He just wants to get at you."

Stashie nodded, wearily. "I got away from him."

"And he remembers." Dasis squeezed Stashie's hands. "Hold me."

Stashie leaned into Dasis's embrace. She felt warm and soothing. This was how they belonged, comforting each other, loving each other, not fighting as they had been.

"I'm sorry," Dasis whispered. "I had no idea how bad things were for you."

"I never told you." Stashie's voice was muffled against Dasis's shoulder. "And I owed you so much—"

"It's okay," Dasis said. "It's okay."

They held each other for a while, Dasis stroking Stashie's hair. Outside the tent, shadows paced. She didn't want to think about what would happen when Tarne returned. Finally she sighed, cupped Stashie's chin and kissed her forehead.

"We need to get out of here."

Stashie's eyes grew wide. "There are a dozen soldiers outside, not to mention the ones at the gate. And all that desert. Dasis, we're trapped here."

"I thought you escaped him once."

Stashie bowed her head. "He thought I crawled off to die."

"Stashie, do you really want to face him in front of the King? We'll be able to do the reading, and then what? Will he kill us because of the things we know? Or because of your memories?"

"Tarne thinks he has a sense of fairness."

"At least, the man you knew years ago did." Dasis got up, grabbed the table leg and held it over the candle's flame. "This was the only weapon I could find, but it should be good enough to get us out of here. Most people fear fire enough to stay away from it."

"No, Dasis," Stashie said. "We need to read. We need to face them."

Dasis set the leg down. Its end was singed. Stashie never argued for the conservative action. Normally she would have wanted them to escape. "Why?" Dasis asked. "Why shouldn't we fight for ourselves?"

"Because." Stashie stood and took the wood out of

Dasis's hand. "I know what they can do when they're crossed. I don't want that to happen again. I couldn't stand it, and I couldn't bear it if anything happened to you. You're all I have, Dasis."

"Nothing will happen," Dasis said, but she wasn't sure if she believed it.

Stashie's smile was indulgent. "I don't even want to take that risk. If we survive this, we can go anywhere we want, do anything we want. That's a reward I'm willing to receive at the risk of a little integrity."

Dasis frowned. "Integrity? What are you talking about, Stash."

Stashie took a deep breath. "Tarne asked you to favor a brother, didn't he? Let's do what he says. It's the easiest and safest for us. No one will know, not even Tarne, because he could have chosen the correct brother. And then we go. We go free and we go safe and we never have to worry again."

"And if he picked the wrong brother?"

Stashie shrugged. "It's not our worry. What does it matter to us who rules this place? We'll still have to suffer their laws no matter what."

Dasis sat down slowly. She felt as if she had walked into a nightmare. "Stashie, you have never wanted to forsake our readers' vows before."

"Our lives have never been at stake before." Stashie looked at her hands. "Who did he ask you to choose?"

Dasis stared at Stashie for a few minutes. Everything seemed to stop. Even the shadows outside the tent had frozen. Stashie's face looked alien. Her eyes were someone else's. Finally Dasis bowed her head. "Ele. He told me to pick Ele."

"Then Ele"—Stashie's voice was firm—"will be our next King."

CHAPTER 25

Radekir's mouth tasted of copper and mud. Her head throbbed. Dirt dug into her cheek and she was cold. Slowly, she pushed herself up, pausing as dizziness swept over her. Someone had hit her. Someone had hit her and made her lose her grasp on Stashie's hand. Someone—

Soldiers. And they had taken Stashie.

Radekir sat up and took a deep breath. The dizziness had to go away. The pain had to go away. She had to find Stashie before they did something awful to her.

The back of her head was sticky with dried blood. They had hit her hard. If the blow had landed in a slightly different position, she might be dead now. She swallowed, realizing that the taste in her mouth was blood. Her jaw ached, and so did her arms. She flexed her muscles, moved her limbs, trying to see if anything was broken. Nothing appeared to be.

She squinted, then opened her eyes the rest of the way. The room was still dark. The door was ajar and no one had come in. Had they said something about dawn? Or had she dreamed it? Her head hurt too badly for her to think clearly.

They had said something about dawn. About reading at dawn. With Dasis.

Radekir moaned. Her desire might have cost Stashie her life. The sexual bond was one all readers were warned against breaking. Perhaps Stashie could read with Radekir. But they hadn't tested it. They didn't know.

The ache in Radekir's head grew worse. She

touched her skull gingerly, as if her fingertips could magnify the pain. Then she gripped the edge of the table and pulled herself up. Dawn couldn't be too far away. She didn't have time to get help. She had to go herself.

She got to her feet and swayed. The effort made the blackness grow thicker and for a moment, she thought she would pass out again. She willed herself to stay conscious. She had to move, had to find Stashie.

Radekir gripped the mud-brick walls. They were cool to her touch. She leaned her forehead on them and waited for the dizziness to pass. She couldn't wait much longer. Finally she raised her head and used the wall to push herself along. And as she moved, a plan formed in her head.

She would go back to her room, wash her face and arms, put on her only other set of clothes, and wrap the turban around her head. That should hide the worst damage and make her presentable enough. And that was all that mattered.

The walk to her room took forever. The torches had almost burned out, and the darkness had grown. She couldn't feel the cold. The air had a midday heat. And the dizziness—the dizziness followed her like a lovesick prison guard, unable to decide whether to envelope her or kill her.

The cushions in her room were still mussed from her evening with Stashie. She touched one, wishing she could go back. She didn't know what she would change—she didn't want to lose the memory of holding Stashie. But even if Radekir had gone back with her, the guards still would have found Stashie, and still would have dragged her away.

She cleaned up, put on her other clothes, and carefully wrapped the turban around her wounded head. Then she grabbed the staff she hardly ever used. It would help her get to the palace. It would also serve as a weapon if it had to.

She was about to let herself out of her room when she stopped. She would never see this place again.

She knew that as well as she knew her own name. She hoped that was because she and Stashie escaped together. She needed to believe in a good future.

Then, leaning on the staff, she stepped outside into air that had grown so cold she thought her entire body would turn to ice.

CHAPTER 26

The Assembly Room was already full when Tarne arrived. Soldiers lined the corridor and the interior walls. The advisers sat in their posts along the floor, dozens of men, waiting to hear who their next ruler would be. The King's sons sat on the dais, trying not to look nervous. Vasenu was succeeding. His expression was calm, his features relaxed. Ele also looked calm, but he kept twisting his hands together in his lap.

The only people missing were the King and the heart readers.

Tarne had given orders that the heart readers should be brought to the Assembly Road shortly after he arrived. He thought it best not to see Stashie until the reading. Even though she knew he was around, the shock of seeing him would help her decide to do what he wanted. His guards had already reported the conversations to him. She was arguing as he had hoped. Seeing him should clinch the fear and ensure that things went his way.

The room smelled of incense and gave off a damp chill, despite the number of people waiting. Tarne nodded to the soldiers as he passed them. Then he took his seat and stared at the brothers until one of them stared back.

Vasenu glanced at Tarne, made a small grimace of contempt, and looked away. Ele looked at his brother, then followed his gaze. Tarne smiled. Ele took a deep breath. Tarne pulled a piece of paper from his pocket and snapped his fingers. One of the guards came forward and took the note.

"Give this to the princeling, Ele," Tarne whispered.

The soldier nodded once, then disappeared. A few moments later, he stepped onto the dais and handed Ele the note. Vasenu watched the exchange. Ele unfolded the note, glanced at it, then handed it back to the guard. The guard put it in his pocket and backed away from the dais.

Tarne could see the effect of the words in Ele's eyes. *It is arranged.* Ele was wondering what had been arranged, hoping that Tarne had arranged his succession. When the readers announced who would be the next king, Ele would know whom he owed his debt to.

So would Vasenu. But Vasenu would have no power.

The back doors to the Assembly Room opened, and the readers came in. Dasis walked proudly, as if the night with Tarne had had no effect on her. Stashie mimicked Dasis's walk, but Tarne could see the fright in the paleness of her skin, the shadows under her eyes. She scanned the room until she found him and then she nodded once. Not the fear-struck reaction he had expected, but one that probably had more safety in it.

They were led to the stairs in front of the dais and commanded to sit. Dasis sat at Vasenu's feet, Stashie at Ele's. Tarne smiled at the appropriateness of the tableau. He leaned back, feeling an ease despite the tension in the room. If they didn't do as he asked, he would punish them. And if they did, then he would let them go. He was fair, when he wanted to be. And they wouldn't be able to hurt him. They wouldn't dare try.

Without fanfare, the doors behind the dais opened. Two servants supported the King and led him into the room. Gasps echoed around Tarne. The King looked twice as old as he had the night before. His skin was sallow, he seemed to have lost weight and his eyes were sunken in his face. It was no wonder he had ordered an earlier reading.

The servants eased the King onto his cushion. He

reached out and took his sons' hands. "Are you ready?" he asked, his voice harsh and raspy.

Tarne could see Ele swallow hard. He glanced at Tarne and Tarne nodded. "We're ready," Ele said in unison with his brother.

The King raised his hands, and brought them together so that both brothers touched as equals for the last time.

"Then let the ceremony begin."

CHAPTER 27

White streaks dotted the horizon behind the distant hills as Radekir approached the palace gates. Her feet hurt, but the dizziness had receded. She felt that if she stopped moving, however, she would collapse on the sand.

Up close, the palace looked no more impressive than the mud-brick buildings that the city was made up of. The giant wall that ran in a circle around the palace itself had small, sunbaked cracks. The torrents beyond looked faded and crumbly. Only the tents, half hidden by the wall, added any color to the landscape at all.

She wiped the sand and sweat off her face. Her clothing was dirty and travel worn. As she walked, she had occasionally felt blood slipping down the back of her neck. Her turban was no longer white, but black with blood.

And she was so tired. Halfway there, she had forgotten for a moment why she was coming. She had only known Stashie for a few days. The woman had meant more of an escape than a lover.

Until the tenderness. Until the warmth. Until Radekir had seen the ancient fear in Stashie's eyes.

The path to the gate had been worn by dozens of feet just the night before. Two guards stood at the gate so silently that at first she thought they were statues. When she reached them, she stopped—and swayed. She had to lean on her staff to keep her balance.

"The King has heart readers with him," she said. Her voice sounded gasping and weak. "I need to see them."

One guard smiled and crossed his arms in front of

his chest. "And who are you? A ghost sent to give them advice?"

She started to shake her head, then thought the better of it. "No. I am partner to one of the readers. I have something she needs, something she wasn't able to take when the soldiers brought her here."

The other guard held out his hand. "I will take it to them."

"No," Radekir said. "It is part of me. Part of who I am. It is nothing that I can give."

"There are two heart readers," the first guard said, "which means, according to my understanding, that both partners are there. Go away. The palace is accepting no visitors today."

Radekir sighed. Her head throbbed and, as the sun moved higher, the desert heat had started to build. "The reading isn't going to happen. I need to see the readers. Please."

The guard laughed. "I was there for the demonstration. I know that these women work well together. Try again."

Radekir bowed her head. She would have to think of something else. "Look," she said. "Send the King a message for me. Have your man deliver it only if the reading doesn't work. Tell him that Stashie's true partner is waiting at the gate."

"Only if the reading doesn't work." The guard's voice was sarcastic. He nodded to his partner. "I suppose we can do that."

His partner disappeared inside the gate. He returned a moment later, a small smile on his face. "Your message will be delivered if it has to be," he said.

The other guard crossed his arms in front of his chest. "If you plan to wait," he said, "go somewhere out of our way. We don't want to look at you all morning."

Radekir wandered off to the side of the gate, toward a part of the wall that looked as if it would provide shade as the sun rose. She sat down. She needed rest and strength. She had to be ready when Stashie needed her.

CHAPTER 28

Dasis's hands were shaking. The room was cold, people were looking at her, and Tarne kept smiling. She wanted to sit beside Stashie, to hold her, and comfort her, but they had to wait on opposite sides of the stairs. She wasn't sure how much longer she could wait.

She and Stashie had had so little time in the tent. They had just started to argue about the ethics of following Tarne's plan when his men arrived. The march across the courtyard was long and the wait for the King even longer. Stashie had gripped Dasis's hand, and Dasis had felt the fear in the sweat on Stashie's normally dry palm.

And then the room. Dasis hadn't been ready for its size nor for the number of dour-faced people who filled it. She had somehow thought that she and Stashie would stand alone before the King and his sons to do the reading. She hadn't expected an audience.

Behind her, the King commanded that the ceremonies begin. Outside the room, young voices rose in an unfamiliar chant. Stashie glanced at Dasis. Stashie's eyes were wide. Her lower lip trembled as if she were about to cry. The room was too full of uniforms and bad memories for her. The experience had to end quickly or Stashie would not make it through.

The chanting sounded magical. Dasis let its feeling run through her, touching her own heart. She had chosen this profession for a reason, just as she had chosen to love Stashie. She had chosen to be a heart reader because she had thought reading would help people. Reading took the veil off people's true selves

159

and allowed them to see who they really were. If they didn't like the look, they had the opportunity to change.

Her mentor had told her that the search for a pure heart was the noblest goal of a heart reader. If a reader found a pure heart, they had found a natural leader, someone who deserved the respect and love of his followers. Dasis had never seen a true heart, although her mentor had described one. And now Dasis sat on the steps in the palace outside Leanda, about to read two brothers, one of whom should have a pure heart.

If neither did, she didn't know what she would do.

The chanting stopped. Through the corner of her eye, she could see the King's servants help him rise. "Let the readings begin," he said and coughed. He put a hand over his mouth, but not before Dasis saw blood spray against his fingers. She shuddered, frightened by his illness and by his closeness to death.

When the King caught his breath, he moved his hand slightly and allowed one of the servants to wipe his mouth. Then he said, "We will let the readers explain the procedure."

Tarne stared at Dasis, his smile gone. The servants helped the King ease back onto the pillows. Dasis got up, held out her hand, and went to Stashie. Stashie rose and met her halfway across the stairs. They turned, and curtsied before the King. He waved them around to face the people sitting on the floor.

"When we read hearts," Dasis said, "we read character. We can tell you how a person has loved and whether or not he feels loved. We can tell you if he's malicious"—she glanced at Tarne—"or merely unlucky. We do not heal, nor do we tell the future."

"We're looking for a pure heart," Stashie said. Dasis forced herself to remain still. She hadn't expected Stashie to speak. "A pure heart knows how to love and how to protect, how to rule without pain. But pure hearts can be shattered, and if we do not find one here, we can make no determination about your future ruler."

Dasis bit her lower lip. Had Stashie changed her mind? Was she saying this so that Dasis would not choose Ele as the King's successor? Or was she exonerating herself and Dasis should Ele become a worse ruler than his father?

The silence grew too long. A few of the men below shifted on their seats. "We read one heart at a time," Dasis said, her voice abnormally loud. "My partner draws the heart with chalk on a slate and I read what she has put there. She does not understand the drawings and I do not know how to draw. That is the magic of heart reading. It takes two to complete the vision."

Stashie ducked her head and tugged on Dasis's arm. "We're ready to begin."

Dasis didn't sit yet. "We will not announce the results until both hearts are read."

Stashie glanced at her. The wide-eyed look was back. Tarne's smile had grown. He looked as if he were happy about the fear he saw.

The brothers stood together, identical men. Only their expressions differed. They came down the stairs side by side. Stashie put a slate on her lap, set out her chalks, and indicated that the men should sit.

They glanced at each other, and Dasis saw her fear reflected in their eyes. Their days as brothers and partners were over. They would now become separated into the ruler and the ruled.

The brothers sat and Stashie took the left hand of the nearer brother. "Your name?" she murmured.

"Ele," he said.

Dasis couldn't suppress a start. This was the one Tarne wanted. That automatically made the man suspect. Dasis somehow didn't believe that Tarne would support the brother with the purer heart.

Stashie closed her eyes, grabbed five chalks and began to sketch. From Dasis's distance, the marks looked like scratchings in the sand. She couldn't even see the chalk colors as clearly as she would like.

When Stashie finished, she set the slate down instead of handing it to Dasis. Dasis took the slate and set it on the other side of her, not wanting to look until both sketches were done.

Stashie held the hand of the other brother, Vasenu. This time she took only one chalk and her lines were smoother. Dasis made herself look away. She didn't want to prejudice the reading. No matter what Tarne threatened, she knew now, as she watched, that she could never pervert this project. To do so would be to sacrifice the magic, and she could not do that.

Stashie set down the second slate, then grabbed Dasis's hand. Dasis could feel Stashie's pulse, hammering rapidly under her skin. She didn't understand the message Stashie seemed to be trying to tell her with that single glance. Dasis offered her partner a half-smile, then grabbed both slates and set them on her lap.

She looked down, expecting to see hearts floating behind ribcages, showing all of their scars, all of the remains of their loves. Instead she saw single colored lines, thin marks, and solid blocks of color. She squinted, but nothing came clear. For a moment, she thought her sight had gone. Then she saw Stashie, biting her bottom lip so hard that a thin trickle of blood ran down her chin.

Radekir. Stashie had slept with Radekir.

The realization hit Dasis like a slap in the face. She felt numb and completely empty. Then the emptiness filled with a rage so deep she wasn't sure she could suppress it.

She had to think. They were all waiting for her, and she had to think.

The easy answer would be to declare Ele as the pure heart. No wonder Stashie had made that suggestion. She didn't have the courage to tell Dasis what had happened. Stashie had only thought about herself and a way out once Dasis discovered what had gone wrong.

The rage gave her power. She set the slates down and stood. "Sire, do you believe in heart readers, in their powers and in their magicks?"

Murmurs rose behind her. Her speech was a breach of protocol.

The King blinked twice. He took a silk handkerchief and blotted his mouth. "If I didn't," he said, sounding confused, "I wouldn't have called you here."

"And you have an understanding of how our magic works?"

A frown creased the center of his forehead. "I believe so."

"You know that it is based on a sexual bond between the two partners. A monogamous sexual bond?"

The murmurs grew in intensity. Stashie tugged Dasis's skirt and she could feel Tarne's gaze sear her back.

"It's not something I like to think about." The King's puzzlement was turning to anger.

"I can't read these slates," Dasis said. "I was afraid that would happen. You see, last night, that man sitting right there"—she turned and pointed to Tarne—"kidnapped me and brought me to his tent. He repeatedly threatened me, told me I had to do what he said or he would kill my partner. And when I refused, he . . ." The lie wasn't going to come as easily as she thought. She forced herself to continue. "He violated me."

The murmurs rose to gasps. Stashie let out a small moan.

"She lies!" Tarne's bellow silenced them all.

"No." Dasis's voice trembled. She brushed Stashie's hand away from her leg. "You can interrogate his men. He brought me, alone, to his tent and kept me there with him—just the two of us for hours. There were men outside, but none of them came inside or had occasion to know what he did."

"I never touched her!" Tarne was on his feet, halfway up the stairs before he stopped.

"So you don't deny that you kidnapped her." Vasenu spoke, his voice tinged with sarcasm.

"Her partner was a spy from the southern lands. I thought I had killed her many years ago."

"And yet you never said anything when we discussed which readers to use. You were pleased at our choice." Vasenu had also risen, his hands clenched at his side. His cheeks were flushed and his eyes snapped with anger.

"I didn't remember until later." Tarne stood directly behind Stashie. She was flanked by two angry men. She had let go of Dasis's skirt, and covered her face with her hands.

"Not true," Dasis said. "He told me about Stashie as soon as he took me into his tent. He told me how he had killed her family to break her spirit and how he had repeatedly raped her when she was little more than a child. And he threatened to hurt her again if I didn't do what he wanted."

"What did he want?" Ele asked.

His tone was so soft that for a moment, Dasis wasn't sure she had heard him correctly. Then she sighed. If she said anything, then she would destroy any chance for a clear reading later on. "I can't tell you," she said. "He wanted a specific result from this reading. And if you get readers to do a proper reading, and you know what Tarne wanted, you will always question the result. The fact that I am standing here and revealing this now should tell you that I will not take the side of that malicious creature, no matter how much he hurts me."

Her words echoed in the room. She had never heard such a complete silence before.

The King put his handkerchief over his mouth and coughed. He gasped for air, his skin turning gray. His servants leaned over him, as if their presence could help, but he pushed them away. He took a deep breath, coughed one more time, and wheezed.

"Why didn't you speak up before we began the reading?"

"I thought rape would not affect my reading." Dasis looked at Stashie as she spoke. "It wasn't making love. It was violence. It wasn't even my choice. I have been and always will be faithful to Stashie. That man's violation should not have affected my reading abilities or my bond with my partner."

Stashie hadn't moved. Vasenu was watching Dasis as if he could determine what she was trying to do by staring at her face. Tarne had frozen in place, his eyes wide with shock. He had probably never had anyone betray him before.

"We need to complete this reading this morning, because I don't have much time left. What can we do?" The King's voice was weak and raspy. He was leaning hard on his servants.

"Sire!" A voice echoed from the back of the Assembly Room. Dasis turned with the others. A guard ran down the aisle and started up the stairs. "I have a message here from a woman at the gate. She said I was to deliver it if the reading didn't work."

The King pushed away from his servants. "Speak."

"She said that she has something one of the partners needs. And that she can make the reading work."

"How would she know?" Vasenu said. "How would she know that it wasn't going to work."

Stashie unfolded herself like a flower. As she got to her feet, she eased herself away from Tarne. "Because," she said.

Dasis reached for her, but Stashie ignored her. If Stashie spoke, she would ruin the little bit that Dasis had been able to salvage. "Because," Stashie repeated, "I made love with her last night. I'm the one who broke the vows. Not Dasis."

CHAPTER 29

Pardu felt his stomach turn. He didn't know how things could have deteriorated so badly since the night before. "Send for her," he said, and allowed a wave of dizziness to overtake him. Two of the soldiers turned on their heels (very ceremonial, Pardu thought), and left through the main doors.

Pardu forced himself to take a deep breath. This was wearing him more than he wanted. He couldn't stand again and run the risk of falling before everyone. They already saw his illness. He couldn't make it worse by a public display of blood and fainting.

"Tarne," he said. "Come here."

Tarne finished climbing the steps. He knelt before Pardu, and bowed his head.

Pardu almost reached out to touch Tarne and then stopped himself. He had known this man for decades, had seen his work, and knew about his cruel streak. He had never thought, however, that Tarne would do anything to jeopardize his relationship with the King.

"Truth, Tarne. I want to know why you brought the heart reader here without my permission."

Tarne kept his head down, his voice humble. "I remembered who the other reader was tonight, sire. I sent for them both, but the guards only came back with one. I wanted to make sure these women were truly loyal. I didn't want them to pervert this process to settle an old vendetta."

"And you used beatings and rapes to determine this information?"

"She lies, sire."

Pardu felt an anger shake through him. He wasn't

166

dead yet. He still had to command loyalties, even if his most trusted adviser had decided to subvert all that he was working for. "Perhaps she does, Tarne, but you lie too. You wanted to mold this process your own way. You're afraid that the son who inherits will demote you and strip you of your power, so you're trying to retain all you have—and perhaps gain more."

Tarne finally raised his head. His cheeks were flushed, but with anger or shame Pardu couldn't tell. "Sire, I—"

"Vasenu has told me of your scheme to help him take my place. I can only assume you approached Ele too. I thought I could dismiss this. I thought my son was overreacting and that I understood that you were only trying to solidify your position for the transition. I explained that talk away. Tell me how to explain this one." Pardu choked on the last word. The cough came back, deep and rumbling from inside his chest. He put the blood-flecked handkerchief in front of his mouth and let the cough destroy his throat. Tears of pain floated in his eyes, and he half wished that death had taken him already.

"Sire, I—"

"No." Pardu forced out the word. He waited for the cough to subside, wiped his mouth, and put the handkerchief down. "You will tell me no more lies. You will sit beside me and watch this reading, and you will serve whichever of my sons will take my place. You have proven yourself untrustworthy. But because you have served me well, I will not destroy you. In return, I am taking from you your power to rule the soldiers. You will be only an adviser now. You will share no part of the rule. And when I die, your fate will be in the hands of my successor. I make no promises to you that will outlive me. If my successor decides to execute you for treason, so be it. That is the choice you have made."

"Sire—"

"Shut up and sit beside me. We still have a reading to watch." Pardu gripped the pillow. The dizziness had grown stronger. "Where is that woman anyway?"

The advisers were staring at him. Some of their faces were gray with fear. Others smiled, as if pleased that Pardu had taken on Tarne. His sons kept their expressions masked. Pardu wondered which of them Tarne would have chosen, and thought he knew.

The heart readers were sitting side by side on the steps, not touching and not looking at each other. Pardu shuddered as he looked at them. He did not understand their magic and he did not understand their relationship. Women gave pleasure and they gave children. They had their own mysterious lives that Pardu did not investigate. But he couldn't imagine maintaining a long-term monogamous relationship with anyone—male or female—and except for the heart readers, he knew of no one who did that. Or perhaps he saw no one who did that. People did not speak much about their lives away from the palace.

The doors to the Assembly Room opened. The guards returned, flanking a tall, thin woman wearing a turban. She limped as she walked and relied heavily on a large walking stick. As she grew closer, Pardu realized she had been recently beaten. He glanced at Tarne, who stared forward as if nothing unusual had happened.

"State your name," Pardu said, "and your reason for standing before us."

"My name is Radekir." The woman's voice was soft and melifluous. "And I am Stashie's new partner."

CHAPTER 30

Radekir leaned on her staff. Her head felt light and twice its size. She wasn't quite sure if she should be here or not. She hadn't expected all the people. The room was cold and smelled of fear. Stashie sat before her, eyes wide and full of pain.

Dasis kept shaking her head. "No," she murmured. "No."

Stashie put her hand over Dasis's. Dasis pulled away.

"Are you saying that you can read the slates?" the King asked. His presence wasn't as commanding as Radekir had expected. She had thought he would be a bigger man, more robust and powerful. Still, the edge in his tone frightened her.

"Yes," she said. She would have to. Dasis and Stashie had failed. Now it was time to test the theory. Monogamous sexual relationship? Or simply a loving sexual contact? She would finally know.

Dasis reached behind her and pulled out two slates. "Stashie already did the drawings," she said. Her hands shook as she gave the slates to Radekir. "Stashie will tell you who each slate belongs to."

Radekir took them with the hand not holding the staff. She limped to the stairs and sat down, setting the staff beside her. For a moment, she closed her eyes, remembering the feel of the magic, the power that seeing slates had held. Then she set one slate down, held the other out in front of her, and opened her eyes.

The slate was blank. She turned it over, expecting a trick. The back was blank also with no drawings on the gray material. She picked up the other slate. It too was blank.

"You've given me the wrong ones," she hissed at Dasis. The woman would trip her up no matter what was at stake. All she cared about was her relationship with Stashie, not that their lives were in danger.

"No," Dasis said. "Those are the drawings that Stashie made just a few moments ago."

"These slates are blank!" Radekir's voice echoed in the silence. She could feel everyone watching her. She didn't like the way that her mouth had suddenly gone dry.

Stashie climbed down the steps and took the slates from Radekir. Then she kissed Radekir's hands and held them to her cheek. "What matters is that you tried," she said.

The pounding in Radekir's head had grown worse. "They're blank," she said, and her words sounded almost like a plea.

"No," Stashie said. "These are the right slates. You can't help us, Radekir, although I appreciate your trying."

"If I hadn't seen you read yesterday," the King bellowed as he rose to his feet—without support, "then I would think this some kind of elaborate scheme to force me away from using the magical choice. But I saw you read. I know that the magic exists and that you can be accurate. This reading must happen today. It must happen now."

Stashie let go of Radekir's hand. Stashie's entire body was shaking. Radekir could see the effort it took for Stashie to stand and face the King. "Sire," Stashie said, "if you want an accurate reading, you must give me time alone with my partner." And then she added, as if realizing the confusion her statement caused, "With Dasis."

The copper taste was bitter in the back of Radekir's mouth. She had wanted so badly for this to work. If she had read with Stashie, they could have disappeared together. Radekir would have had a partner again and Stashie would have had someone who understood her.

"So be it." The King clapped his hands. "But should you fail, this woman"—he pointed at Radekir—"will die. Take her from here and hold her until the readings are done."

The guards who had brought Radekir grabbed her arms. This time, their touch held no gentleness. Bile rose in her throat. "Wait, sire, please," she said. There was no guarantee that Stashie and Dasis would ever be able to read again. "Please. I have done nothing wrong."

The King didn't look at her. Stashie reached for Radekir's hands, but the guards pulled her away too quickly. Halfway up the aisle, she began to fight. She kicked and struggled and bit. More men surrounded her. Sharp pains shot through her head and her dizziness grew. They grabbed her legs, pinned her arms to her sides, and carried her away.

CHAPTER 31

The room the King had given them was a small, unused chamber off the Assembly Room. Someone had hastily thrown cushions on the floor, and set a pitcher of water in the back corner. Stashie sneezed at the dust-filled air. She waited until Dasis entered before closing the door.

"I'm sorry," Stashie said.

Dasis nodded. Her entire body had wilted.

Stashie stepped over to her and started to put her arms around her, but Dasis pushed her away. "I really don't want you to touch me," Dasis said.

"We have to touch," Stashie said. "We can't read if we don't."

Dasis shrugged and sat down. Her sandals had left tiny prints in the dust. The cushion barely sank under her weight. Stashie sat beside her, and Dasis moved to the next cushion.

"Dasis, please."

"How could you?" Dasis whispered. "We've lost everything. Our love, our business, our connection. How could you, Stashie? Don't you know I love you?"

Stashie glanced down at her hands. This wasn't going to be as easy as she had hoped. "I know," Stashie said. "But you wouldn't listen to me."

"And Radekir did?" Dasis got up, turned her back and wrapped her arms around herself. "You never told me why you didn't want to face the soldiers. You never told me what was so hideous about Leanda. I had to find out from that—that man—that awful man—"

"I'm sorry," Stashie said. "I—"

172

"Sorry?" Dasis whirled. "You're sorry? You don't try, you go to another woman, you probably have gotten us killed, and you're sorry?"

Stashie took in a deep breath and then bowed her head. It had all seemed right when she had done it. And with Dasis's anger after the audition reading, Stashie had thought that she couldn't bear the misunderstandings any longer. "Dasis, look," Stashie said, "I couldn't face coming here. I didn't want to see any soldiers ever again. When I see them, I remember how they felt on me, how happy Tarne looked when he—cut off my brother's head. This whole place is filled with ghosts and horrible reminders of things I would love to forget. I begged you not to bring us here. I asked in as many ways as I knew how—"

"Except you never told me the truth about what happened to you."

"You didn't seem like you cared."

Dasis's mouth drew into a thin line. "That's not fair," she said. "I never pried. I was waiting for you to tell me."

Stashie shook her head a little. She thought she had never stopped talking about it. She thought Dasis had grown tired of hearing about Stashie's past. "I told you everything."

"You told me nothing. You told me that your family was dead, and I could see when you arrived that someone had hurt you, but you never told me what happened, not ever."

"Never?" Stashie's voice sounded weak, even to her own ears.

"Not ever," Dasis said.

"I thought about it all the time. I thought I was telling you."

Dasis shook her head. She sat down on the cushion, far enough away that she and Stashie couldn't touch. "Your eyes would glaze over and sometimes you'd flinch if I touched you. That's how I knew you were remembering. But you never told me, Stashie. I wouldn't have forgotten. I may not have understood everything, but I wouldn't have forgotten."

Stashie forced herself to take even breaths. Things had been a lot simpler when she could blame Dasis for not understanding. "I told Radekir," she said in a low tone, "and she sympathized with me, and held me, and comforted me—"

"And maligned me," Dasis said.

"No." Then a memory flashed through Stashie's mind. "Yes. I guess she did. I'm sorry, Dasis."

"Don't be." Dasis took Stashie's hand. The action made Stashie melt a little. "Radekir is a lonely woman. She wanted you to take that loneliness away. She took all those skills at watching people, all the things that make her fortune-telling work, and applied them to you. She got you to tell her. And then she acted as if it were my fault that you never had the chance to speak before. It was both of our faults, Stashie. Mine for not asking and yours for not telling."

"I wanted to tell," Stashie said.

"And I wanted to ask." Dasis smiled, just a little. Then the smile faded. "But I still don't understand how you could have gone with her, broke our vows, and touched her. . . ."

A shudder ran through Stashie at the repulsion in Dasis's tone. "I— It was after the reading. I thought I was going to go crazy from those soldiers. I thought you were going to force me to continue. And Radekir was there and she held me and I didn't want to stop her—" Stashie's breath hitched, but she stopped herself. She didn't want to cry. "I guess I was trying to hurt you, Dasis."

Dasis took her hand away and put it on her lap. "You have, Stash."

Her words sent a panic through Stashie. She had caused her family's death and now she was hurting Dasis. She buried her head between her knees, and let the shivers take her.

A hand stroked the back of her head. "But I understand." Dasis's voice was soft. "I just want you to promise me it'll never happen again. We have to talk to each other, Stashie, both of us."

Stashie raised her head. Dasis's face was beside hers. Stashie leaned into a kiss, and the kiss began to build. "I love you, Dasis," she said.

"I love you, too," Dasis whispered.

"I promise you," Stashie said against Dasis's ear, "that I will never hurt you like that again."

"You better not," Dasis said, "because I can't bear it. We may have lost everything."

"No." Stashie burrowed her face in Dasis's neck. "I think we've managed to regain each other."

CHAPTER 32

Tarne paced the corridor. He could hear the murmur of voices from the Assembly Room. He didn't have to be there to know what they were discussing. The King had gone to his chambers to rest, but the others waited and talked.

Tarne clenched and unclenched his hand. The bitch. He had never been crossed like that before, nor had he ever been so effectively ruined. Even the appearance of the other bitch, the one who had really caused the problem, didn't affect the contempt that had risen in him. Stripped of his power. Stripped of the King's trust. With one sentence, she had ruined him.

She would pay.

He wasn't sure how yet. Killing her would be too easy. He didn't want to do that. He wanted her to suffer. Yet if he did it in an unsubtle manner, the King would go after him. Unless he waited until the King died.

Tarne whirled and started down the stairs. He still had power. He had loyalties and he knew secrets. Those mattered much more than titles. He could still get people to do precisely what he wanted, exactly when he wanted.

He went down to the guards' barracks, ready to make plans.

CHAPTER 33

Pardu leaned back on his cushions. Someone had cleaned up his rooms. They smelled fresh, and the cushions were new. The air was cool. He drew a coverlet over himself and closed his eyes. He had wanted the reading to be over by now, and it had yet to begin.

He let himself doze, knowing that he had to be fresh when the readers reappeared. Even though his body relaxed and his breathing grew heavy, his mind didn't quit. He reviewed the entire attempted reading and let the disappointment fill him.

He had always trusted Tarne, always believed that Tarne would support him, because he thought Tarne cared for him. All of Tarne's actions over the years—good and bad—could be explained away with a mention of Tarne's affection for Pardu.

But if Tarne had truly cared, he would never have compromised the reading. He would have waited until the correct son had been revealed and then worked with that son to consolidate his power. Pardu had always seen Tarne's manipulative nature. He had never thought it would be applied against him.

The room grew too hot, almost stifling in the midday heat. He kicked off the coverlet and snapped his fingers. A servant began to fan him. The heat didn't ease, but the breeze cooled him a little.

The problem was Pardu couldn't trust the readers now. And if they brought in new ones, he would worry that Tarne had compromised them as well. He had to settle things with these readers. He had to get his faith in them back.

Then he opened his eyes, his fingers clutching the pillow.

"Sire?" Aene's face contained too much worry. Had Pardu passed out? He didn't think so.

"Are the readers ready yet?"

"No one has reported," Aene said.

Pardu closed his throat. The cough threatened again. He wished he could be free of it, wished that the pain and ache in his joints would end. "I want them brought here when they're ready. I would like to see them first."

"Yes, sire."

Pardu closed his eyes, and this time he slept.

The hand on his shoulder sent a searing pain down his side. Pardu groaned and tried to move away. The room was too hot, and the sleep felt good.

"Sire." Aene's voice was insistent. "Sire, the readers are here."

He didn't care. He wanted to continue his rest. He felt better than he had all day. But the hand on his shoulder shook again, and this time, the pain shot down to his feet. He opened his eyes. The room was spinning. He closed them again, willed the room to stop, and then opened one eye. The spinning had stopped, but Aene's face filled his vision. Aene's frown lines had grown deeper. The servant really cared for him—

Or perhaps he cared like Tarne.

The thought snapped Pardu into wakefulness. He eased himself up, limbs trembling, and head light. "Water," he said. His voice scratched out of his throat.

Aene nodded and snapped his fingers. Another servant brought a full goblet, droplets falling off its sides. Pardu took it, relishing the coolness on his hands, placing the goblet against his face. The chill felt so good. He took a sip and savored it for a moment before he sent the water down his traitorous throat. The tickle eased, but only for a moment.

"The readers are here," Aene said.

"I heard you the first time." Pardu took another sip of water, swallowed, and waited for the cough to come. It didn't. "Clean me up."

Aene helped Pardu off the cushion, removed his robes and gave him new ones. Then Aene brushed his hair and with a cloth dipped in the fresh water, wiped the sweat off Pardu's face.

"Ready, sire?"

Pardu sat cross-legged on a cushion, another cushion propped against the wall so that he could lean back. The aches were fiercer than they had been before he slept. "Send them in."

The women looked rumpled and frightened. The heavyset one's face was tear-streaked; the willowy one looked as if she had been shattered inside. He beckoned them to sit. They did, cross-legged, across from him.

"Can you conduct a reading?" he asked.

They glanced at each other. "We believe so," said the heavyset one. "But we've never had this experience before. We don't know."

He nodded, wishing the lightness in his head would go away. "Then we'll test it here."

"And what if we can't read?" The willowy woman shook as she spoke. Pardu despised her fear. No matter what had happened to her, she needed to remain calm in front of him, and she wasn't.

"We'll worry about that then." He held out his left hand. "Read."

The willowy woman's eyes grew wide. "You, sire?"

Pardu bit his lower lip. He had had enough of these delays. "I have been read three times before. I would know if you were lying."

She nodded once and grabbed his left hand. Her palms were clammy, but her fingers were dry. He closed his eyes. He could feel the energy seeping from him. A new experience, probably caused by his growing weakness. Every other time he had been read, he had been strong.

Chalk scratched against slate. The energy kept flowing from him. His heart felt as if it were being poked and prodded. The aches grew, and he wanted to sleep . . .

Then she let go of his hand. He sighed once, and opened his eyes. The heavyset woman had taken the slate and was staring at it intently. He leaned forward. As with all the other times, the slate looked blank.

She glanced up at him. She licked her lower lip, a nervous gesture.

"Nothing again?" he asked.

"No." She took a deep breath. "I can see your heart."

"Then tell me what you see."

She adjusted the slate. She didn't want to tell him and for a moment, he didn't think she would. "Your heart is thick and ropy with scars, many of them cracked and bleeding. It looks as if your heart once erupted from the inside out and what I see is no longer representative of what you once had. Your heart has been broken too many times to count, and every surface area has been damaged at least once. You have a strong man's heart, but it is fading now. It is gaining a weakness that is common with age and too much pressure. If your illness doesn't kill you, your heart will."

Pardu had been expecting the words, but they still hurt. He closed his eyes, trying to picture the scarred and ropy thing that no longer wanted to keep him alive. He couldn't see it. He wondered if the heart readers could see their own hearts.

He opened his eyes again. The readers were watching him with intent, fearful expressions. "It is time," he said, "for the actual reading to begin."

CHAPTER 34

The conversation stopped when Tarne entered the Assembly Room. The advisers watched him walk down the aisle and to his seat. He sat down, feeling the room's chill more than he ever had. On the dais, Ele stared at his hands. Vasenu kept his gaze on Tarne, a half-smile on his face.

Tarne would have given anything to wipe that smile away. He hadn't had a chance to approach the heart readers as he had hoped. He wanted to remind them he still had power, but by the time he had returned from the guards' barracks, the readers were gone. They weren't here either, but one of the pages had told him to report.

The slates still sat on the dais where they had been left when Radekir arrived. The thought of her made Tarne smile. He hadn't been able to threaten the readers, but they would feel his power nonetheless.

The door behind the dais opened and the readers entered. They kept their heads down as they walked around the brothers and down the stairs to the slates. Tarne could see no evidence of unity, but knew there had to be for the readers to reappear.

The King followed them, supported by his servants. His walk was slower than before, his movements even more painful. Tarne had never seen a man deteriorate in a single day. He didn't think the King would live through the week.

Tarne glared at Dasis, wishing she would look up. He wanted to remind her with a gesture or a grimace that she still needed to chose Ele for him. Yet she didn't move. He wondered if she would no matter what he wanted.

The servants held the King upright. He cleared his throat. The sound echoed in the overlarge room. "We shall begin again. If Dasis cannot read the already drawn slates, Stashie will redraw them. If I have a son with a pure heart, he will lead. You all will follow him and not question his rule."

Dasis picked up the slates. Then she took a cloth from her pocket and wiped them off. The advisers gasped. "Sire," she said, her voice faint, "I believe we should do new readings. I can see these hearts, but I don't remember which is which."

Ele's hands clenched into fists. Tarne gripped his knees. Vasenu hadn't moved. He looked as if he were expecting this development.

"Vasenu," the King commanded, then sat down quickly, too quickly, as if his legs would no longer support him.

Vasenu stood, walked down the dais, and nodded at Tarne. Tarne did not nod back. The arrogance of the man. Just because he thought he had won. Vasenu thought that the King's ruling meant something. Tarne would show him. He would show them all how much power the King had in his last few days.

Vasenu sat before Stashie and extended his left hand. Stashie pulled chalk from its container and sketched rapidly on the slate. Then she set the slate aside and let go of Vasenu's hand. "Thank you," she said.

"Thank you," he responded with a sincerity that Tarne didn't believe. Then he stood and returned to his seat on the side of the dais. Ele stood next. His trembling was visible even from the floor. He took the stairs carefully, as if he were afraid that, in his nervousness, he would trip. He knelt in front of Stashie like a supplicant, and extended his left hand.

She took his hand and removed chalk almost instantly. The sketch seemed simpler. She made fewer strokes and finished quicker. Tarne felt his heart pound against his chest. Maybe his humiliation was for nothing. Maybe Ele was the one with the purer heart.

"Thank you," Stashie said to him.

Ele nodded at her, stood, and returned to his seat. Dasis studied the slates before her. After a moment, she reached out and took Stashie's hand.

"We have two brothers," Dasis said, "identical in form, with the same birthdate, and living the same lives."

Pardu looked even paler than he had before. Tarne wondered if the sickness had grown worse or if Dasis's words were affecting him.

"Yet they have very different hearts, complementary hearts—as if one were given a part the other lacked. One brother has never understood love. His heart is unmarked and empty. He has given affection and allowed affection to come to him, but nothing has touched him inside. Nothing affects his heart."

Ele twisted his hands together. Vasenu hadn't moved.

"The other brother has loved every day of his life. His heart is marred, pocked, and scratched. He understands how to give and how sometimes even giving can grant hurt. This brother has a pure heart, for he understands that love cannot exist without pain."

Dasis set the slates down. They clunked against the stairs. She stood and pulled Stashie up beside her. "Vasenu," she said, "your heart is pure, and you know how to love."

Ele let out a strangled cry and half rose to his feet. Tarne didn't move. Damn women. They had probably chosen Vasenu to spite him. He glanced at one of the guards near the door and nodded. The guard nodded back and left.

The King snapped his fingers and the servants helped him rise. "Vasenu." The King extended a hand to his son. "As of today, you will bear the name of my heir and successor. You will take my place when I die, and rule fairly until your son replaces you."

Vasenu took his hand, and stood beside his father. Ele sank back onto his cushion, his expression blank.

"My son, Ele," the King continued, "shall inherit my brother's lands east of the palace. He will hold a place as Vasenu's most trusted adviser, and he will retain all the respect due a king's son."

Tarne crossed his arms in front of his chest. Ele was angry. Tarne could feel it from even this distance. Vasenu might hate Tarne, but Ele never had. Ele might consider redressing his father's betrayal.

"As for my advisers," the King continued, "I expect you to treat Vasenu as you have treated me, with courage, honesty, respect, and loyalty. This kingdom holds our futures. We must do everything we can to make sure that it survives."

The heart readers gathered their possessions and moved to the side of the dais. "Enough speeches," the King said. He clapped his hands. "Let the festivities begin."

Outside, the choir began again, this time voices lilting in a rousing, joyous tune. Tarne wanted to strangle the notes out of their throats. He didn't feel like celebrating. The damn women had made too much work for him. He stood, only to be shoved by advisers pushing their way toward the dais, trying to be the first to congratulate the new king. Ele stood off in the corner with the readers, forgotten and lost. Tarne pushed his way toward Ele. Stashie saw Tarne coming and scurried out of his way.

Tarne took Ele's hand, and squeezed it once. "Luck can be changed, you know."

"How?" Ele asked.

But Tarne didn't answer him. They couldn't be seen talking in front of this group. He would bide his time, and make his plan known when he felt it safe. Until then, he pushed his way forward, ready to congratulate Vasenu on his new, very short, reign.

CHAPTER 35

Stashie grabbed Dasis's hand. They had to get out of there. They had to leave before something else could happen. Tarne had gotten too close to them a moment ago, and all of the people—the King's people—were pressing against her. She couldn't stand it. She needed to get away.

She started down the stairs, when Dasis stopped her. "We haven't gotten paid yet." Dasis almost shouted the words above the din. The cold room had suddenly gotten hot with the press of bodies.

"I don't care," Stashie said and tugged at Dasis.

Dasis still didn't move. "What about Radekir?"

Stashie's heart froze. She had forgotten about Radekir. In her concern for herself, she had forgotten all about the woman who was imprisoned because of her mistake.

Stashie dropped Dasis's hand, and steeled herself. She pushed her way through the throng that had gathered around the King and his son. The other son, the impure one, watched her, eyes haunted.

"Excuse me, sire."

No one looked at her except the man next to her. His expression told her she was out of place. She shouldered past him and tried again. "Sire!"

The King glanced up. He did not look pleased. At his movement, the conversation ebbed.

She bobbed a little, trying to show respect. "Excuse me, sire, but we have a friend who is still imprisoned. We did do the reading. Could you set her free?"

Dasis had shoved her way to Stashie's side. "And, please, sire. We haven't been paid either."

Her voice rang in the now quiet hall. "Impudent peasants," someone whispered. The silibant sounds repeated themselves over and over, each time the derision sounding worse.

The King started to speak, then doubled over in a racking cough. His heir grabbed him and held him tightly. Blood seeped through the King's hands. A servant handed him another handkerchief, which the King used to wipe at his hands and face. He rose slowly, as if the movement were painful. "See to it that they're paid, Aene. And free that woman." He swallowed, then addressed Stashie and Dasis. "Thank you for your services. I am sorry for the actions of my adviser. Be assured that no one will bother you again."

Dasis nodded. "Thank you, sire."

Stashie bobbed again. She didn't believe the King's words, but she saw no reason in confronting him. She was a peasant, as someone had said, and peasants were always bothered by royalty and royalty's people. Nothing would ever change that.

The King's servant, Aene, came down the stairs beside them. "I will get your money and help you release your friend," he said.

The voices started up again. Dasis followed Aene closely, wending their way through the crowd on the stairs. Stashie lagged a little, getting trapped behind person after person.

Someone grabbed her arm. She wrenched it away, only to have it grabbed again. She looked up. Tarne stared at her, his cheeks flushed, eyes glittering. "Don't think you can betray me and survive this easily," he said. "I still have a great deal of power, more than anyone thinks."

Stashie yanked her arm away. "You have nothing to gain by terrorizing us anymore."

"I can let people know that they shouldn't cross me. Imagine your partner's head on a spike. A little sample of what might be to others who try your tricks."

"You wouldn't."

Tarne shrugged. "Probably not. That's too obvious.

I'm better known for doing the unexpected. And don't worry. You will pay for what you have done. I guarantee it."

Stashie shoved him away from her, and forced her way through the crowd. She glanced back once. He didn't follow her. He stood at the foot of the stairs, smiling, as if the entire afternoon and his humiliation had never happened.

The aisle was thinning, and it took her only a moment to catch up to Dasis and Aene. "You okay?" Dasis asked. "You're pale."

"I'm fine," Stashie said. She walked with determination, careful not to let Tarne see that he had frightened her. Once they were free of the palace, she would talk Dasis into leaving Leanda. Tarne couldn't touch them if he didn't know where they had gone. She would ask Dasis to take Radekir too, at least part of the way. She didn't want Tarne to interrogate Radekir to find Stashie.

Aene led them out a side door in the Assembly Room, and into a narrow corridor. He took them down a flight of steps into a small, rounded hallway. A torch burned beside the door at the end of the hallway. Aene grabbed the torch, and knocked five times in a repeating pattern. Then the door swung open.

Candles burned on tables inside the room. The room smelled of smoke and sweat. Four men sat at those tables, copying figures and counting coins. The King's money house. Stashie had heard of it, but had never thought she would see it.

"I need payment for the heart readers," Aene said.

One of the scribes got up. He went to the back of the room, opened a small door and disappeared. A moment later, he returned carrying four small pouches.

"I've broken it up, easier to carry," he said.

Aene took the pouches and handed two to each woman. Stashie was astonished at the weight. Dasis opened hers. Gold glittered. Stashie tied hers to the inside of her skirt, so that the pouches would pound against her leg. Dasis did the same.

Aene thanked the scribe and led them out of the room. "Don't think you can reenter," he said. "The knock-code changes daily, and if you try to get in on your own, you will be killed. Is that clear?"

Stashie nodded. Murder, terror, and intimidation. She hated the way these people operated. Dasis clutched Stashie's hand. Her palm was damp.

"What about Radekir?" Stashie asked.

"They took her to a room off the Assembly Room. Come." Aene returned the torch to the wall, and led them up the stairs. Once inside the corridor, he turned left. The corridor got darker and had a musty smell. Poor Radekir. All she had tried to do was make sure that nothing had gone wrong. She had come even though Stashie had treated her so coolly when she left. She believed in Stashie and was now paying the price for that belief.

The corridor seemed endless. It grew dank and chill. A single torch guttered in the weird, thick air. Aene glanced at it, and Stashie thought she caught a sense of unease.

"Come along," he said. His voice held an urgency that hadn't been present before. He picked up his stride.

Dasis and Stashie did too. Perhaps he just didn't like to be in this hallway. Perhaps something about it spooked him. They had gone another few feet when Stashie saw the torch holder. It was empty, and the entire area was dark. A smell had seeped into the air, thick and rank, a familiar scent, one that made her think of—Tarne, and her brother Tylee.

"No," she whispered.

"Get that other torch," Aene said.

Stashie had already turned. She was running down the corridor, away from the smell, away from Dasis, away from everything that reminded her of the past. Then Radekir's face rose in her mind, the soft touch of her hand, and the sweet smile she had had just the night before. Stashie made herself slow down. When she got to the torch, she took it out of the holder.

The torch had burned halfway down and was warm against her hand. She had to move cautiously because each time too much wind caught it, the torch threatened to go out. As she approached the other two, she saw what was alarming Aene. The torch holders were all empty. The corridor should have been well lit. They hadn't put Radekir in a dungeon at all. They had just put her in a fairly comfortable place to guard her while she waited. But there was no light. And there should have been.

"Where is she?" Dasis asked.

Aene licked his lower lip. "She should be in the room up ahead," he said.

Stashie's torch illuminated the ground in front of them. Burnt-out torch husks were scattered across the floor. She kicked one aside, and it hit another, rolling until they bumped against the wall.

"Radekir?" Stashie's voice echoed. She sensed no presence other than theirs, no warmth that would respond.

Aene took the torch from Stashie. He held it before him like a sword. "There should be guards here," he said.

The chill had seeped into Stashie's bones. Dasis grabbed Stashie's hand, but Stashie shook her away. She didn't want to concentrate on anyone else. She had to find Radekir.

Aene stepped into the room. His hand shook, and the torch guttered. Dasis took it from him before he dropped it. He turned away, and vomited against the wall. Dasis put her hand over her mouth and backed out of the room. Stashie took the torch from her and walked forward. She could handle what was in that room. She had seen almost everything.

The rank smell was even stronger here. The walls were black with blood, and the floor sticky. Stashie stood in the center of the room and stared at the thing before her. Its face—her face, Radekir's face—had been left intact, but the rest of her body had been spread across the room like festival decorations. Some parts had been burned so that they would fuse against the wall. Stashie ignored that and walked forward, staring at Radekir's head. Her eyes were wide with fright, her mouth pulled into a line of pain. Stashie touched Radekir's cheek. It was still warm. She hadn't been dead long.

I'm better known for doing the unexpected. You will pay for what you have done.

Stashie balled her free hand into a fist. Tarne. This time she was not frightened, but angry. This time he had taken her through everything, the worst of everything. And he was wrong.

This time, he would pay.

PART THREE

Four Months Later

CHAPTER 36

The stables were warm and smelled of horses. Vasenu rubbed down Misty, cleaning the sweat off her black hide. He liked doing this kind of work. It made him feel a part of the cycle, and remember how life had been before his father had gotten ill. Sometimes Vasenu wondered if the heart readers hadn't been wrong. He didn't enjoy the busy work of ruling. He hated the small decisions, each with the power to alter lives. Perhaps it would be better to have someone who didn't care, someone who made the decisions lightly, instead of agonizing over every change and every detail.

The horse nickered. He reached in his pocket, but had nothing to give her. One of the grooms came over and provided her with a sweet. Vasenu smiled his appreciation.

"Sire?"

Vasenu turned. Since his father's illness had gotten worse, everyone treated Vasenu as King. He was still not used to being addressed with the same respect people had accorded his father, but he at least answered to it now.

Aene stood at the stable door, his face flushed. He was breathing heavily, as if he had come a long way. "Your father, sire. He needs you."

Vasenu handed the brush to the groom, then hurried out of the stable. The midafternoon sun was fierce. It reflected off the sand and made him squint. He hated the heat, hated the sunbaked warmth of this place. He didn't understand why the palace hadn't moved north, where the air was fresher and cooler, and every event seemed like less of an emergency because the heat didn't make things worse.

Aene led him past the barracks, through a small copse of trees, and around the back of his father's wing. The servant said nothing, but he moved with a rapidity that surprised Vasenu.

"What is it?" Vasenu asked.

"He's dying." Aene opened a side door. "I'll fetch your brother, if you like."

Vasenu nodded. "Ele needs to be here."

He went on ahead as Aene ran off in the direction of Ele's quarters. His father's wing smelled of blood and sickness. Vasenu always grimaced when he entered it. He couldn't stand coming, but he forced himself to show up every day, even though his visits probably didn't matter. His father had stopped talking shortly after the reading. Then he began to sleep all the time. Last week, he had mumbled gibberish, and this week, he had lain on his pillows, staring straight ahead and drooling.

Vasenu hated to watch the deterioration of this once-powerful man. When his father ceased speaking, Vasenu only let close advisers, a few servants, and Ele see the King. And in the past few weeks, no one had come on their own. No one except Vasenu.

He pushed open the door to his father's chamber and went inside. The sickness smell was stronger here. His father looked like a pale ghost resting against the cushions. His skin was translucent, and the bones jutted prominently in his face. He had aged decades in the past few weeks. Now the man that Vasenu had known had become an elderly doddering corpse, waiting for the breath to leave him.

"Father?" Vasenu knelt down and took his father's hand. The fingers twitched weakly. The King's eyes were closed.

Vasenu couldn't see what had caused Aene to seek him out, but something about the King's demeanor had frightened the servant. He had not called Vasenu away from his tasks before.

"Father, it's Vasenu."

The twitching continued. The King's tongue lolled out the side of his mouth. His cheeks were flecked with blood. Vasenu smoothed the hair off the King's forehead.

"I'm here, Father."

The King didn't move. Aene appeared at the door, Ele beside him.

"What's changed?" Vasenu asked.

"I give him water and he does not swallow." Aene's voice trembled. "I put food on his tongue and it stays there until I clean it off. His breathing has gotten very shallow. I do not think it will be much longer."

"It could be days," Ele snapped. He had been angry since the readings.

"No." Aene knelt beside Vasenu. "He told me how his father died. Explained the symptoms and the progression. Hours, maybe, but not days."

"Thank you." Vasenu kept his grip on his father's hand. Hours. The word sent a chill through him, a chill that ended in an emptiness. He had been expecting his father's death, welcoming it, because he hated seeing his father suffer. But he was not ready for it. If he had been ready for it, the emptiness would not have appeared.

Vasenu closed his eyes, remembering the stern man, the powerful one with the deep voice, the father who had raised them and kept them by each other's side. As a boy he had adored that man, doing everything he could to get his father's attention and his father's praise.

A hand brushed Vasenu's arm. He opened his eyes. Ele sat beside him, and caressed his father's face.

"He was always such a strong man," Ele said.

"He still is," Vasenu replied, "or he would not be clinging to life like this."

"He's not clinging. He's dying." Ele pushed himself away and went to the other side of the room. "I don't know why you need me here. You can do the death-watch alone."

The rhythm in the twitching fingers remained constant. Vasenu didn't look at his brother. "I need you to show him you care."

"Why should I care about him? He abandoned me."

Vasenu squeezed his father's hand, then let it go and turned to face his brother. "He did not abandon you. We both knew that one day we would have separate tasks. He prepared us for that from birth."

"He always made it clear that he favored you."

Vasenu stood. "Let's go outside."

Ele shook his head. He sat on one of the pillows. "We're going to stay right here."

"I don't want him to hear this fight. He doesn't need it."

"His brain died a long time ago." Ele leaned back, but didn't look relaxed. He crossed his arms in front of his chest. "And if it didn't, he needs to know how I feel."

Vasenu crouched beside Ele's pillow. "He did not always favor me. He treated both of us equally. You're not thinking clearly."

"He favored you," Ele repeated. "And when it was clear that the reading wasn't going the way he wanted, he pulled the heart readers aside and told them what to say. He didn't have the guts to make his choice in public. He had to hide behind two women and some fake superstitious nonsense."

Vasenu rocked back on his heels. His stomach felt hollow. "Who told you that? Tarne?"

"It didn't take anyone's help to make that clear to me. I believe in your right to rule, Vasenu, as much as I believe that he loved me." Ele extended a hand toward his father and froze. Vasenu followed his gaze. The King's body was shaking twice as badly as it had before. His lips were working, as if he were trying to speak.

"Stop this," Aene said. "You're upsetting him."

"We'll finish this conversation some other time," Vasenu said. He hurried to his father's side, and took one of the twitching hands. "Father, it's okay. We're okay. We'll settle everything."

The King shook his head from left to right. Vasenu

couldn't tell if the action was a voluntary movement or not. Ele got up and stood over them, looking down. "I upset him, huh?"

"I hope not," Vasenu said. "Quick. Take his other hand. Let him know you care."

"What, and lie? I can't love, remember?" Ele made a half-laugh.

"Ele, let it go. He's dying."

Ele clasped his hands behind his back. "We're talking about my future here. The future he destroyed. I'm not going to let it go. And I'm not going to tell him I love him when at the moment I hate everything he stands for. And I'm not going to do what you tell me to, not ever."

He walked out of the room, back straight, hands clasped so tightly Vasenu could see the knuckles turning white. The King's shaking had grown even worse.

"This is not good for your father," Aene said. "Brothers fighting at his deathbed. His soul will not rest."

"It's all right, Father," Vasenu said, running his hand along his father's brow. The King kept moving his head from side to side. "You must trust that we'll settle it, Ele and I. We will. I promise."

"No!" The word exploded from the King's mouth in a spray of spittle and blood. He shook so hard it seemed as if he were going to fall out of his skin. His lips moved again, but Vasenu could hear nothing.

"We will." Vasenu felt his own hands shaking. He took one of the handkerchiefs from the cushion beside the bed and wiped the King's mouth. "I promise. I'll rule this land as you did, Father, and I'll make sure that there is no strife. I'll get Ele—"

"No." This time the word was fainter.

Vasenu looked at Aene. The other man shrugged and kept patting the pillows around the King, as if those would hold him in place.

"Father, please, believe me," Vasenu said, feeling all of three years old and very frightened. "I will do everything I can—"

The King let out a huge sigh. His body jerked once

and stopped moving. His eyes half opened, showing the whites, and his teeth clamped down on his tongue.

Aene placed a hand on the King's chest, then brought it under the King's nose. "He's not breathing," Aene said. "And I can't find his heartbeat."

Vasenu stopped breathing himself for a moment. The lack of oxygen filled the hollow area in his stomach with a tightness that almost felt good. He wanted to shake the old man, bring the life back into him, have his father sit up and yell at him for not controlling Ele. He wanted his father to take back his job, to take his power and handle the world around them. He reached out and touched his father's face. The skin was still warm, but the touch felt empty.

He took a deep breath, then got up slowly. "Prepare the banners," he said. "And have someone say chants over my father's body so that his soul rests properly. We need to make the final transition of power smooth and easy."

"Yes." Aene wasn't looking at him. He had cupped the King's face and was holding it as if he wanted to pull it forward and clutch it against his breast.

"I will notify my brother," Vasenu said. He turned his back on the corpse and its servant, and left the room. As he stepped into the corridor, he felt as if the stench of sickness clung to him. He wiped his hands and brushed off his sleeves. He was trembling and barely breathing. He couldn't close his eyes for fear of seeing his father's twitching body, hearing that final *no!* resound again. Was his father saying no to death? Or was he saying no to Vasenu's words? Either way, it unnerved him.

He leaned against the wall for a moment, feeling the coolness of the mud brick soothe him. He hadn't expected to fight with Ele. He had thought everything was settled. Ele was bitter, but Vasenu would have been bitter too. But to fight, to doubt what they had been raised for? Vasenu shook his head. He stood and squared his shoulders. He was King now. He didn't have time to mourn. He had to keep the kingdom running smoothly, and he had to settle this trouble with his brother.

His father had demanded peace between them. Vasenu needed that peace. The family had been changed by his father's illness and death, but Vasenu wouldn't let it be destroyed. He couldn't. He and Ele were brothers. Their love would remain constant forever.

CHAPTER 37

The sun had reached its height. No shade appeared on the side of the buildings. Stashie wished she had put a canvas over her table. The turban made her head sweat, and her table had grown warm. She sat cross-legged on top of it, trickles running down her cheeks. No one visited the bazaar. They were all at home sleeping, or carrying on business in the cool, dark confines of the mud-brick buildings.

Her dice were hot. She wondered if she dared crawl under the table to sleep. The shade would ease some of the pressure on her arms and legs.

She unwrapped herself from her swamilike position and eased under the table. Her skin tingled with the memory of heat, but she could already feel the relief. Just a short nap. She checked her pouch, attached to her side, and lay down on the rug, ignoring the little grains of sand that had rolled on it with the morning's wind.

She hadn't expected to be so lonely. When she sent Dasis away, she had thought she wanted to be by herself. But the nights lasted forever and when she closed her eyes, she still saw Radekir's face holding the shock of her death. She hadn't loved Radekir. She loved Dasis, but Dasis couldn't be part of her revenge against Tarne. Stashie couldn't bear to lose the only person she loved.

Dasis hadn't understood. She had cried and begged, promising to hide and to not get in the way. But Stashie had stayed firm. She had finally walked away from Dasis, and stayed away, even when Dasis tried to approach her. That had been almost four months ago, and she hadn't seen Dasis since.

She also hadn't taken any action. She felt dead inside, more dead than she had felt after crossing that desert the year Tarne murdered her family. All she wanted was revenge. And she couldn't think up a plan.

"Stashie, soldiers."

She must have dozed. The shade had moved from under the table, leaving half of her body exposed to the sunlight. She squinted, and covered her eyes with her hand. Ytsak crouched near the table's edge, his patch reflecting the sun.

She pushed herself up on one elbow. "Soldiers?"

"Near my booth. Come on, get up. You'll need your strength."

Stashie ignored his outstretched hand and brushed the sand off her cheek. She felt even hotter than she had when she crawled under the table. She adjusted her turban and rolled out from underneath into the sunlight. The tabletop was searing, but she sat on it anyway. Ytsak smiled at her.

"This is your chance," he said.

She shrugged. He handed her a few dates and wandered back to his booth. He had kept watch over her since she sent Dasis away, and he knew about her desire to get Tarne. Ytsak seemed to have his own reasons for wanting revenge, although he never spoke of them outright. He just managed to be there every time she needed something, or could use support.

Five soldiers clustered around his booth. His partner was haggling with them over some bit of fruit. Stashie ate the dates. They were cool against her throat. She hadn't realized how thirsty she was.

One of the soldiers laughed and left the group. He was more weatherworn than the others, older, perhaps, and more seasoned. Wrinkles creased his sun-darkened face, but his eyes had the freshness of youth. Stashie watched him weave in and out of the booths, touching cloth samples, lingering over the food tables, flirting with some of the young girls. She clutched her

ankles and was amazed at her lack of fear. The fear
had left her with her decision to get Tarne. She probably knew, somewhere in the back of her mind, that
he could not hurt her worse than he already had.

Unless he got Dasis.

The fear rose, and Stashie pushed it down. He
wouldn't get Dasis. Dasis was gone, far away. Somewhere not even Stashie knew.

The soldier had worked his way to the magic side
of the bazaar. He glanced at the tarot reader, ignored
the new heart readers off in the corner, and came
toward Stashie.

"Dice reading, huh?" His voice was soft, with more
flirtation than sarcasm in it. "Do you do palms, too?"

"My friend two rugs over reads palms," Stashie
said.

His smile faded a little with her coolness. "How
much for a reading?"

"The simpler the reading, the cheaper the price."
Stashie wiped the sweat off her face. The sun hadn't
eased during the time she slept.

"How about letting me know if I can get one of
these pretty ladies around here to spend time with
me?"

Stashie smiled. "I can do that without reading. The
answer is no. No one here sells her body. You have
to go to the taverns for that."

"What if I'm merely looking for companionship?"

"Why would a man want companionship from a
woman?"

He shrugged. "Because the man isn't from Leanda
and doesn't believe in this land's artificial
boundaries."

Stashie pushed at her dice. The surface was hot,
almost too hot. "Most of us already have
companions."

His gaze seemed to miss nothing. "You sit alone."

For a moment, Stashie thought he could see her
loneliness, her aching for Dasis, and her regret over
Radekir. Then she realized that he was merely search-

ing for someone to fill his lonely time with. "My companion vends fruit."

"The young gentleman?"

"The one with the patch."

The soldier squinted, as if he could tell she was lying. He flicked a gold coin at her. "For your time," he said.

The coin clattered on the table. Stashie didn't touch it. "I don't take coins unless I perform work."

"You gave information."

"Freely. And it was of no help."

His smile half faded. "It confirmed that I have to adapt to the culture here. It won't adapt to me. That's helpful, although not in the way I wanted."

Stashie picked up the gold piece and held it out to him. "I don't want your money," she said. "I would rather trade information for information."

He did not take the gold piece. Instead, he crossed his arms over his chest. She would have to tread lightly.

"What do you want to know?" he asked.

"Does Tarne still act as your lord and commander?"

The soldier's mouth tightened. With his posture change, she suddenly realized that he could be difficult. "He hasn't commanded us since the King took away his title weeks ago."

"Oh." Stashie looked down and shook her head. She felt a flush rise into her cheeks. "Then you don't know how to find him."

"What business have you, miss?"

She had thought of the story before, but she had never planned to use it. "I was his woman once, when he campaigned through the southern lands."

"And you seek him out?" The soldier's surprise registered in both his face and voice. He knew then, about Tarne's practices with women.

"There is a child, a son," Stashie whispered. The lie practically choked her. The idea of bearing Tarne's child filled her with horror.

"Leandan women." The soldier spit onto the sand next to the rug. "Honor and duty before pleasure.

Have you ever had a man give you pleasure? Men and women can talk, can spend time together. They don't need this artificial barrier between them. In my land—"

"I talk to Ytsak," Stashie said. The truth came easier than the lie had.

The soldier stopped, let out a sigh. "And he told you to tell Tarne about his son."

"No. He says I need to keep the boy away from here."

The soldier nodded. "Tarne is not the kindest of men. He will bend your boy into his own image."

"His son is already the image of his father."

The soldier laughed, but the laugh was bitter. "No wonder you want to rid yourself of him. The Lord Tarne tours the barracks daily, just after dawn. He advises the men and constantly assures us that he will regain his old position. All we must do is remain loyal, a task some of us will achieve easier than others. Should you want to see him, you could probably find him there, if you want to brave the soldiers."

"I've braved soldiers before," Stashie said.

"Then I wish you only the best of luck." He bowed his head and turned away.

"Wait!" Stashie cried. "Your gold piece."

He shook his head. "You need it more than I do." He walked away, head down, the laughter gone from him. Stashie wondered what about the conversation had dulled his mood. Then she sighed and tucked the gold piece in her pouch. She hadn't earned much more than that all day. Dice reading had very little profit—just enough to keep her in room and board. She had hoarded the money she made from the King. She figured she would use that—Radekir's blood money—to get revenge.

Stashie smiled and stretched. Suddenly revenge seemed like an option again. Tarne at the barracks at dawn. Perhaps she could meet him there, or have Ytsak do so. Tell him the same lie she had told the soldier and let Tarne come to meet his son. He would meet a blade instead.

She didn't want him to die right away, though. She wanted him to suffer like she had. And she didn't have a plan for that. If she let him live too long, his soldiers would come after her and all who helped her. She wouldn't condemn any more of her friends to death. She needed to kill Tarne, but slowly and painfully. He needed to use his last breaths to plead for a mercy he would never receive.

Stashie grabbed her ankles and rocked a little. The other soldiers made their way through the bazaar, eating dates and laughing. Their leader would die. She would kill him. And if she survived, she would find Dasis and live free of fear for the first time in her entire life.

CHAPTER 38

Ele sunk into the baths, the tepid water caressing his skin. He shook inside. He half imagined his body to look as his father's had, trembling on all levels, nothing to stop the shaking until his eyes rolled up and his tongue lolled out.

The old man had deserved his fate. He had hated Ele from the start.

Ele leaned against the bath's marble edge. The smell of incense made his nose tickle. Vasenu didn't understand. And yet, he would have felt the same way if he had been the one who lost. Raised together, groomed to be kings, only to have the dream yanked from him. Ele knew how to rule as well or better than his brother. Love had nothing to do with it. Pure hearts had nothing to do with it. Men who could make decisions without worrying about the consequences were the best leaders of all. Ele should have been chosen, and his father had destroyed that.

The bathhouse door creaked open. "This is private!" Ele shouted.

The door closed. He sighed and moved a little, feeling the water lap around his neck. Behind him he heard clothing rustle.

"I said this—"

"This is private, I know." Vasenu's voice. It sounded curiously flat.

Ele turned. His brother had taken off his clothes and was striding, naked, toward the water. Their bodies had once been identical, but years of living had separated them. Vasenu had a scar running along his stomach from the time he had tried to save another man in a knife fight. A number of white crescents marred his left leg from the folly of an afternoon when he had fought for a horse's life, only to be stomped near to death himself by the horse.

Vasenu slipped into the water. He was trembling visibly. The sight made Ele's trembling return.

"What do you want?"

"Father's dead." Again the flat tone. Vasenu sunk under the water, and came up, spraying water in the air like a geyser.

"He's been dead for weeks now."

"No." Vasenu pushed the wet hair off his face and found a seat at the corner of the bath. "He stopped breathing. He's not alive anymore."

Ele stopped moving. He felt something curious flicker and die within his breast. Hope. He had actually hoped for his father's improvement, and that this nightmare would end. He had wanted his father to get well and make it all right again—reunite him with Vasenu, and take the power from both of them.

Vasenu was King now.

"So?" Ele said, hoping that he kept his voice cool and disinterested.

"I thought you would want to know."

Ele lowered himself a little more, so that the water touched the bottom of his chin. "I don't really care," he said. "Nothing has changed."

Vasenu slapped water on his face, as if he were trying to make sure he was awake. "Everything's changed. He heard us fighting. He yelled 'no,' and then he died."

"It was just a reflex. He couldn't think anymore." But Vasenu's words chilled Ele. Always the ungrateful son. Then he had proved his father right, in any case. He slid under the water, feeling the pressure against his eyes, his forehead. He stayed there until his lungs felt as if they were going to burst, and even then he didn't rise. He let out some of the air, felt the bubbles as they passed his cheeks, and waited until his chest started burning. His body floated upward of its own accord. He would have to force himself to die, if that was what he wanted to do. Die and be with his father.

Ele broke the surface and gasped for air. The air tasted sweet—of incense and salt. "He's dead, huh?"

"Yes." Vasenu hadn't moved. He wouldn't have saved Ele, if Ele had started to drown.

"And you're King."

"That's what the heart readers said. That's what we agreed to accept."

"And you think I'm backing down now."

Vasenu sighed. The sound echoed across the water. "I don't know what to think. Why did you fight me in front of Father? To get him to change his mind?"

"He had no mind, remember?"

"I don't know what you were doing." Pain had etched itself across the lines in Vasenu's face. Ele wondered if he looked like that. "He wanted this transition to be smooth. He wanted the kingdom to go on as before."

"It can't." Ele spoke softly. "He's dead. You'll be a different ruler."

"You would have been too. Look," Vasenu moved a little closer. Ele resisted the urge to move away. "You're supposed to be my closest adviser. It was the best he could do without making us both rule. If we work together, we will run the kingdom together. I'll be King in name only."

"Until you disagreed with me, and that wouldn't be long." Ele cupped some water in his hand and poured it into the bath. "We never did agree on policy matters. You were always too soft."

"You never understood that there were people involved." Vasenu grabbed Ele's hand. "If we work together, we'll balance."

Ele pulled away. "We'd balance only if we were both in charge."

"But then we would never make a decision."

Ele shrugged. He put his hands on the side of the bath and eased himself out of it. Water sloshed all over the marble, sliding down toward a depression, where a small dirty puddle had formed. He grabbed a towel and wrapped himself in it. The bath had made him cold.

"Are we going to fight each other?" Vasenu asked.

"Does it matter? Neither of us will ever get what we want." Ele dried himself off, then set the towel aside. He got dressed quickly and stepped out into the scorching midafternoon heat.

The desert shimmered in front of him, more lasting than power, more lasting than anything else he would know. A thousand campaigns had been fought on that soil, a hundred rulers had come and gone. His father had ridden across that sand, with his father and brother, and then with his sons. Ele had always loved those times. He had always imagined riding across the sand with his sons, preparing them to rule in his place.

His father had given him a dream, without any real hope of ever fulfilling it. Vasenu mourned a man's life, but Vasenu had a future. Ele had no father, a brother he envied to the point of hatred, and nothing to hope for in all the coming years of his life. His father had destroyed his dreams, destroyed his family, and destroyed his future all within a few weeks. And now his father was dead, not even giving Ele a chance to redeem himself.

Ele had to create his own future. He had to carve something out of the nothing his father had left him. He had no friends, no support, and no true idea of what he wanted.

CHAPTER 39

Dasis sat in the shade of the building, her hat brim low over her eyes. The men's clothes that she wore itched. She hated the constriction around her legs, and the way the heat intensified. So far, however, Stashie hadn't noticed her—or if she had, she hadn't realized who was watching.

Dasis sighed and leaned back against the cool mudbrick. From this angle, she had a direct view of Stashie's table, and she could see most of the bazaar. The soldiers made her nervous, but Stashie hadn't looked a bit frightened. Their roles had reversed since Radekir died. Stashie had taken charge, and Dasis felt as if she had lost everything.

She understood why Stashie sent her away. Stashie wouldn't be able to take her revenge with Dasis around. Only Dasis didn't believe that Stashie could attack Tarne alone. Dasis had a stake too in Tarne's death. She would be there to help.

The last few weeks had been hell. Stashie had disappeared into herself with Radekir's death. Dasis knew that Stashie hadn't loved the woman, but still, the loss affected them both. Stashie never said a word, retreating into the quiet, haunted woman that Dasis had first met. Only this time, Dasis's touch and her silent support meant nothing. Stashie kept pushing her away until she finally commanded Dasis to leave.

And in anger, Dasis had left. She had gathered her things, leaving the slates and chalks behind, and set out across the desert alone, seeking another town, a place she could live peacefully as she and Stashie always dreamed. She traveled for miles and found quiet towns, but soldiers lurked in tents at the outskirts. Every time Dasis saw one of the soldiers, she remembered Stashie's look of fear, and Tarne's hatred. She saw Radekir's dead face, and knew that if Stashie died the same way, she would never forgive herself. So she turned back.

She knew that Stashie would never let her stay. Dasis didn't even approach her. She watched from a distance, a silent guard, whom no one knew and no one cared about. Sometimes entire days went by when she never spoke a word. Her loneliness was deep, but not as deep as Stashie's was. Stashie had spent her days just as she had so long ago, sleeping and gaining strength.

The fact that she had taken on Radekir's old work didn't bother Dasis. She felt it appropriate somehow. But Dasis did know that if Stashie didn't make a move soon, Dasis would go back to her and demand their reunion. If Stashie wasn't going to take action, then the separation wasn't necessary.

Dasis felt in her pocket for a gold piece. She would get herself a nice midday meal and then continue her vigil. She started to get up, when she saw the soldier approach Stashie.

Dasis sat back down. The conversation was animated, the soldier shocked. Stashie was calm, almost too calm, and when she appeared emotional, Dasis recognized the pretense. The scam had started. Stashie finally had a plan.

Dasis clutched the money tightly in her palm. The gold piece dug into her skin, like a small sand creature biting to save its life. She hadn't believed that Stashie would do anything. She had somehow thought that Stashie would give it all up, that they would be reunited soon.

Dasis should have known better. Stashie never forgot and she never forgave. Dasis bit her lower lip. She could go to Stashie and try to talk her out of it, but that wouldn't work. Stashie would only get angry. No. Dasis had to watch even more carefully than before. And she had to be ready. For anything.

CHAPTER 40

Ele slipped inside the tent. The shade brought no relief from the midday heat. A table, ornate chairs, and beautifully embroidered pillows furnished the tent. The faint scent of day-old incense rose in the air. Uniforms hung against the far wall, half a dozen of them for all occasions, all of them worthless now.

His wasn't the only luck that had changed with the readings. Tarne had lost everything too.

"I didn't expect a visit."

Ele whirled. Tarne stood behind him, holding up the flap to the tent. He looked older somehow, more tired. "You heard?" Ele asked.

"That your father finally died. Yes." Tarne hadn't moved. His entire manner was cold.

"Vasenu's in charge now."

Tarne let the flap down. "What do you want?"

Tarne's anger made Ele take a step back. "I wanted to talk to you. I tried to talk with Vasenu, but he won't listen to me."

"Why should he? He's King now. He doesn't have to listen to anyone."

"We're brothers—"

"You are whining. He doesn't have to take anyone seriously, especially not someone who whines."

Ele took another breath. "I came to talk to you, Tarne."

"Then talk." Tarne went over to one of the chairs and sat down. He looked up, as if he were waiting for Ele to sit too.

Ele continued to stand. The chill he had received in the bath hadn't left him. "I was wondering if we could work together, like you were talking about before."

"That was before. Your father is dead now. My connections are shattering. I have no power." Tarne adjusted his boots and then crossed his feet on the other pillow. He leaned back on his elbows, the posture almost too casual for his words.

"You said you would always have power."

"And you let me believe that you didn't need me." Tarne brushed a strand of hair off his forehead. "What do you want, Ele?"

Ele. No "Your Highness" or title of respect. Just Ele. The name made a flush of anger sweep through him. "I want to be King."

"You'd have to kill your brother to do that."

"There has to be another way."

Tarne shrugged. "Then talk with him."

Ele shook his head. He had been wrong to come here. Tarne couldn't help him. Only his father could. And his father was dead.

Tarne stood and took a step toward him, hand outstretched. "You want to be King?"

"That's what I was trained for."

"Then I can make you King."

Ele studied Tarne's face, unable to read it. This was what he had come here for. This was the kind of support he needed. "How?"

Tarne smiled. "We have a lot of choices. You could kill your brother outright—a duel, a fight for the throne. The people would understand. No one completely believes that women should decide the future of Leanda, no matter how superstitious the people are. Then, of course, you would be the one covered in blood, the one who remembered your brother's last word, last breath—and last glance."

No, his father had said and shivered to death. That was what Vasenu had said. His father had yelled *no*.

"And our other choice?" he asked.

Tarne closed his eyes and leaned back. "A public murder, an assassination by a crazed man, someone we can kill quickly who won't talk. Or in the middle of the night, my men would go in and slaughter him, stab him to death, cut off his head. We'd claim it was a military coup and we'd then kill the new head of the soldiers as well. You would take command and save the people from an awful rule. There are a lot of options. But the options aren't the issue."

Ele finally sat down. Sweat was running down one side of his face, even though he still felt chilled. "I don't understand."

"Of course you don't. You're a king's son. You've lived an easy life, no matter how many campaigns you've gone on. You've had people wait on you and say 'Your Highness' and tend to your every whim. You've never had to make a difficult choice. Even now, you're coming to me, expecting me to have the solution to your problem."

"I thought that's what you offered."

"I know that's what you thought. I'm offering ways that we can both obtain power. Something completely different."

Ele couldn't swallow. He had made a mistake in coming here. "I don't want to kill my brother."

"It's the only way you can be King."

Ele shook his head. "There has to be another way."

"Look." Tarne took Ele's hand. Ele pulled away. "If the situation were reversed—which it will be if you take over from him—he would kill you. You are no longer brothers, no longer close. Now you're enemies—"

Tarne's words opened the rip forming in Ele's heart. He couldn't lose his father and his brother on the same day. Not even for a kingship. He and Vasenu had had the same training. Their rules would be similar. He couldn't fairly say that he would be a better king than his brother. And he couldn't kill his brother for his own gain.

Ele stood up. "I made a mistake in talking with you. I thought you would have reasonable ideas. It shows how muddled the events of the past few weeks have made me to allow me to think *you* would be reasonable."

Something flashed across Tarne's face. Panic? It disappeared too quickly for Ele to be certain what the emotion was. "We need each other," Tarne said.

"No," Ele said. "You need me."

He grabbed the flap of the tent and let himself into the sunshine. The soldiers looked at him as if he were a curiosity. He walked past them to the edges of the wall and peered through one of the openings. He loved this land, deep down. It was as much a part of his family as his brother was, as his father was—had been. If he were to fight Vasenu, he would lose his entire family. His brother would become his enemy, as Tarne had predicted. And the land would curse him, because too many people would die.

Ele wiped the sweat off his forehead. His father was dead. He needed to view the body, say chants, and hope the spirits would convey his apologies to his father. Maybe his father's spirit would forgive him.

Maybe he would forgive himself.

CHAPTER 41

Tarne watched the tent flap fall shut. He had failed. He had pushed too hard with both brothers, and he had failed. He closed his eyes and leaned back against the pillows, feeling the softness against his back. Without a brother's support, he had nothing.

Nothing except himself.

He remembered the joy of riding into a village, the fear on the peasants' faces, the way they listened to him. He had had real power then, not this political maneuvering based on intrigue that operated at the palace. In the villages what Tarne said was law. He wanted that again.

In the middle of the night, my men would go in and slaughter him, stab him to death, cut off his head. We'd claim it was a military coup and then we'd kill the new head of the soldiers as well.

Tarne sat up. He hadn't thought of the implications of those words, not until now. He had a lot of options. He could kill Vasenu and make everyone think that Ele had done it. There were witnesses to Ele's visit to the tent. It wouldn't take much to make Ele into a scapegoat. And then Tarne could either kill Ele or control him, use the incident to take power from him, and manipulate Ele however he wanted.

Tarne let out a long sigh. He didn't need to wait for others. He could act on his own. Should Ele gain power, he would do the same unless Tarne made himself invaluable. Perhaps Ele would have a short rule too. Perhaps Tarne would have to take over to prevent the country from falling into chaos and civil war.

He had never thought of himself as a hero. He had

never wanted that kind of adulation. But he could gain adulation from fear—fear of the future. And he would become a savior.

Tarne laughed. For the first time in weeks, he felt strong.

CHAPTER 42

Stashie took the gold piece from the young woman. Sometimes she wished she could waive her fee. She felt as if she were cheating them somehow, even though people had been taught from childhood that most of the magicks in the bazaars were not real.

Stashie watched the woman make her way through the crowds. The day wasn't as hot as some had been, but Stashie wished she were somewhere else. She hated lying to these people, telling them that the dice saw good fortune in their futures or wealth or the cure to some hideous disease. She was amazed that more of her clients didn't return in anger, wanting to hurt her somehow. Yet many came week after week for another dose of luck and prophecies for the future.

Shouting echoed from the other edge of the bazaar. Stashie turned. Ytsak was climbing out of his booth. The crowds were thinning—running. Stashie got off her table as a soldier rode by. His white tunic blazed against the black hide of the horse. He had his sword out and was slashing at the people and the booths.

"The King is dead!" he shouted. "Long live the King!"

Other soldiers, also riding black horses, followed him. They rode among the tables, scattering the crowds and knocking over booths. Stashie grabbed her dice and her money pouch and ran.

"Best run, mistress!" one of the soldiers shouted after her. "The bazaar is closed. There should be no merriment on the death day of the King!"

She tripped over a rug, but kept running. People surrounded her. The air smelled of sweat and fear.

Behind her, she heard screams and crashes as booths fell over. Ytsak caught up with her, his hands stained with crushed dates and his forehead streaked with blood.

He grabbed her arm. "Come on," he said.

He pulled her through the crowd sideways so that they weren't moving with the group. They ended up at the side of a building, half in the shade. The crowd flowed past them, screaming and running. The bazaar was a mess: booths destroyed, tables knocked over, rugs pulled up. Some of the merchants were on their hands and knees trying to pick up their wares. The soldiers were weaving their horses through the mess, trampling people as they went.

One of the horses careened toward them. Stashie cringed and Ytsak cast about for a place to go. Another hand grabbed Stashie's. A young man in loose trousers, his face half covered by his hat, pulled her into the crowd. She grabbed Ytsak and they all swung around a corner and into the building itself.

The building smelled of ale. Stashie blinked. Dust motes rose in the thin stream of sunlight coming in the door. They were in a tavern and it was empty— odd, even at midday. The building shook as people ran past. The screams faded and grew, faded and grew, but the clip-clop of horses' hooves slowly passed.

"Thank you," Stashie said to both of her benefactors over the din. Her voice warbled. She took Ytsak's arm. "Your partner?"

Ytsak shook his head. "He wasn't here. We had sold a lot of fruit this morning. He was getting more."

Stashie could hear the worry in his voice. She squeezed his arm and turned to the young man—

—who was walking toward the door. She recognized the walk. She had seen it every day for years. "Dasis?"

The boy broke into a sprint and hurried out the door. Stashie broke away from Ytsak. She ran to the door, but saw only the frightened crowd shoving its way past on the packed street. No hat, no slightly rotund figure. No boy. No Dasis.

"Did you see that?" Stashie asked.

Ytsak nooded. "He helped us both."

"That was Dasis."

Ytsak put his arm around Stashie and pulled her close. She let him, but remained stiff in his grasp. "You sent Dasis away," he said.

"She came back."

"She would have told you."

Stashie stared out for a moment at the chaos in the street. A cry went up and faded at the sound of splintering wood. Dasis might not have said anything. Dasis had been so hurt when Stashie had sent her away. And Stashie had been right. She hadn't expected the riot, but she knew that people would be hurt. She knew that things were going to change. And she didn't want Dasis killed.

"I have to find her," Stashie said.

"No." Ytsak smoothed the hair on her forehead. He smelled of dates and sunshine. "That boy helped you and now he's gone. He wasn't Dasis. You would only get hurt if you went back out there."

Stashie took a deep breath and moved away from Ytsak. He was right. She was seeing Dasis because she missed her so much, because she wanted Dasis to rescue her. Only, Dasis was gone. Stashie needed to be alone to get her revenge and to protect the last person she loved.

"Why did they wreck the bazaar?" she whispered.

"I don't know," Ytsak said. He wiped his stained hands on his tunic. "But things are going to be different now."

"Vasenu is King," Stashie said, more to herself. She remembered his calloused hand in hers, the calm manner in which he had gazed at her. His brother had been nervous, but Vasenu wasn't. She wondered if he was nervous now.

"Let's hope he gets this controlled and quickly."

Stashie glanced at Ytsak. His patch was blood covered and his visible eye looked red. It wasn't exhaustion. It was fear. Ytsak had been near soldiers out of control before.

Stashie shuddered, remembering the yipping, the cries of elation as the soldiers had taken the village well all those years before. "Yes," she said quietly, "let's hope this only lasts the night."

CHAPTER 43

Tarne pushed himself off the pillows. He ran a hand through his hair, untangled his beard and changed into one of his lighter uniforms. The tunic belted at the waist, and the pants were looser than they had been. He had lost weight since the southern campaigns. He thought of this as his war clothing. And he was about to start a war. On two fronts.

He pushed back the tent flap and stepped outside. Most of the men had dispersed. In the distance, he could hear shouts and cries. Dust hung in the air—not from a sandstorm, but from the movement of too many horses at once. The soldiers had gone into the town to announce the King's death. Tarne smiled. Vasenu's first failure. He probably didn't know that soldiers loose with horrible news were likely to do terrible things. He would learn.

Or maybe he wouldn't have time. Tarne crossed the sand, nodding at the men who remained. Some sat listlessly against the fortress wall, and more than a few had red-rimmed eyes. A group near the main doors shared a jug of mead and were getting quietly, seriously drunk. Tarne watched them, noting faces, matching names. Loyalists. He hadn't expected so many of the men to be affected by Pardu's death.

He rounded a corner and slipped into the barracks. The mud-brick building smelled of too many closely packed human bodies. He sneezed, then noted the lesser scents of incense and alcohol. Discipline had declined in the few short weeks that he had been away. He never would have allowed alcohol in the barracks. The men wouldn't be fresh should a surprise attack occur outside the palace.

His footsteps echoed as he walked across the hard-packed floor. The barracks felt empty. He couldn't believe that all of the soldiers were gone. He pushed back a curtain covering one door, noted the neatly covered pillows and the dress uniform hung against the wall. At least some discipline remained.

A hand touched his shoulder. Tarne's heart pounded, but he didn't jump. He made himself turn around slowly.

The man behind him wore two scarves like bandages around his head. His black hair stood in well-oiled spikes. Scars criss-crossed his cheeks, leaving gaps in his beard and giving his face a half-decorated look.

"Didn't expect to see you sneaking through here," he said.

"Didn't expect you lurking in the shadows." Tarne reached out a hand. "It's been a long time, Kendru."

Kendru took his hand and squeezed it in a motion that had meant a lifetime of loyalty a long time ago. "You didn't see us when you were relieved of command."

"I had other plans." Tarne took Kendru's arm. "We have some talking to do."

Kendru nodded. "We're alone. Come to my room. We'll have even more privacy there."

He slipped around a bend in the corridor so silently that if Tarne hadn't been watching, he wouldn't have known where Kendru went. The hallway was narrow, the curtains drawn back revealing empty rooms. The torch holders were empty, and sooty stains rose on the walls where torches had stood. Kendru led him through the hallway, around a number of twists and turns, and into a back room that stood by itself at the end of the corridor.

They went inside. Tarne reached for the curtain to bring it down, but Kendru caught his arm. "Leave it up. We want to know if anyone arrives."

Tarne did as he was bid. Kendru's room was filled

with momentos of dozens of campaigns. Tapestries from the southern lands covered the walls. Pillows, woven in the east, were scattered on the floor. The rugs were handmade and covered with gold incense burners, wine goblets, and eating trays. The wealth here astonished even Tarne, and it must have registered on his face, for Kendru smiled.

"No one takes anything because they know I'll kill them," he said.

Tarne nodded. He remembered Kendru's ruthlessness from their very first campaign. They had ridden into a village that sat at the mouth of a large river. The village had controlled the waterways for decades and demanded that all traveling people pay tribute. When the village leaders approached the soldiers with the same demand, Kendru had swept a small boy into his arms. He took out his sword and placed it under the boy's chin. "Is leaving him alive tribute enough?" Kendru had asked. When the elders didn't answer immediately, Kendru ran the sword through the child's chin, into his skull, and out the back of his head. He pulled the sword free and tossed the child's body in front of him. "I guess not," he had said. "Then perhaps all of your lives are." That time, the villagers agreed. The soldiers had stayed in the place free of charge for weeks. And later, when Pardu had decided to take the eastern lands, Kendru and Tarne had no fight at all when they came to capture the village.

Tarne had remembered that lesson in terror and used it many times, often to greater effect.

"The King is dead," Kendru said, "and you no longer command the soldiers."

"I will soon," Tarne said. He sat on one of the pillows and picked up an incense burner. It had been carved in the shape of a cat with pointed ears and with a wide opening in its belly for the incense itself. One of the village gods, but from which village he could not remember.

"I expected you to come to me after you lost your post."

Tarne shook his head. "It would have created more problems than it solved then."

Kendru waited. He understood violence, but not politics. That was why Tarne had moved up in the ranks and Kendru had not. Kendru didn't appreciate the need for subtlety.

"How many good men do you have, completely loyal to you?"

Kendru sat too. He frowned. "Four that I would trust with anything."

"Good. We'll need them tonight."

"You'll be with us?"

Tarne shook his head. "I need to be completely innocent of this one. It's going to be blamed on Ele if it fails."

The implication became clear to Kendru. He paled, then rocked back. They had always discussed a coup and Kendru had sworn his loyalty to Tarne. But Tarne could tell from Kendru's expression that deep down he had never really expected to act on it.

"Do you have a special plan for how you want this done?"

"Not detailed." Tarne's mouth had gone dry. He longed for a taste of the mead he had seen the soldiers drinking. "I want you to kill Vasenu tonight in his sleep, and I want it to look like a sloppy unprofessional murder."

"You want to eliminate both brothers in one act?"

"I want that option," Tarne said. He still felt the chill of anger around his heart. Ele would learn who knew the most about power.

"And what do we get?" Kendru asked.

"The satisfaction of a job well done."

Kendru didn't smile. "I can't pay men in satisfaction."

Tarne knew that. He wondered what had happened to the early closeness they had had, the one the handshake symbolized. The old Kendru would never have asked for a payment. But the old Tarne would never have killed a sovereign.

"You will become my number one in command.

Elite guards, higher pay, easier hours. There will, of course, be difficult jobs that will take a lot of risk, but they will be rare."

Kendru nodded. "I plan the details then."

"I don't want to know what they are," Tarne said.

"All right." Kendru held out his hand. "You have guts, my friend."

Tarne took Kendru's hand, but did not shake it. "I take advantage of opportunities," he said. And in this case, he would make sure he had more opportunities than anyone ever dreamed.

Elita parade, higher pay, easier hours. There will, of
course, be difficult jobs that will take a lot of risk,
but they will be rare."

CHAPTER 44

Vasenu pulled all the curtains down in his chambers.
He unrolled tapestries that he hadn't seen in decades.
He wanted privacy. He needed a shell around himself. He
felt so fragile that he was afraid he was going to break.

He took the glass of wine he had brought with him
and set it on the silver table beside his plush, ornate
lounge. He piled pillows against the back and put a
silken blanket at the foot. Then he climbed on the
lounge, settled in and covered himself as if he were a
little boy again, waiting for someone to tuck him in.

Long day. A day he never wanted to repeat. Every
time he closed his eyes, he saw his father's trembling
form, the last-minute anguish and then the shaking
stop. Somehow the end of the shaking was more horrible than the shaking itself.

And Ele. Ele's cool "So?" when he learned of his
father's death. Vasenu used to go to his brother for
comfort when something went wrong. He and Ele had
done everything together. He half suspected he saw
Ele in the baths not to spread the news, but to regain
that trust that they had lost with each other.

And Ele had walked out on him. The room had
been filled with anger, hostility, and more than a little
fear. Vasenu had never expected in all his years of
imagining that he would approach his father's death
alone.

He hadn't expected to lose the rest of his family
either.

He leaned back and grabbed the wine glass. It felt
as fragile as he did. A little bit of pressure applied to
the right place and the glass would snap into a thou-

sand pieces. All day he had been hearing questions—
*How would you like the burial, sire? Should the body
be cremated or should we dress it for state? Would you
like me to notify neighboring kingdoms, sire? We need
to let the people know, sire, that you now lead them.
Let me take your tunic, sire. You're not wearing the
right colors for a ruler.*

The wine went down easily, burning slightly at the
back of his throat. He wished he had brought in the
entire bottle. Perhaps that would hush the voices in
his head. He rested against the pillow, but didn't close
his eyes, afraid of what he might see.

He thought he was prepared for his father's death.
He had thought, with the prolonged illness and the
succession preparations, that he knew what to expect.
He hadn't realized that the absence of his father's
presence, that the absence of his father's life, would
affect him so deeply. He had been away from the man
for years at a time. He didn't need his father like a
child did, for survival and affection. But that didn't
explain why he was lying on his lounge now, drinking
wine and feeling about three years old and very, very
lonely.

He supposed he had to get used to the loneliness.
His father had warned him that rulers never had true
friends. They were never able to trust anyone.

Not even their brothers.

He took another sip of the wine. If he wasn't careful, it would become more of a friend than he wanted
it to. He could imagine himself on this lounge night
after night, slowly drinking down the wine cellar. He
wondered if that would make the fragile feeling go
away. He suspected it would make the feeling worse.

A small rustle sent a chill down his back. He had
asked not to be disturbed. He froze, listening as
closely as he could. He thought he felt another presence—a strong one—somewhere near him. He
glanced at the glass, using only his eyes. The contents
were barely gone. He could drink an entire bottle by
himself without losing control. It wasn't the wine. It
was something else.

He inched his hand down his side until it rested on the hilt of his dagger. He hadn't taken it off when he had come into the room—something about that fragile feeling had left him wary—and he was glad of that now. Then he closed his eyes almost all the way, staring through his eyelashes at the ceiling. He made his breathing regular, and he listened over it for movement.

There were none. The quiet seemed too quiet.

Before his eyes, the image of his father rose, as he had been when Vasenu was a boy—young, powerful, strong. His father had had a solidity then that he had lost in later years, a sturdiness that made him seem all powerful, all knowing.

This is not a job for the weak, he had said, *for there will always be someone to hate you, someone who wants what you have. All you can do is the best you can do. You must remember that people depend on you and you must make the right choices.*

Something rustled again, and Vasenu steeled himself not to open his eyes. He couldn't see anything, but he felt his entire body become alert. His heart was pounding so hard he was afraid that someone else could hear it. It was hard to keep his breathing steady. It had a ragged edge. Anyone listening closely would have heard his nervousness.

A slight scraping noise, nearer than he imagined. He opened his eyes and rolled into the noise as a dagger came down and slashed the pillows where he had been lying. Feathers rose and clouded the air. Vasenu crashed into his assailant, knocking him back. Another dagger rose and fell near him. Vasenu kicked and rolled off the man, grabbing his own dagger and standing with his back against the wall.

Four of them, all dressed in black, their faces covered with the traditional veils women had worn when he was a child. They stood as warily as he did, daggers out, free hands poised. He was surrounded and he didn't dare move.

He hadn't expected anything this quickly, but it made sense. If he died now, before he consolidated his power, no loyalties would be lost to him. He wondered who had sent them, and felt suspicion rise as hot as bile in his throat.

One of the men grunted and brought his dagger up in a forward thrust. They expected him to roll sideways as he had before, but this time he came forward and off to the side, kicking at the dagger to the left of the man who had used his. The other dagger hit the wall with a thump. Vasenu's foot connected with the dagger hand of the man before him, but the dagger stayed in place. The two remaining men came toward him, but Vasenu dove beneath them, rolled and hit the table. The glass fell off and crashed against the floor. Wine-covered glass shards surrounded him. He grabbed a handful, not caring that the glass dug into his palms and threw it at the eyes of the men before him.

One man screamed and clutched his face, blood oozing between his fingers. Vasenu scrambled backward, got to his feet, and pushed aside a curtain. He hoped no one else was waiting on his balcony. He got outside and the cold air hit him like a shock. "Guards!" he screamed. "I need assistance, now!"

He could hear the response to his shouts on the ground below. He crouched to the side, his own dagger extended, free hand poised, ready to battle with the people who had invaded his room, but they didn't emerge. He felt half-paralyzed, his cut palm throbbing, and a headache joining its rhythm.

The curtain pushed back and he stiffened, prepared to fight. But Jene, his own servant, stood there, looking sleepy and confused. Guards rushed beside him, checking to see if Vasenu was all right.

"Sire?" Jene asked.

"Assassins in my room. Four of them. I think I blinded one," Vasenu said. He didn't move from his crouch. Somehow he didn't think it was all over yet.

"The room is empty now, sire, except for the mess and the blood."

"I want them found," Vasenu said. "They didn't come through here."

Some of the guards disappeared back through the doors. The others combed the room. Jene sent one off to get other servants to clean the mess.

"Why would anyone do this?" he asked.

His naivete startled Vasenu. Vasenu put his dagger back into its scabbard and entered his room. It smelled of wine and sweat. He sat on one of the pillows and stared at the mess. Someone had tried to kill him. He opened his palm, watched it shake with a dispassion that startled him. Two glass shards stuck out of the skin. He grabbed them with his other hand and yanked. The first shard pulled free, and blood welled in the cut. He pulled out the other shard and watched the same thing happen.

The only person who would gain from his death was Ele. But he and his brother had done everything together. They had defended each other on campaigns, held each other after lost loves, promised each other fidelity. He couldn't believe that the boy he had grown up with would betray him.

But the man, the cold man who had been in the baths might.

Vasenu had to pull himself together. He was King. Someone had tried to kill him. That meant treason. Someone wanted his rule. He took slow, deep breaths, working on calming himself.

Outside the room there were shouts. Vasenu didn't move. If the trouble grew, he hoped his people would deal with it. Jene crouched beside him, clutching a wet cloth and a basin of water.

"Let me clean off your hand," he said.

Vasenu extended his wounded palm, noting that it didn't shake anymore. He was all alone now, completely alone. No father, no brother, no true adviser. He hadn't prepared well enough for this. He should have had his own guards, his own advisers, and his own friends. Somehow he hadn't thought it through, despite his father's warnings. He had always assumed that he and Ele would remain bound for life.

Jene scraped against something sharp in Vasenu's palm. "Ow," he complained.

Jene pulled back, glanced at the wound. He gently picked out more glass slivers.

The shouting grew closer. Finally the curtain in front of the door swung back and two guards that Vasenu had dispatched earlier came in. They dragged a man garbed in black behind them, holding his elbows because his hands covered his eyes. They pushed him forward when they saw Vasenu and shoved him to his knees.

"Uncover your eyes," one of the guards said.

The man didn't move.

The guard yanked the hands away. One of the man's eyes was slit in half, blood running down his cheek. Broken glass was embedded in his brows and forehead. He glared at Vasenu with his remaining eye.

"Who sent you?" Vasenu said.

The man said nothing.

Vasenu felt a slow burning anger. This man had come into Vasenu's rooms on the worst night of his life and had tried to take the last thing he had left—his life. "I want to know who sent you."

The man didn't move. A drop of blood ran down his cheek like a tear.

"Who is he?" Vasenu asked the guard.

"He's a lower lieutenant, works with Kendru."

Kendru. Kendru. Vasenu squinted, trying to remember. He had worked with Kendru once, on a western campaign. Kendru had been ruthless and violent. And at night he had told stories about his campaigns with Tarne.

"Did Tarne send you?"

The man remained motionless. Not a flicker betrayed his thoughts. If he was from Kendru, Vasenu's words wouldn't frighten him. The only thing that frightened him was the threat of Kendru's retaliation. Unless Vasenu could make things seem worse.

You'll hate the choices you must make as King, his father had said. *That is why you must have a pure heart to begin with, so that it will survive the shattering.*

Vasenu pulled his hand away from Jene. He took out his dagger, grabbed the man's hair and held the dagger against the edge of the man's good eye. "I took your other eye. I will blind you if you don't talk to me."

He could feel the man shivering beneath his hand. Vasenu shook him once. "Have you a tongue?"

"He can speak," the guard said. "He was calling for help loud enough when we grabbed him."

"And you saw no others?"

"None, sire."

Vasenu let the tip of the blade dig into the loose skin near the man's eye. "Tell me who sent you."

The man's trembling grew worse. He bit his lower lip.

Vasenu slowly sliced along the cheekbone. The man whimpered. His breathing grew labored. Vasenu brought the blade closer to the man's nose before the man whispered, "Stop."

Vasenu stopped cutting but didn't move the blade. His stomach was turning. He had never done anything like this before.

"Who sent you?" he asked again.

"I came with Kendru," the man said.

Vasenu brought the blade down. "Yes," he said. "But who sent you?"

With a shaking hand, the man touched the cut that Vasenu had made. He brought his hand away slowly and examined the fresh blood. "Kendru is working with Tarne."

"And?"

"And?" The man blinked and then winced. His voice was cracking.

"Who else?" Vasenu inched the dagger closer to the man's face.

The man leaned back as far as he could. "Your brother," he whispered.

Even though he had expected the words, Vasenu nearly doubled over with pain. He stood up and walked to the balcony. Outside the night air was chill. Torches illuminated the courtyard and the desert beyond. Below, soldiers paced in front of the gate. Everything was going on as it had before, and yet nothing was the same.

"Kill him," Vasenu said.

Jene gasped. Vasenu was not known for his harshness.

Vasenu turned. Everyone had frozen, as if his words had carried a power none of them had expected. "I cannot tolerate treason in any form. If I'm lenient now, the attempts on my life will never end. Kill him and make him an example to any other who might try to overthrow me."

One of the guards reached down and yanked the man to his feet. The man extended his hands. "Sire, please."

Vasenu cocked his head. He felt empty inside. "Yes?"

"I can tell you where Kendru is and what Tarne plans. Please, let me live and I will help you."

"I know what Tarne plans. I know that my brother is aiding him. All you can give me are details and your life isn't worth those. You're more valuable to me dead." Vasenu turned his back and stared out the balcony doors. His headache had grown worse.

"Sire—"

The man's voice faded as the guards led him away. Vasenu's palm itched and he rubbed it against his trousers. Jene came up beside him.

"Sire?" Jene's voice had a new tone to it, a deference that it had never had before.

Vasenu glanced at him, surprised to find Jene's gaze averted, as he used to do with Vasenu's father.

"Let me finish with your hand."

Vasenu held out his palm and winced as Jene applied ointment to it. "I want my brother here, now," Vasenu said over his shoulder to the remaining guards. Two left hurriedly, as if afraid to disobey him.

That was the price he was buying: power instead of affection. After tonight everyone would treat him with a bit of wariness, a touch of surprise. No one had expected him to kill a man on his first night as ruler. But then, he hadn't expected to fight for his own life.

The ointment stung. Vasenu tried to pull away, but Jene held tightly. "The men won't like this change in you," he whispered.

"I don't like it either." Vasenu spoke in a normal tone. "But I have no choice. I'm no longer a child, and no longer my father's son. I'm the one in charge here, and I have to be respected."

"But not feared."

The words pierced through the emptiness in Vasenu's stomach. There was pain behind it, more pain than he wanted to acknowledge. "What would you have me do?"

"Imprison him. Lock him away forever. But don't slaughter him. That's not civilized."

"And what do I do the next time?" Vasenu asked. He pulled his palm away and stared at the grease covering the cuts. Minor wounds for such a serious event. "Put the next one in the dungeon and the next and the next, hoping that they'll die of their own accord before the place fills up? Or perhaps I should have finished the job of blinding him and let him wander the streets to live off the charity of others until he died of starvation. Which is the most cruel? And which is the most effective?"

Jene said nothing. He took his ointments and set them aside, then moved the basin away. The remaining guards continued their cleanup as if nothing had happened. The pain in Vasenu's stomach felt like a rotted melon about to burst. He wanted to go to his father and have his actions confirmed. His father would have told him what to do, how to handle the situation. *Each problem has more than one solution,* his father used to say. *But some of the solutions are more valuable than others.*

"Sire?"

Vasenu turned. He hadn't heard the two guards come in, the ones he had sent after Ele. They were alone.

The guard who had spoken dropped his gaze. He looked nervous. "Sire," he repeated, "your brother is gone."

"As is Tarne, Kendru, and half the soldiers stationed at these barracks." The other guard met Vasenu's gaze. Vasenu saw the fear there, and the expectation of fairness.

Vasenu nodded. "I had thought so." He sighed. "I want a meeting in the Assembly Room in an hour of the advisers and the remaining ranking soldiers."

He turned his back on them all, so that they couldn't see the panic move from his chest to his eyes. This was what his father had feared. This was why his father had yelled *no* just before he died.

No one had moved behind him. "Leave me," Vasenu said.

He could hear the footsteps. His father had put the kingdom first. Ele wouldn't rule with Vasenu as his father had wanted, and they couldn't rule together as joint sovereigns, not after this. Vasenu would never be able to trust Ele again. Other solutions. He could abdicate and give his brother the power he wanted. But Ele was thinking of himself and not Leanda. If he had been thinking of Leanda, none of this would have happened. But if Vasenu fought Ele, would he be working for Leanda or himself? He didn't know. Either way, the discord was not good for the country. No matter what happened, he had already lost.

CHAPTER 45

He was strangling, his air gone. Ele reached a hand
to his throat, found a thick and hairy wrist. He jerked
awake, saw a face above his, half-hidden by a black
veil.

"You're coming with us."

Ele kicked and his assailant fell aside. He rolled,
only to be caught by other hands, stronger hands, and
to feel the prick of a dagger against his throat.

"One more move and I will kill you. Nothing would
please me more than to gut you and watch you die."

Tarne. Another dagger pricked Ele's back. His
room was too dark, the candles burned out. He could
see a shape huddled in the corner, its feet at an odd
angle, and realized they had already gotten to his servant. He couldn't tell if the man was dead.

"What do you want?" Ele kept his voice calm.

"You," Tarne said. He snapped his fingers. Ele's
original assailant grabbed Ele's wrists and yanked
them behind his back. Ele kicked and was about to
push away, when the dagger at his throat pushed
against his larynx.

"I said I will kill you." Tarne's voice was low. "I
mean it."

Ropes bit into his wrists and cut off the circulation
in his hands. "What's so important about me now,
Tarne?" It hurt to talk. The pressure against his throat
caused the words to jumble up behind his tongue.

"Your brother thinks you just tried to kill him. If
you're going to stage a coup, you need to leave the
palace tonight. I could care less if you leave it alive."

Ele tried to swallow. More hands grabbed his feet,

237

pulling them together, stringing another rope around his ankles. "If I were going to kill Vasenu, I would have succeeded."

"Perhaps." Tarne removed his blade from Ele's throat. "You know the same maneuvers. He rolled into his assailant too. My men weren't prepared for that."

The fact that Tarne didn't rise to the taunt upset Ele more than he thought it could. "You may as well kill me now, Tarne, because I'm not going to cooperate with you."

"Yes, you are. You just don't know how yet." Tarne took a silk scarf from his waist and handed it to another of the men. The man shoved it into Ele's mouth, then tied another scarf over the first. The angle was odd, and his skin pulled. Ele tried to spit them out, but couldn't.

"Get him out of here," Tarne said. "Quietly."

They lifted him up as if he weighed nothing. Ele wriggled, but the men held him tightly. He felt panic rise in his breast. Vasenu would think Ele betrayed him after that conversation in the baths. Tarne had manipulated him, and he hadn't even realized it. Ele would get no help from his brother—or from anyone else. Tarne's men were Tarne's men. Ele hadn't fought for any support, hadn't built any base because he thought he hadn't needed one. Such a mistake. A major mistake.

He was alone now, completely. One more mistake and he would die.

CHAPTER 46

Vasenu pulled open the door to the Assembly Room. He was using the King's entrance, which he had used a dozen times before, always following his father into the room. He could almost see his father's swaying form moving ahead of him. Vasenu shook his head slightly. Exhaustion and panic were making him weaker than usual. He had to get a grip on himself.

Torches spread along the walls gave the room almost a campfire feel. If Vasenu closed his eyes, he could imagine the open air, the stars above, and the whinnies of horses behind him. The room still had a bit of a chill—it had been closed for weeks—and it smelled faintly of smoke.

The advisers looked sleepy. Many of them wore robes casually belted, their hair askew. The soldiers were all dressed in clean white tunics and trousers, with boots going up to the knee. The swords attached to their waists did not have the dress hilts. Yet many of these men also looked exhausted, their eyes red-rimmed as if they'd been crying or drinking.

Vasenu paused a moment before taking his father's place at the dais. He didn't know who half these men were and didn't, for a moment, think he could lead them. What if he gave them an order and they didn't obey? He couldn't execute them all.

The thought made him wince. More than once, he had gone to his door to rescind the execution order. Each time he had stopped. His argument with Jene still seemed valid in his own mind. He had to show his strength right at the beginning. He had to prove that he would never tolerate treason.

Even from his brother.

Vasenu sat cross-legged on the satin pillow. The advisers looked up. All but Tarne had shown up. Only about fifteen soldiers had appeared, however.

"For those of you who don't know," he said, "my brother Ele made an attempt on my life tonight. He was assisted by Tarne and one of Tarne's men, Kendru. They have since left the palace on their own accord, destination unknown."

No one moved. They had heard.

"I want this discussion to be frank," Vasenu said. "We're at the early stages of my rule. The decisions we make here could affect decades to come. Anyone who feels that he can't be honest and that he cannot keep this discussion secret should leave now."

One of the soldiers near the back shifted slightly. Vasenu watched him. The man didn't leave.

"All right." Vasenu took a deep breath. He was tired and he wished he could get some sleep. "I believe that my brother and Tarne are planning to overthrow me. My brother has not kept his agreement made before this assembly and my father, to abide by the heart readers' decision. When he discovered that our father had died, he left me and refused to talk to me. He went immediately to Tarne, and arranged this evening's assassination attempt. Clearly he believes that he should rule."

"The heart readers said he could not," said Arenu, an elderly man who had advised Vasenu's father for decades.

"No," said Vasenu. "The heart readers said he did not have a pure heart. The concept behind the pure heart is that it can withstand the decisions a ruler has to make without breaking, and still maintain a love and interest in the people it serves. I may have already destroyed my purity. I ordered a man executed this evening."

The gasps echoed in the room. Most of the men had not heard that news.

"He was one of the assassins. I needed to set an example."

Arenu nodded. Some of the others did as well. The soldiers toward the back remained motionless. Vasenu wondered if he could trust them.

"My brother wants this rule, enough so that he will kill for it. He will risk everything. And I am at a loss. Am I as bad if I go to war to defend my position? We must decide first if I am to rule and to what cost."

Vasenu's words sent a murmur through the room. He strained, but could only catch phrases. He held up a hand. "Please," he said, "discuss this with me."

Salme, one of the younger advisers, stood. "Your brother has given no thought to Leanda. If he had, he would have avoided this struggle at all costs. I think his actions prove the heart reading. He cannot make choices based on the needs of the people, only upon his own needs."

"So I must act for the people. But I'm not sure which course is the wisest," Vasenu said.

One of the soldiers stepped up from the back. General's bars ran along his sash. "A battle now will cost hundreds of lives and will pit friend against friend," he said.

Vasenu wished he knew the general's name. He would have to ask as soon as he could. "So you believe I should abdicate to my brother."

"No, sire. Your brother will take hundreds of lives over the years and will do as much harm as King as he is doing now. If you can find him and kill him before the war starts, then the problem is solved."

For a moment, Vasenu couldn't breathe. Kill Ele. That was the option he hadn't seen, that he hadn't wanted to see. And yet he had already acted upon it by killing the assassin Ele sent. Perhaps that was why Vasenu couldn't stop that execution. He had to practice—to get a death done with before he killed his brother.

"Have you a plan?" Vasenu asked. His voice remained calm, although his heart was pounding.

"Yes, sire." The man stepped into the light. His face was weary, leathery from decades under the sun. "The only defensible positions outside the palace are the caves west of the city. I'm sure that Tarne took them there. We need to draw your brother out, bring him here, and execute him."

"It'll still cost lives," Arenu said.

"Yes." The general spoke softly. "But maybe dozens instead of hundreds."

One of them Ele's. "We would need Tarne as well, and all the others involved in the assassination plot." Vasenu cleared his throat. "Are there other choices?"

"Certainly, sire," Salme said. "We could let your brother rule or fight him in battle or you could choose not to fight at all and weather assassination attempt after assassination attempt. You need to consolidate your rule. You would have had to do it no matter what. You just have to do it early, that's all."

Early and against the only remaining member of his family. Vasenu clasped his hands together and twisted them slightly.

"No matter what, sire," said Arenu, "we're better off under your rule than your brother's. Ele has proven that this night."

The murmurs in the room sounded like agreement. Vasenu felt twenty years older. He had half hoped that they would excuse him, apologize for their mistake, and take Ele on as ruler. But they hadn't—and they wouldn't. Vasenu was his father's choice. And in many ways, his father's word was still law.

"Then I want a force heading for those caves," Vasenu said. "And I want my brother and Tarne before me as soon as possible."

He stood, swayed a little, and nodded toward the group. They nodded in return. Then he went out the door and leaned on it in the narrow hallway. He didn't know how much more he could take. And yet he would have to go on. He would have to take control of his rule, of the kingdom, and of his brother's life.

242   Victoria Ashwood Pierce

the caves west of the city, I'm sure that Tarne took
them there. We need to draw your brother out, bring
him back, and execute him."

CHAPTER 47

Ele's hands chafed and his mouth was dry. The horse
jolted him and he had trouble maintaining his balance.
He hadn't realized how much he relied on his arms
and legs when he rode.

The desert was cold in the darkness. The company,
a hundred in all, rode silently. Tarne's displeasure
stung as much as the chill air. The only sound that
accompanied them was the crunch of hooves on sand.

Tarne was taking them to the caves. It was the only
place he could build a defense on short notice. But
Ele didn't expect Tarne to run away and defend himself. The man was too cunning for that. Tarne's
scheme to kill Vasenu and blame Ele would have removed any support that Ele would have had within
the palace. Ele would have had to rely on Tarne—if
Tarne let him live. Tarne could also kill him and claim
that he had done so to protect his King.

Ele glanced back at the palace, a dark mountain on
the face of the plain. His brother was probably awake,
steering advisers, leading a force to attack Ele. Tarne
was brilliant.

Tarne rode beside Ele, his black tunic and trousers
blending into the darkness. He stared straight ahead.
He hadn't paid any attention to Ele since they had
left the palace.

Another horse rode up beside them. A man, also
wearing black, glanced at Ele and Ele recoiled from
the scar tissue covering the man's face.

"What do you want, Kendru?" Tarne didn't look
at the man, but the man didn't seem upset.

"I don't think we should go to the caves." Kendru's voice was gravelly. He kept glancing at Ele.

"Oh?"

"I don't think we should trap ourselves there."

"What gives you the right to express your opinion?" Kendru sat up even taller in his saddle. "You asked me to help you."

"I asked you to kill a king. You failed."

"He sent for the guards."

Tarne finally faced Kendru. Tarne's glittery gaze also took in Ele. "You should have killed him before they arrived. I thought you said these men were loyal to you. Loyal men would have died in the service of their leaders."

Kendru patted his horse's neck. Ele could see anger in his movements. "You never said anything about sacrificing ourselves."

"I thought you were smart enough to figure it out. Men do not kill kings easily or lightly. There's always a price."

Tarne's words echoed in the cold air. The crunch of hooves on sand continued, the only sound for miles. Ele took a deep breath. The air smelled of horses, sweat, and fear.

Kendru glanced back. Ele did too, and even in the darkness could see the trail the horses left.

"They'll find us," Kendru said.

Tarne didn't look back. He clucked at his horse and moved a little ahead of Kendru. "They won't find us tonight. And tomorrow they'll be too busy to think about catching us."

"You've made plans. You didn't tell me any plans."

Tarne placed his horse in front of Kendru's. The entire troop stopped. "You're not in my confidence. You are an old soldier past his prime looking for easy answers. You had promised to help me and you failed. It's only for old times' sake that I don't kill you now."

"Perhaps that would be better." Kendru's hand fluttered over his sword.

"Perhaps," Tarne said. "For you. I need you to guard our little princeling here. When Vasenu's soldiers arrive, they'll have no qualms about killing you. You're clearly a traitor. You can stay at the caves and defend yourself, or you can try your luck with the desert."

"And what do you plan?"

Tarne weighed the question. Ele tried to swallow, hating the dryness in his throat. His jaw ached from the pressure of the scarf, and his tongue felt thick. Finally Tarne sighed. "A number of soldiers went into town today to proclaim the King's death. We'll meet those soldiers before dawn, and set up the first skirmish. After that, we'll keep Vasenu so busy, he won't have a chance to search for you. And if he does, he will find you—and kill you for aiding his brother. Unless, of course, you're smart enough to fend him off."

"I thought we were old friends and partners," Kendru said.

Tarne guided the horse's reins and started riding again. "So did I," he said.

Ele tried to spit the gag out of his mouth. Vasenu had never fought in an expected manner. That's how he always won the war games. He didn't think like a normal commander. Tarne was going to surprise Vasenu, but Vasenu would probably try to surprise Tarne.

And Ele would be stuck—helpless, roped, and gagged—in the middle.

CHAPTER 48

Stashie finished wrapping the turban around her head. She hated getting up before dawn. Darkness was for sleeping and yet every morning she had been at the bazaar, she had arrived before the sun came up to set up her table and be ready for early morning customers.

She hadn't slept well. She wasn't sure if she should even go to the bazaar this morning. After the events of the day before, she was afraid that the soldiers would do worse today. They had made it clear that the bazaar should close out of respect for the King. But, as Ytsak had reminded her, the city depended on the bazaar for its food and trading. To shut down the bazaar was to shut down the city.

Still the bazaar didn't need its magicians. She could, if she wanted, spend the day in her room, away from the noise and bustle. She could sleep and think.

But then she wouldn't see Dasis again. If indeed that young boy had been Dasis. Ytsak didn't think so, but Stashie had been with Dasis half a lifetime. She should recognize her partner's movements, no matter what the disguise.

Stashie tucked a free strand of hair under her turban, adjusted her skirt, and patted her pouch of gold. She still had a lot of money from the reading, some of it stashed in the pockets of her skirt, but the bulk of it in the pouch she wore around her waist. Someone would have to get close to her to take the money away—and she wasn't going to let anyone she didn't know well get that close.

She grabbed her dice and let herself out of the

room. It had taken her nearly two hours to find the dice after the soldiers tore up the bazaar. Ytsak had begged her to stop looking, to buy new dice, but she had refused. These dice had belonged to Radekir, and they were all Stashie had left. She wasn't about to forget a woman who had died for her, and she would keep the momentos as long as she could.

The corridor was quiet, as it usually was this time of morning. The late night revelers had all gone to bed, and most of the workers were not yet up. She went out the back door and onto the street.

The torches had burned low, and in the east a tinge of color touched the sky. She had to hurry. Her table had been undamaged in the attack, but others hadn't. She could set up and then she wanted to help all the other people who had helped her—particularly Ytsak, whose booth had been demolished.

The city was unusually quiet. She didn't even hear the scurry of rats on their early morning foraging or the snores of drunks against buildings. The entire place seemed to be waiting. She thought she heard a footstep behind her, but when she stopped she could hear nothing.

Her hands were shaking. The attack the day before had left her more frightened than she wanted to admit. When she closed her eyes last night, she had seen fires everywhere, had heard women screaming, and her brother yelling. The memories had been on the surface since she and Dasis had come to Leanda, and now they were even stronger.

A door banged behind her and she jumped. She stopped for a moment, put her hand on her heart as if that would calm her panic. She hated soldiers, hated their unpredictability. She would have expected them to act with caution and decorum when their king had died, not participate in a revelry.

But then she would have expected them to have the decency to spare children when they attacked a village, and they hadn't.

The light in the east had gotten brighter by the time she reached the bazaar. People were already moving.

Some looked as if they had spent the night repairing their booths and rugs. Ytsak was there, his tunic streaked with dirt. His partner, Pare, was covering the booth with cloth, hiding the gaps in the structure left by the previous day's attack. Stashie stuck her dice in her pocket and walked over to them.

Ytsak didn't say a word. He handed her a date and she took it, welcoming the fruit's sweetness. She hadn't realized how hungry she was. "I keep wondering if we should do this," she said.

"We're not going to let a few wild men on horses scare us away." Ytsak gazed in the distance as if he expected the horses to return. "Does it seem quiet to you this morning?"

Stashie nodded. "I'm not sure if it's because I'm on edge or because the entire city is."

"It was quiet the morning they attacked my village."

Stashie glanced at him in surprise. He had never before spoken to her about his past. She waited, knowing better than to ask.

"I was ten, too young to fight." He smiled and touched his eye patch. "Sometimes too young doesn't matter, though."

"I know." Odd that they were both thinking about the same thing this morning. She wasn't sure if it was caused by the attack or by the silence.

Ytsak put his arm around her. She leaned into him. "Come on," he said. "You don't need to be here today."

"I want to be."

"No, you—"

Half a dozen shouts drowned his words. Soldiers sprang from corners. Others rode down the main thoroughfare, plucking torches out of their holders as if it were a game. This was different than yesterday. These soliders weren't out of control. They moved with a purpose, as if everything had been planned. The foot soldiers disappeared into the taverns. The others rode by buildings, tossing torches onto the roofs.

Ytsak's grip tightened on Stashie. He tried to push

her to the ground, out of the way, but she wouldn't let him.

"We're not safe here," she shouted.

Pare stood and watched as the soldiers came forward. The air was full of screams and battle cries. Smoke poured off the roofs, smoldering big and black, tickling the back of Stashie's throat. She watched them—

(They came in on horseback, almost peacefully. Tylee had watched the growing cloud from the window and slipped out the door alone. He wouldn't let Stashie go with him. "I'll take care of this," he said.)

—the melee moving in a circle around her. Ytsak had the same faraway expression on his face that Stashie felt on hers. Pare tugged his hand. "We need to leave."

Her own words. She'd said them to Tylee and he'd yelled, "No one abandons their village. No one."

"Yes," she whispered. "We do. Ytsak."

She took his other hand and pulled him forward. Pare glanced at her, as if she should lead. She didn't know where to go. In a few short minutes, the soldiers had surrounded the bazaar. Smoke came from all parts of the city. Other soldiers, bleary eyed, half-dressed, carrying only swords, had emerged from the inns and were fighting in a daze. She didn't know who was fighting whom. They all wore the same uniform, all had the same technique. It was as if they were fighting brother against brother. . . .

"Oh no." She didn't realize she had spoken aloud until Pare looked at her. But she couldn't tell him. This was her fault, hers and Dasis's. If they'd lied as Tarne wanted, the morning would be clear. No smoke would be clogging the bazaar. People would be working instead of screaming and fighting.

"We need to get out of here." She pulled harder on Ytsak. "Come on."

He heard her this time. She and Pare put their arms around him and pulled him forward, running back toward Stashie's inn as if that would make a difference. The streets were clogged with running people, fighting men, and screaming children. Stashie longed to scoop them all up and carry them away before they lived through the things she and Ytsak had. They pushed past people, the three of them serving as a battering ram. But they moved deeper into the confusion instead of away from it. The smoke had gotten thick, blocking the light. Stashie's lungs burned.

"This isn't getting us anywhere," Ytsak said.

But Stashie didn't want to stop moving. If they stopped, they would get hurt. She couldn't bear to see anyone else hurt. And they didn't dare go into a building like they had the day before. The smoke had turned into flames on many roofs and the buildings were disintegrating, the wooden beams charring and cracking the mud-brick.

Yesterday. She had forgotten Dasis. That young boy who saved her, the one who moved like Dasis. Stashie stopped and turned, but Ytsak dragged her on.

"Come on," Pare said.

"Dasis," Stashie said.

"If she's here, she'll have to take care of herself. Finding her will be impossible."

Stashie only heard half of Ytsak's words, but enough to know what he was saying. She knew he was right, but she didn't want to believe him, any more than she believed that Dasis had stayed out of the city. The smoke was making her eyes water. Ahead, a clash of soldiers had huddled around each other, circling like hungry dogs. Pare eased Ytsak and Stashie onto a side street.

Stashie took a deep breath. The air wasn't as sooty here. "Where are we going?" she asked.

"We need to get out of the city. The fighting must be everywhere," Pare said.

"We can't go toward the palace," Stashie said.

Both men looked at her. Horses pounded by—more shouting soldiers. Stashie cringed against the wall, but they weren't looking for civilians. They were looking for other soldiers. Ytsak stared at them, then at Stashie, and suddenly understanding filled his face.

"The King—"

"—is dead," Stashie finished for him.

"The twins?" Pare asked.

Stashie nodded.

"There's nowhere to go then. No escape."

"Except north," Stashie said. "They've been fighting in the north. They'll turn the troops around."

"That's not going to help us now," Ytsak said. People crowded past them, most too terrified to scream. Licks of flame poured down the building they were near and the street had already grown hotter than it was at midday. "I think we're trapped."

POINT BLANK

dren, crying, the did wonderful and cacophonous at
the same time.

Tarne recalled a curtoe and found himself facing
the Senate.

CHAPTER 49

Tarne's horse pranced beneath him. His white tunic was already turning gray with smoke. The entire city was in flames. The men were frenzied, battle lust thick. Already swords were bloodied and bodies covered the ground.

Tarne led his horse into the mess. Men fighting hand to hand on the ground. The advance troops, on horseback, had set the fires, adding to the confusion. He didn't care who killed whom at this point. He just wanted that arrogant Vasenu to know who had the power. Vasenu's men were disorganized and startled. Tarne's were in control.

He put a scarf over his mouth and nose to protect himself from the rising dust. The smoke dug into his eyes, but he didn't care. Soon the whole city would be burning. Vasenu would lose the center of his kingdom in a single day.

Ele had already lost his chance at ruling. The stupid bastard hadn't even planned on fighting for his own birthright. He didn't know how to use power to his advantage. He didn't realize that war was destruction—necessary destruction—and peace was rebuilding. The man who could come in after a war and give the people prosperity could be King forever, no matter what his lineage.

Ele didn't have that ability. Tarne did.

A man slammed into his horse and bounced away. The horse kept moving as if nothing had happened. Tarne always made sure his mounts were battle trained. He couldn't have them spooking at the first sign of disturbance. People were screaming and children crying, the din wonderful and cacophonous at the same time.

Tarne rounded a corner and found himself facing the bazaar.

It was not in flames, just disarray. Most of the merchants had run, leaving their wares behind. A few remained, using swords to protect their goods. Tarne rode past a booth, reached down and took some fruits from the baskets, then kicked the booth over. He wasn't going to fight, not yet. But he was getting ready. His biggest fight would be with Ele. If he couldn't convince Ele to listen to him, to be a puppet ruler, then Ele would die.

He chuckled softly and pushed a woman away with his sword. It was a beautiful morning. He hadn't felt this good in a long time.

CHAPTER 50

The screaming woke Dasis up. She rolled off the rug, pushing it away from her. She was too hot and she had gotten dust in her throat. She coughed—the air was thick—and wiped her eyes.

Her fingers came away dirty.

She sat up. She'd been sleeping outdoors for too many nights. She shouldn't be so filthy. She blinked. The air *was* thick, thick with smoke. Screaming was going on all around her.

She brushed herself off and peered out through the crack between the buildings. She had found this small space near the bazaar days ago. It was too narrow to be an alley, but wide enough for her to huddle comfortably, away from prying eyes.

Something snapped behind her and she whirled. A large piece of burning wood landed on her rug, setting it aflame. She squealed and folded the rug over, trying to smother the flame. Then she looked up. The roof was on fire—on both buildings. If she didn't move quickly, she would be trapped.

She squeezed out of the opening and onto the street. People poured past her, screaming, shouting, searching for loved ones. Soldiers chased one another through the crowd, while men on horseback stabbed at random. Dasis stayed near the walls, afraid that the fire would hurt her as much as the men could. She pushed her way to the bazaar. It had to be past dawn. Stashie would be there.

Movement was difficult. People seemed to be going in a hundred different directions. More than one grabbed her hand, as if she were someone they knew, only to glare at her in surprise. She squinted at everyone who passed, looking for Stashie and not finding her.

Finally Dasis rounded the corner into the bazaar. It looked worse than it had the day before. Layers of smoke clouded the scene, but nothing burned. The booths had been trampled, and two bodies lay across tables. She swallowed, nearly choking on the dryness in her throat. Stashie couldn't be one of them, could she?

Dasis used her elbows and fists to push people aside. She didn't care who she hurt. She was running, running, until she reached the first table. The body was too big, bulky, male, but she had to be sure. She grabbed the bloodstained shirt and pulled the body over. It was the wine merchant, his grizzled face frozen in anger. She let him go and his body flopped against the table, too newly dead to be stiff.

Food and money crunched beneath her feet. She hurried to the other table. This body was slight, slim, wearing a long skirt. It was far, too far from Stashie's table. But Stashie talked to Ytsak—Ytsak who loved her and would never accept Stashie's love for women. Ytsak, from a strange land where men and women spent time together and cared for each other, or so he claimed.

Dasis's hands were shaking as she touched the woman's blouse. Gently, she lifted the woman's head, saw white streaks through her black hair, the open brown eyes wide and frightened, the gash that nearly separated the head from the neck.

Not Stashie. Not anyone Dasis recognized.

She sighed with relief and a matching fear. If she had found Stashie here, wounded, she would have at least known where she was. Now Stashie could be anywhere in a city filled with people who were frightened and angry. Trembling rose in Dasis's body. She was supposed to be watching Stashie, to know her every move. She should have gotten a room in the same tavern, risked being seen. She had risked it the day before to get Stashie out of the bazaar.

The screams had all blended into a single roar. Dasis clung to the table beside her, trying to calm herself. She was dizzy from the smoke and dust. Her eyes hurt and her body ached from being jostled.

Across the street a roof caved in with a sea of sparks. Screams grew louder for a moment, and then faded. Dasis swallowed bile. People had been inside.

She had to think. She had to get out of the city. If she stayed too long, she would be killed. But she had to find Stashie. Stashie might be overcome by memories or old angers and try to fight back. Stashie might get herself killed.

Think. Dasis crouched beside the table, using it as a buffer between herself and the chaos around her. Perhaps Stashie hadn't come to the bazaar. Perhaps she had stayed in her room, unwilling to face the soldiers for a second day.

That meant she was trapped inside one of those burning buildings, unable to escape, panicked and frightened by the scene below. Dasis uttered a small cry and ran forward, then was stopped by the crowd. That's where Stashie was. That's why she wasn't in the bazaar.

Dasis pushed through, pushed through, not caring that she shoved people into each other or caused them pain. They wouldn't move fast enough for her. She had to find Stashie and get out of here. Didn't they know that?

A horseman plowed through the crowd. Dasis had to jump aside with the rest. This man wasn't fighting, even though he clutched his sword tightly. She glanced up, saw the white tunic of a general, and then looked into his face. Tarne. And he seemed to be enjoying himself.

The horse slipped through the crowd before she could throw herself after it and drag him from its back. Right now, she would kill him if she had to, just to stop Stashie's obsession and get her out of the city. He veered off, away from Stashie's tavern, and Dasis paused, uncertain whether to follow him or try to find Stashie.

Sparks flickered around her. Another roof had collapsed. That decided her. She had to find Stashie—and she would.

CHAPTER 51

Vasenu's eyes burned. He lay on his pillows, but sleep eluded him. Every time he closed his eyes, he heard a noise, a scrape, something that made him leap up, knife in hand. He would scan the room, note that it was empty, and lie back down.

The sun had come up a short time ago. Already the room was too hot. Still, he didn't move, preferring the comfort of the pillows to the decisions that awaited him outside.

The double curtain pulled back. Jene came in with a breakfast tray. "Sire, your advisers wish to see you."

Vasenu sighed. He pushed the food aside—he wasn't hungry—and rolled off the pillows. He took his sleeping robe off the rack and slipped it on before Jene could help him. "What do they want?"

"There's fighting in the city."

A chill ran down Vasenu's back despite the heat. He went to the balcony and looked out. Smoke rose on the horizon. He couldn't see the buildings of the city. He stood there, body trembling, and smelled the acrid scent of fire on the air.

"Send them in," he said without turning around.

His fingers, clutching the cool rail, had turned white. He didn't believe so many disasters could happen in such a short period of time. Half of him believed that he would wake up and discover his father laughing in the next room. *Why do you believe in dreams, Vasenu?* his father would chide. *Because they have so much power,* he would respond.

"Sire?"

Arenu's voice calling his father. Vasenu willed himself out of sleep.

"Sire?" A hand touched his shoulder lightly, hesitantly. Vasenu turned. He wasn't dreaming. They were speaking to him. Salme, Arenu, Jene, and the general Vasenu had met the night before whose name, he had later learned, was Goddé.

"The city's on fire," Vasenu said. His voice sounded raw. He wondered if it was the effect of the smoke, but decided he was probably too far away for that.

"Your brother's men attacked before dawn," Goddé said. "The fighting is fierce. One of my men escaped and rode here to report. They want reinforcements."

Before dawn. The maneuver was too cunning for Ele. He always played war games in a straightforward by-the-book manner. But Tarne had conquered half the eastern and southern provinces and had done it using surprise as his main weapon.

"Our men are fighting our own men." From this distance, the burning city looked so small that Vasenu could extinguish the flames with a touch of his hand.

"Yes, sire."

"And none of them really know why or who's who."

"Yes, sire."

Vasenu leaned against the balcony railing, half wishing it would give way. Then Ele and Tarne would get their way, and the country would be at peace again. So many lives would be lost in this confusion. So many probably had been already. "What do you recommend?"

Goddé glanced at the others. Arenu stepped forward. "We need to stop this fighting quickly," he said. "We need to move into the city and crush the rebellion."

"How would we do that?" Vasenu asked. "This isn't a peasant revolt. These are our soldiers fighting each other."

"We reclothe our men," Salme said. "Give them

something so that they can recognize each other on sight. Then we send them in there."

"A hat, a sash, anything will do as long as a man can glimpse it through dust and smoke," Goddé said.

"Given that we have the time and materials to do this," Vasenu said, "what do we do about the men already in there helping us? Kill them too?"

Salme looked down at his hands. "Some of them."

"No." The smoke rose in plumes against the blue sky. The day would be a fair one, but the smoke looked like rainy season clouds looming on the horizon. Vasenu marshalled all his reserves. He had to think clearly. "They're fighting us with surprise and cunning because they have a smaller cadre of men than we do. In time, and if we were willing to lose a lot of lives, we could subdue them."

He turned. The others were watching him with the kind of polite awe that they used to reserve for his father. The looks made him pause, but then he took a deep breath and kept going.

"I'm not willing to lose a lot of lives."

"I don't see any way to fight them except on their own terms," Goddé said.

"I know," Vasenu said. "And that's what they expect. Fought that way, on their terms and losing a lot of lives, even if we win, we lose. I'll never have the popularity my father had and I'll never be able to sleep at night."

A shudder ran down his back. He could see himself, years hence, still jumping at every scrape, every nighttime noise. He didn't want to live like that.

"We don't have a lot of time to come up with alternate ideas," Arenu said.

"I know. We don't need them, at least not yet." Vasenu leaned his back on the railing and wiped his hands on his robe. They felt sooty, as if he were standing in the thick of the smoke instead of miles away from it. "You said last night that they had probably gone to the caves—"

"But the attack this morning proved me wrong," Goddé said.

"No, it didn't." Vasenu glanced again at the city. "Cunning. You're thinking what they want you to think. My brother would never go into the thick of the fighting. It frightens him. He's always been terrified of leading troops into battle. He is probably the backup general, the one operating out of a safe place. He's too important to risk in a melee. So he's stashed in the caves with a minimal force. Tarne is out leading the troops, expecting our people to swoop on the city at any time. We don't swoop. We let the city take care of itself. We have our people there and the townspeople themselves. They will either flee or attack soldiers—any soldiers. Why send more into the fray?"

The others seemed confused, but Goddé was with him. "We capture their King, and take their morale."

"Right. Once Ele is taken care of"—Vasenu couldn't bring himself to say "dead"—"we worry about the city itself. A number of soldiers should come back to us, shouldn't they? Tarne doesn't have that many personal loyalists."

"He has quite a few," Goddé said, "but not if they thought he was going to be king. Tarne is a brilliant general, and a cruel man. Soldiers want him to lead them into battle because they know he'll win. They don't want his cruelty directed against them. That's why he had so many problems in a peacetime army. He should never have become an adviser. He should have stayed in the field."

Vasenu sighed. "That's what I had hoped. Then here's what we do. Goddé, I want you to lead a large force to those caves and capture my brother. Bring him here for me to deal with. I always want the remaining army to stay here, guarding the palace. Tarne could be even more cunning than I thought, getting our men out of here and attacking the palace. I don't think so, but I don't want to risk it."

Goddé nodded.

"Arenu, Salme, I want you two to get the advisers together and come up with as many alternate scenarios as you can. I don't want this fight to drag on, but if it does, we need to be prepared. Is that clear?"

They nodded also.

"Good. I'll want reports as you have them." Vasenu turned around, dismissing them. He waited until their footsteps receded off the balcony before he spoke again. "Jene?"

"Yes, sire?"

"Throw out that breakfast and leave me for a short time. Have the cook prepare something light for me just before the sun reaches its zenith."

"Yes, sire."

Vasenu watched through the corner of his eye as Jene left. Then he went back inside his room and lay on the pillows, unwilling to move. In some ways, Ele had already defeated him. Vasenu no longer wanted what he had. The future, no matter what the outcome of the battle, looked bleak, gray, and lonely.

CHAPTER 52

"We need to keep moving," Stashie said. Her voice sounded small against the shouts and screams around her. She felt sick from lack of food and too much smoke. "We can't stay here."

The heat from the building had grown intense. The streets weren't safe. Roofs were collapsing, sparks flying. She had seen more than one person slap out flames that had sprouted on their clothing.

"But where to?" Pare asked.

"The bazaar." Ytsak was looking up. He must have been thinking the same thing Stashie was. "It's at least open there."

They moved forward, three as a battering ram, shoving their way past screaming people. Children ran loose, excited and frightened at the same time, as if the fighting were some kind of strange holiday. Some of the men got between the soldiers, joining without knowing the issue or the sides. Women were moving in circles, hunting for children and a way out.

As the three neared the bazaar, a man on horseback loomed out of the smoke. For a moment, Stashie thought she was seeing an illusion. Then she froze, causing the others to stop.

"Tarne," she whispered.

Ytsak followed her gaze. Pare tried to pull them forward. Stashie shook herself free, but Ytsak grabbed her arm.

"That's Tarne," she shouted at him.

"He's on horseback. He has an advantage."

"I have surprise."

"And you're not battle hardened. You're leaving him alone."

She had left him alone once before and he had murdered her entire family. Then she left him alone when she went before the King and he had murdered Radekir. "No," she said. "I'm going to kill him."

"You have no weapon, no plan. He's on horseback."

"I know," Stashie said. "Get me a sword, Pare. Ytsak, you and I will get him down."

Pare looked confused. "I thought we were going to the bazaar."

"Soon," Stashie said. "Get me a sword."

Ytsak nodded at him and Pare moved through the crowd. "How're you going to get him down?"

"Watch me," Stashie said. She pulled the dagger from Ytsak's belt and shoved her way through the crowd. Her breath was coming in gasps and her chest felt heavy. She elbowed people, ignoring the screams and cries around her.

Tarne was smiling as if the entire show were for him. She went behind him, swung the knife, and shoved the blade as deep as she could into the horse's rear leg. The horse screamed and kicked, nearly hitting Stashie. She backed out of the way. Tarne gripped the horse, struggling to keep his seat.

Pare came up, clutching a blood-covered sword. Ytsak was beside him, holding another sword. He had seen what Stashie had done. He hurried around the flailing horse, and chopped its remaining back leg. The horse kicked again, its squeals rising above the human cries of pain. This time when it landed, it stumbled, then toppled, taking Tarne with it.

Stashie took the sword from Pare, startled at its weight. People had moved away from Tarne and were running in various directions. Smoke blew across the scene like a southern mist. The horse fell, landing on Tarne's leg. Stashie stepped beside the horse and, using both hands, brought the sword down on Tarne's exposed leg.

He screamed and grabbed his dagger, his expression fierce. Stashie worked her blade free, then held it above her head, feeling the blood dripping onto her hands.

"Remember me?" she asked.

CHAPTER 53

Ele was stiff. The circulation had left his hands, and his feet hurt. They had placed him in the far corner of one of the caves, against the dirt wall. The air was cool here, and he could barely see the sun through the cave's mouth. The cave was wide and had several alcoves, as well as one long dark tunnel that led even deeper into the earth. At least five soldiers guarded the outside. He could hear their laughter rise faintly on the breeze.

Tarne had left before dawn, and since then Ele had caught a touch of smoke on the air. He wondered what they were doing. One of the guards said it looked as if the city were burning. Perhaps Tarne was winning after all. Perhaps he had gotten Vasenu to fight Tarne's battle.

A soldier came through the entrance, carrying a pouch. He crouched by the rock, reached in the pouch and pulled out dried fruit and meat. Then he set a cup beside it, and poured water into it from his own canteen. He reached forward, and slit the scarves from Ele's mouth. The man smelled of tobacco. Ele spit the scarves out. His tongue felt heavy and his lips ached.

"Don't feed me," he said.

The soldier frowned. Ele realized that the soldier didn't understand. "Don't feed me," he repeated, careful to enunciate clearly. Speaking hurt too. He couldn't get moisture into his mouth. "Let me feed myself. I'm not going to try anything. I can't. I'm too hurt."

The soldier glanced over his shoulder. "Lean forward," he said.

Ele did so. The soldier undid the ropes from Ele's wrists, then retied Ele's left hand to his belt. "You can use one hand."

Ele twisted his wrist, wincing at the pins and needles as the feeling returned. Tentatively he reached forward and picked up the cup. The water was warm and stale, but it was wet. He had never had anything so good. He licked his lips and took another sip, pleased to have control of his mouth again. Then he took a piece of meat and chewed it. He hadn't realized he was so hungry.

One of the guards leaned into the cave and beckoned the soldier. "Shenu."

Shenu looked up, obviously reluctant to take his gaze from Ele. "What?"

"You have to see this."

"Don't try anything," Shenu said. He got up and walked to the cave's mouth. "What's that?" he asked as he emerged.

The answer was lost outside. Ele shoved more food in his mouth, chewed quickly and swallowed. He kept his eye on the cave opening and carefully untied his left wrist from his belt.

No one had come back inside. If there were only five men, he could take them, if he had an element of surprise. And if he took them, he could take a horse and ride back to the palace. Somehow he would get past the guards at the gate and see Vasenu. Vasenu would have to listen.

He got his left hand free, shook it, and sighed as the blood rushed into it. The pain brought tears to his eyes. He took another drink, forcing himself to think of something else. He could hear shouts outside. He paused, keeping his left hand against his waist in case someone came in, but no one did. He waited a moment, then reached down, and untied his feet.

Still no one came inside. The shouts had diminished. He forced himself to finish eating, and allow the circulation to return to all parts of his body. Then he rose carefully, and made his way around the side of the cave.

When he reached the mouth, he saw what the men were looking at. A dust cloud had risen on the desert, a cloud that could only have been made by horses carrying a large troop of men. Tarne? If so, why were his men in such a panic? Ele glanced at the city, saw the smoke billowing to the sky. No, the dust cloud hadn't come from there. It had come from the palace. From Vasenu.

CHAPTER 54

Dasis felt battered. She had been pushed, shoved, and attacked with a sword. She had managed to cross the streets despite crowds going the other way. Screaming children clung to her before they realized that they didn't know her. People grabbed her arm, inquiring after other people. She didn't answer anyone. She just shrugged them off and kept moving until she reached the inn where Stashie had been staying.

The roof had caved in. Wisps of smoke rose from the open ceiling and mingled with the cloud that hung in the air. The door stood open. Dasis coughed—she wasn't breathing well—and walked in the open door.

Most of the roof had landed on the dirt floor and lay smoldering. A bench toward the back of the tavern glowed red, but she could see no real fire. Most of the room doors stood open—people abandoning them in their haste—and a few torches still burned against the wall. Dasis picked her way across the debris, feeling the heat against her ankles, trying to avoid the hot places with her feet.

Stashie had had the far room toward the back, one of the handful that innkeepers reserved for women traveling alone. Dasis's heart was pounding. She half wanted to find Stashie in this empty place, and half didn't. She didn't know what she would do if Stashie were unconscious or injured. Drag her into the panicked crowd? Treat her here, where the smoldering ruins could turn into flames at any moment?

She heard a snap above her and a piece of flaming wood fell from the ceiling. It knocked one of the torches off the wall and they landed together in the dirt, inches from Dasis. She jumped away, a scream tucked in the back of her throat. She glanced up, but could see no more flames. The roof was precarious though. It could finish its collapse at any moment.

She hurried across the remaining floor. Stashie's door was closed. Dasis pushed on it, but it didn't budge. "Stashie?"

No answer. Dasis rattled the door, wishing that Stashie had chosen to stay at a cheaper place that used curtains instead of wasting rare and precious wood. Dasis pushed with her entire weight. She heard something snap and then the door flew open.

The ceiling had collapsed on the pillows. They were still smoking, little licks of flame teasing along the edge. Dasis stepped over a beam and into the room. It was hotter than the rest of the building.

"Stashie?" she called again.

She didn't see anyone on the floor, and the debris was too small to hide a body. Dasis pushed at the pillows with her sandaled foot, wincing as a bit of flame nipped her toe. She pulled away, turned, and saw a slate underneath some of the burnt wood. She crouched down and touched it. It felt cool despite the room's heat. She tugged at it and it came free easier than she suspected.

Half a slate, broken perfectly. Tears came to her eyes. "Stashie," she whispered, "where are you?"

The heat in the room grew. Dasis dropped the slate and backed out. She took the side door out of the corridor.

The street seemed even more full than it had before. The buildings were traps so people had gone outside, into a place filled with dust and chaos. Dasis crossed her arms in front of her and pushed through the crowd. She had to get away from the inn, had to find Stashie. Maybe she hadn't combed the bazaar well enough. Or maybe Stashie had left town during the middle of the night, unwilling to face the soldiers one more time.

Dasis coughed and pushed. She would go back to

the bazaar. She would find Stashie, or someone with word of Stashie. And if that failed, she would take the only choice left her.

She would leave.

CHAPTER 55

Blood spurted from Tarne's leg. Stashie couldn't get her sword free. Tarne reached forward and grabbed her arm. She fell into the horse, her face next to Tarne's. He shoved his dagger under her chin.

"Of course I remember you." His eyes glittered. She remembered the look. He had it before he had killed Tylee. She struggled, unable to free herself. Her skirt was getting wet with Tarne's blood. She pushed at his chest with her free hand, but he pushed the point of the dagger tighter against her neck. She felt hands on her back—Ytsak and Pare—but Tarne glared at them.

"Touch her again, and I'll kill her."

They let her go. The horse shook itself, and tried to rise, unable to move its legs. Tarne was trapped, his face growing pale with the shock of the blood loss. Stashie slammed her knee into his groin.

His grip loosened for a moment and she pulled free. He grabbed her again, but she hit him with her own head. Pain shot through her skull. She had to get away—

(Tylee telling her to go inside, his face stuck in a grimace)

—but she couldn't. She was here to kill Tarne, not to flee from him. He had loosened his grip and she snatched the dagger from his hand. He tried to grab for her and missed, his hands closing on open air. She couldn't think. She had to act, had to destroy this man who had destroyed her, make him pay for everything he had done. She reached inside his tunic, his trousers, searching until she found the dagger by his hip. She tossed it to Ytsak.

Tarne leaned forward, grabbing for Stashie's hand. She slashed at his face. He dodged and hit his head on the saddle horn. His back probably hurt him, at the odd angle he was at. She brought the knife down again, missed and hit the horse. The horse screamed, and Tarne grabbed Stashie's arm. She heard an *oof* of pain behind her and turned to see Ytsak on his back in the crowd, Pare bent over him, the horse's hooves caked with blood. She couldn't help them now. She had to get Tarne. She had to help herself.

Tarne was reaching for the dagger, his hands impossibly strong. She pulled the dagger free of the horse, and brought it down again, this time catching Tarne in the shoulder. He rolled away too late, his right leg still trapped under the horse's weight. He lay still and Stashie bent over him, about to bring the blade down into his head, when he swung around, clutching his sword. The broad, flat side caught her, and she staggered sideways, falling to her knees.

The air had left her. She saw visions of her mother, her baby sister, her brother, and all those soldiers above her, hurting her. She was dizzy, her head throbbed. The sword came back, hitting her again, and this time she felt the blade slice into her skin. He would win. He always did. He would—

No. She looked up, saw the sword coming again, and shoved her dagger forward into the open space under his arm. The blade dug into his side just above the hip, and he grunted with pain. He was more difficult to kill than she had expected. She thought, somehow, that he would die the moment the blade hit him. But he didn't. And neither had her family. They had been tortured. She had been tortured—and he needed to be tortured.

Tarne had dropped the sword and was reaching for it. Stashie stabbed at his shoulders, his arms, making slight contact. He grabbed at her, turning his attention away from the sword. The confidence had left his face.

He knew now that she meant to kill him. He was combat trained, and fighting for his life.

He grabbed for her wrist. She dodged, brought the blade back, and then at his face. He moved, but not far enough. The dagger sliced through his eye.

This time he did scream. He brought his hands up to his face, then held them back, as if he couldn't believe what she had done. His movements became more frantic, more hurried, but the strength was leaving him. Her skirt was matted with blood. The horse was covered. Tarne was bleeding to death through his leg. And she wasn't through with him.

She got on top of him, wrested open his trousers, and pushed his weakening hands away. With a swift movement she grabbed his penis, and shoved the blade into it, as deeply as it would go. He screamed again, sounding like the horse, thrashing and kicking, spraying blood in the air.

Passing people glanced at them, but did nothing in their haste to escape. Stashie pulled the blade free and brought it down again and again, until the lower half of his body was mush. The blood was covering her, drenching her, and it felt good, it felt right.

"This is for my brother," she said, and slashed.

"My sister," she said.

"My mother."

His body was covered with blood. He didn't move much. Only his good eye watched her, and she thought she saw comprehension in it. "I never forgot," she said. "And I never forgave."

She put the tip of the blade against his remaining eye. "And this," she said, "is for Radekir."

Only she didn't slash yet. She stared at him, while he stared at her. She had hated him all her life and now he would die. "This will be the last time I will touch you," she said. "And for the first time I'm going to enjoy it."

Then she brought the blade down with all her strength.

CHAPTER 56

Ele grabbed a rock and eased himself out of the cave. The troop was visible now, over one hundred horses and men in full armor, all carrying the King's flag. Vasenu's men. Ele had been right. His brother wasn't going to play by Tarne's rules. Vasenu had come after Ele, the man he considered the true traitor.

Ele's guards had taken one look at the full troop and were scrambling for their horses. Five men against a hundred didn't seem to them like fair odds. Ele could see the general ahead, signaling half his troop to follow the men on horseback. Ele limped out of the cave and dropped the rock. He now faced the troop alone.

He half wished he could go back inside and tie himself up, proving that he had been an unwilling captive. But he couldn't. So he waited. He climbed on the edge of the rocks outlining the cave and stood there, a single figure, alone.

The general reined up in front of him, the rest of the troop behind. Dust choked Ele and made his eyes water. The pungent scent of horses filled the air.

"I want you to take me to my brother," Ele said.

"My orders are to kill you."

Ele swallowed, but worked at not showing his nervousness. "My brother would never order that. At least give him the honor of killing me himself."

The general looked hesitant.

"This is not a trap," Ele said. "You can have your men inspect the caves. I'm alone here. Tarne kidnapped me last night and left me here with a handful of guards—the men you saw riding away. If you catch them, they'll corroborate my story. Also, there are ropes inside, and rope burns on my wrists and ankles. Check if you like. I'm weaponless."

The general snapped his fingers. The soldier to his left dismounted and went inside the cave. A moment later, he emerged, carrying rope. He took Ele's hand and looked at the wrist. The rope burns were red and ugly. He ran his finger across them and Ele winced.

"He is burned and injured, sir," the soldier said. "And the ropes bear out the story."

A scream echoed across the sand. Ele glanced over, as did the general. Another dust cloud rose not too far away. A horse shrieked, and one bolted, running riderless into the desert.

"They'd better agree to your story."

"They will," Ele said. "They have nothing to lose."

But he did. He had everything to lose. Vasenu could have him killed without even seeing him.

"Tie him up," the general said, "and bring him with us. No man touches him until we talk with the King."

Ele stood as they bound his hands and feet. The ropes cut into the wounds on his wrists and ankles, but he said nothing. This was his last gamble, a gamble he had to win.

CHAPTER 57

A little girl ran screaming by, blood running from a cut on the side of her head. Dasis dodged out of her way, wondering where her own compassion had gone. Once she would have gone after the child, to see if she were all right. But not now.

Men were pulling torches off building walls and throwing them into the open doorways. The smoke had grown thicker and half the city was on fire. Dasis moved slower than she wanted to. She felt as if she were slogging across deep sand.

When she reached the edge of the bazaar, she stopped and caught her breath. Breathing was difficult in the thick air and each intake made her want to cough. Even so, she couldn't stand moving anymore, as if each action made her breathlessness worse. She rubbed her eyes, but that seemed to grind the smoke particles in them instead of dig them out.

She walked, head down, pushing people away from her. A small crowd had gathered around a fallen horse. She shoved her way into it, hearing moans and encouraging shouts. When she reached the front, she stopped in surprise.

Stashie straddled a blood-covered man. She clutched a knife in hoth hands and she was talking, although Dasis couldn't hear the words. Stashie herself looked as if she had been dipped in blood. Her hair was matted to her head, her skirt was saturated, and her arms were dripping. With a movement that looked practiced, she brought the knife down into the man's eye.

He shuddered, then didn't move. Stashie rolled off him. Dasis grabbed her, ignoring the blood and gore.

"Stashie!"

Stashie's eyes were wild. She brought the knife back up and Dasis caught her wrist. "It's me. Dasis. Stashie, stop."

Stashie froze. She took a slow breath, then shuddered and wrenched her arm free of Dasis's grasp. "I told you to go away," she said. "I didn't want you to see this."

Then Dasis understood. That was Tarne down there, trapped, bleeding and dying under his horse. She would have thought that she would take the knife and slash his other eye, but she couldn't. She felt no more hatred for him, only pity.

"Finish him, Stash," Dasis said.

Stashie shook her head. "I did."

Dasis stared at Stashie. She was almost unrecognizable under all the blood. Dasis could still feel the bloodlust humming through Stashie's fingers.

The two men who had befriended Stashie were behind her, looking as shocked as Dasis felt. Ytsak slowly got to his feet. Dasis couldn't stand their scrutiny. They would have done the same, if they had lived like Stashie. Dasis would have.

Dasis put her arm around Stashie and led her forward to the bazaar, feeling a sadness she didn't know possible. They were heart readers, a profession, she thought, geared toward healing. But what had they done, really? The readings told people who they were, and allowed the people the opportunity for change. Most people never took the opportunity. The brothers hadn't. That was clear from the wreck the city had become.

Stashie was limping. Dasis supported her with more weight. The crowd was thinning on this edge of the bazaar. Most of the people must have been like her, circling, searching, caught in the battle, and seeing no escape. Escape was just beyond the ridge. She would take Stashie away from the city, away from soldiers, away from the past. They would live on the money they had and then they would find a new profession, something that was easy and safe. Something that allowed them to build a home and stay together, in silence if they had to.

"Do you hate me?" Stashie asked.

Even though she spoke softly, Dasis heard the plaintive note over the crowd noise. "No," she said. "I could never hate you."

Stashie stopped, ripped off part of her ruined skirt and wrapped it around her ankles. Then she wiped her hands on her blouse, but they still didn't come clean. "I'm just like him now," she said. "He made me just like him."

"No, Stash," Dasis said. "You chose to do that."

"Just like him." She glanced around, as if she saw the mess for the first time.

"You were provoked," Dasis said. "He was never provoked."

"Maybe he thought he was. Maybe he thought what he was doing was right." A man ran into Stashie. She swayed, but didn't move.

Dasis wasn't sure how she felt. She did know that Stashie couldn't live with herself if she believed that she was just like Tarne. "But you didn't enjoy it."

Stashie brought her head up for the first time. There were deep circles under her eyes. Her cheeks were streaked with blood and soot. "For a moment I did. I should have stopped sooner, but I liked his struggling. I liked that he was frightened of me. I liked his pain, Dasis."

Dasis didn't move. If anyone drew a picture of her heart then, they would see something wrapped in gauze, hidden away. Dasis made herself breathe the foul air. She couldn't let this freeze her. She had to reach out.

"You're not going to do it again," Dasis said. "And that's different from him." She put her arm around Stashie.

Stashie shrugged her away. "I can't go with you," Stashie said. "Not after this."

"You need me more now," Dasis said.

Stashie shook her head. She wouldn't budge. This was how it had been before, after Radekir died. Stashie wouldn't let Dasis close, at least not for Stashie's sake.

People were walking past, carrying their belongings on their backs. In the background, the screaming and clashing of swords continued.

Dasis grabbed Stashie's arms. They were bone thin. "I love you," Dasis said. "I will always love you and I always want to be with you. I need you, Stashie, not to read with me, but to be with me. Please, let's leave. Please, let's find a home."

Stashie stared at her for a moment, as if she hadn't heard at all, and then she crumpled into Dasis's arms. Dasis stroked her matted hair, whispering soft things into her ear, and wished.

She always thought the reading was enough, but it was only the beginning. She had seen hearts that were wounded, unloved, destroyed. Their owners already knew in some way about the damage. The reading had just confirmed it. Heart readers failed because the reading wasn't enough. Healing had to start, somehow. And Dasis had no magic for that. She wished she did, because then she would use it on Stashie and everything would be all right again.

"I love you," Dasis whispered and hoped that in the end, love would be magic enough.

CHAPTER 58

Vasenu paced back and forth in the Assembly Room. It seemed too large to meet his brother here alone, just the two of them. He should have chosen another place, but they all seemed too personal. His own chambers, Ele's chambers, gave one brother power over the other brother. Vasenu didn't want that. Instead he chose a neutral place, the last place where they had been equal.

His heart had been pounding in his chest since he learned that Ele had surrendered. He had heard about the kidnapping, spoken to the guards, but wasn't sure if he believed the story. Ele was cunning enough to make the guards speak for him and to put the rope burns on his arms. But Tarne was cunning enough to double-cross both brothers. Vasenu could order his brother's death now and no one would think anything of it. He could pull his troops together, crush the rebellion in the city, and then rule with an iron fist. People would say that Leanda had remained strong and that its King was tough and powerful.

His father would have done that. His father would have made the difficult choice and lived with it for decades. He probably had. Perhaps that was why his father wanted to control the succession, because of the pain he felt at causing his own brother's death.

Vasenu clasped his hands together tightly. He couldn't bear to live with the thought that he might be wrong.

The main doors to the Assembly Room opened. Two guards brought Ele in, his hands bound and his head lowered. His clothes were dirt covered and his hair matted against his skull. He looked as if he had been away from the palace for years instead of hours.

"Untie him," Vasenu said, "and leave us."

"Sire—"

"Leave us." Vasenu made his voice powerful. It echoed in the large, empty room. The guards undid Ele's hands, then backed out of the chamber. Vasenu stared at his brother. Ele looked as if he hadn't slept either.

"The death chants for Father are tomorrow," Vasenu said.

"I would like to be present for those." Ele rubbed his wrists.

Vasenu nodded. "He was afraid of this, you know."

"I know," Ele said.

"He wanted us to work together."

"But he trained us both to lead."

Vasenu turned his back. His throat had gone dry. He surveyed the room for a moment, thinking how meaningless the rule was to him, alone. Then he unsheathed his sword and whirled around. Ele cringed. The fear in his brother's eyes made Vasenu hesitate.

"He trained us to work together," Vasenu said. "We don't work well apart. But"—he tossed the sword to Ele. Ele caught it with one hand—"if you want this rule so badly, take it. Kill me here and no one will question you. You will be able to rule, no matter how I die."

Ele stared at the sword in his hand, and then looked at his brother. Vasenu didn't flinch. He had thought about this for hours, knowing it to be the only way. If Ele killed him, then Ele wanted to be King badly enough to protect it against anything. Vasenu didn't have that desire. He held his hands at his side.

Ele took a step forward, sword out. He took another step, so close that all he had to do was place the tip against Vasenu's stomach and shove. Ele lifted the sword, tested its weight, and then dropped it. It clanged against the marble floor and skittered off to one side. Neither brother watched it go.

"I was angry when I didn't get the kingship," Ele

said. "I'll not lie to you about that. You would have been angry too. But I never betrayed you. Tarne asked me to and I said no. He ordered your death. And he kidnapped me. Do you think that if I were leading those troops I would have been alone in the caves, undefended? Would you have done that?"

Vasenu glanced at the sword at his feet. He would have thrown his entire self into the rebellion if he had been leading it. And he would have been angry at not getting the throne too. They had been raised together. Each was the other's closest companion. They complemented each other. Even the heart readers had said that when they did their reading. One heart was the exact opposite of the other. Vasenu had felt as if he had been operating without one half of himself—and he had been.

"I'll be your adviser," Ele said, "or I'll go away, whichever you want. I even understand if you want to kill me as an example. But know that I never betrayed you."

Something had changed him in during the night, something as strong and powerful as the change that had come over Vasenu. "I'm not going to kill you," Vasenu said. "And I don't want you to leave. I can barely handle our father's loss. If you go too, I'll lose all of my strength."

Ele nodded. His face crumpled, and Vasenu could see the pain that had hidden behind the mask. "I'm sorry I got so angry—that I even provided the opening for Tarne."

"I'm sorry too," Vasenu said. He took a step toward his brother, and suddenly they were in each other's arms, holding each other tightly. They hadn't done that since they were boys, and Vasenu hadn't realized how much he had missed such a simple touch.

"There's still fighting in the city," Vasenu said after a while. "We have to stop that. We have to stop Tarne."

Ele pulled away. "He's in the city. If we send in all of our troops, then perhaps we can stop it."

"We have to surround it and stop the fighting somehow. All the innocent lives. We have to do something Tarne doesn't expect."

"I know his plans. Let me work with the advisers," Ele said. "That is, if you give me leave."

"I don't have to." Vasenu took his brother's hand and led him forward, to the dais where their lives had changed. "You have the power to do that now. I'm not going to rule alone. We're going to share this title, as we should have from the beginning."

"But Father—"

"Is dead," Vasenu said. "And I've been thinking about this. Haven't you wondered why twins were always born to the royal household? One with a pure heart and one without?"

Ele frowned. "I just thought that was the way of things."

"So did Father. But you and I have always worked together—your strengths compensating for my weaknesses, my strengths covering yours. Then heart readers come in and say I'm pure. Yet I killed a man for crossing me yesterday and you have been saying no to death. Perhaps I am the pure one, the one who understands the consequences, but you're the one who takes action."

"You're saying that we're supposed to rule together."

Vasenu nodded. "And I think Leanda will be stronger for it." He clapped his hands. "It's time to tell the others, and to get things moving as they should."

Jene peeked his head in the side door.

"Send in the advisers," Vasenu said. He took Ele's hand and squeezed it. Ele squeezed back. And as the advisers came in, the brothers faced them, together.

EPILOGUE

Ten Years Later

Vasenu stepped into the birthing tent. The air smelled of blood and sweat. It was hot, so hot he wished he wasn't wearing his formal tunic. Ele already stood against one side, looking awkward and out of place.

Dania was naked, her distended stomach and swollen breasts heaving. A pillow had been placed at the edge of the couch to catch the little prince when he appeared. Vasenu stood beside his brother, feeling as out of place. They had shared the woman so that paternity would not be questioned. Now they would share the birth.

The midwives hovered around her. Dania clutched one of their hands and pushed as they commanded. Vasenu could see a bloody head appear between her legs. He took a step forward, but Ele held him back. Birthing was not his place. They were only present due to the grace of the midwives.

Dania screamed and Ele turned away. Vasenu watched, his hands clutched together. The shoulders appeared next, and then the baby slid into wizened hands that placed him gently on the pillow.

Dania's stomach hadn't lost much of its size. She had been a thin woman and the pregnancy had bloated her into odd proportions. Both brothers had hovered over her like the midwives did now, making sure she ate well and took care of the baby inside her. She had laughed at them and their fussing, but had taken it well. Vasenu liked her, as did Ele, and they had decided not to banish her from the baby as their father had done with their mother.

Vasenu tapped Ele's arm and his brother turned

around again. Vasenu moved toward the baby, but the midwife held him back. She cleaned the baby's eyes and nose with one finger, then stuck another in his mouth and emptied it. Vasenu wanted to hold the boy, blood and all, but Ele's grip on his arm tightened.

Another head had appeared between Dania's legs. Twins. Vasenu glanced at Ele, who had gone white. Dania moaned as the shoulders poked through, then another midwife guided the baby next to his brother. Two boys. Twins. Just like every generation before them.

Dania moaned one final time, and this time, a large bloody mess exited her body. A third midwife caught it, cut it away from the babies and took it out of the tent. Dania leaned back, her entire body covered with sweat.

Vasenu came forward, kissed her, and then took his son. Ele took the other boy—his son too, since they couldn't know who fathered them—not caring about the blood that smeared his tunic.

The fourth midwife turned to open a tent flap.

"Where're you going?" Ele asked.

"To get the womb caster," the woman said. "We need to know which child will rule."

"No fortune-tellers, no superstitions," Vasenu said. He clutched the warm squirming baby against his chest. "They'll decide their own future."

"Together," Ele added.

Then they took their sons and brought them to Dania, placing one in each arm. She held the babies against her breasts, closing her eyes in contentment.

Vasenu crouched beside her, feeling contented too. The future was assured. He wished, for a moment, that his father was here to see it, but then he decided that his father wouldn't have understood. They were a new generation with new ways. And they had new sons.

He took one of the baby's curled fingers, feeling the tiny grip. He smiled at Ele, who was holding the other baby's hand. Vasenu could see his own pride and pleasure echoed in his brother's face. They would share these children, as they had shared everything. And it would be good.

ROC   **⊙ONYX**   (0451)

TERRIFYING TALES